ONE UNDER

Recent Titles by Cynthia Harrod-Eagles from Severn House

A RAINBOW SUMMER
ON WINGS OF LOVE
EVEN CHANCE
LAST RUN
PLAY FOR LOVE
A CORNISH AFFAIR
NOBODY'S FOOL
DANGEROUS LOVE
REAL LIFE *(Short Stories)*
DIVIDED LOVE
KEEPING SECRETS
THE LONGEST DANCE
THE HORSEMASTERS
JULIA
THE COLONEL'S DAUGHTER
HARTE'S DESIRE
COUNTRY PLOT
KATE'S PROGRESS

The Bill Slider Mysteries
GAME OVER
FELL PURPOSE
BODY LINE
KILL MY DARLING
BLOOD NEVER DIES
HARD GOING
STAR FALL
ONE UNDER

ONE UNDER

A Bill Slider Mystery

Cynthia Harrod-Eagles

This first world edition published 2015
in Great Britain and 2016 in the USA by
SEVERN HOUSE PUBLISHERS LTD of
19 Cedar Road, Sutton, Surrey, England, SM2 5DA.
Trade paperback edition first published
in Great Britain and the USA 2016 by
SEVERN HOUSE PUBLISHERS LTD

British Library Cataloguing in Publication Data

Harrod-Eagles, Cynthia author.
One under. – (The Bill Slider mysteries)
1. Slider, Bill (Fictitious character)–Fiction.
2. Police–England–London–Fiction. 3. Cold cases
(Criminal investigation)–Fiction. 4. Murder–
Investigation–Fiction. 5. Detective and mystery stories.
I. Title II. Series
823.9'2-dc23

ISBN-13: 978-0-7278-8556-2 (cased)
ISBN-13: 978-1-84751-665-7 (trade paper)
ISBN-13: 978-1-78010-719-6 (e-book)

All Severn House titles are printed on acid-free paper.

Severn House Publishers support the Forest Stewardship Council™ [FSC™],
the leading international forest certification organisation.
All our titles that are printed on FSC certified paper carry the FSC logo.

Typeset by Palimpsest Book Production Ltd.,
Falkirk, Stirlingshire, Scotland.
Printed and bound in Great Britain by
TJ International, Padstow, Cornwall.

ONE
Two Under

A suicide is a detective sergeant's shout. Fortunately for Atherton, who was 'it' that Monday, the British Transport Police did the immediate graft. Unless there turned out to be anything suspicious about it, he was only required to attend, in both senses of the word, and write a report afterwards.

Shepherd's Bush has an Underground station at either end, one serving the Hammersmith and City Line and the other the Central. It was at the Central station that what was called – in the arm's-length language beloved of policemen – the 'incident' occurred. The BTP, like all railway people, called it a 'one under'.

'Eastbound platform,' said the BTP sergeant, Jason Conroy, who met Atherton at the top of the escalators. The ticket gates were locked open; the entrance gates were locked closed, and outside a small crowd had gathered, five-eighths pissed off that they couldn't catch their train, three-eighths hoping for some excitement in their lives, and a chance to capture something unusual on their mobile phones.

'Where did he travel from?' Atherton asked.

'Oh, right here. He lives locally. Addison Way.' It was a two-minute walk from the station. 'Name of George Peloponnos. We got his wallet from the tracks. Various bits of ID, including this.'

It was a laminated pass for a local government building. No one looks entirely human in an ID-card photo, but he was probably looking better there than in real life, after his argument with the business end of a speeding locomotive. The picture showed a man in his mid-forties with thinning, light-coloured hair over a rather large skull, a high forehead and a pleasant, mild, perhaps weak face.

'I took a photograph of the body on my tablet,' Conroy went on, 'if you want to see it, but it's not much help. His face got a bit messed up.'

'Pity,' said Atherton. It was Standard Operating Procedure to match the photo against the corpse – there were unfortunately many reasons a person could have someone else's documents on him to trip the unwary. When there was any doubt about identification, it meant getting a partner or relative involved to specify other identifying marks – never a happy task.

But Conroy said cheerfully, 'No worries. We got it all on CCTV. He looks like the photo on the pass. It's him all right.'

'And did he definitely jump?'

'Oh yeah. No doubt about it. D'you wanna see the MPEG? I haven't edited the whole tape yet, but I've downloaded the jump.'

Since the terrorist attacks, Transport for London – as London Transport had wittily renamed itself – had installed some of the best CCTV kit with the widest coverage in the business. Furthermore, Shepherd's Bush station had been completely remodelled in 2008 when the vast new Westfield shopping centre had been built next door, so it had modern lighting too. Conroy cued up the video clip and turned his tablet for Atherton to see. There was the brightly lit eastbound platform. Conroy pointed to the tallish, lean figure in a dark overcoat waiting among the other travellers – not so many of them, since the rush hour was over. He was standing a little apart, staring straight ahead, his hands down by his sides clenching and unclenching. Then he turned his head towards the tunnel mouth, presumably hearing the train approaching, and the camera got a good view of his face. It certainly looked like the man on the ID card.

Then 240 tons of 1992 BREL/ADtranz rolling stock hurtled out of the tunnel and it was all over.

Atherton handed it back. He had jumped. Nobody had pushed him. So far so good.

'Witnesses?' he asked.

'We've interviewed the people standing nearest him. Not that they were much help. As you could see, one was reading the paper and two of them were messing on their mobiles.' He cued the video again and froze it just before the jump, and showed it to Atherton again. 'There was this bloke,' he said, pointing to a young-looking man standing with his hands in his pockets and the leads of an iPod protruding from his ears. 'But he wasn't looking.' He was, indeed, staring absently in the other direction. 'He says the first he knew, there was this scream, and the bloke with the newspaper stepped back on his foot and nearly knocked him over.'

'Who screamed?'

'Woman further down the platform. She saw him jump. The paramedics are treating her for shock. Do you wanna talk to her?'

Carole Parkinson, sitting in a cramped little office behind the concourse, was sufficiently recovered to ensure that Atherton took down her first name correctly, 'with an e'. Indeed, wrapped in a cellular blanket and clutching a mug of tea, she seemed more stimulated by the attention she was receiving than devastated by what she had witnessed.

She was aged forty-six and was a waitress in a West End restaurant. She had been on her way to work at what was her normal time.

'I'd just missed a train – it was pulling out just as I reached the platform – so there was no one else there except him. Well, I didn't think anything about it, obviously. Didn't really notice him or anything. But when I heard the train coming in, of course I looked that way, and I saw him jump.'

'Did he jump, or could it have been a slip, or a stumble?'

'Oh no. He jumped all right. Straight out in front of the train.' She sipped. 'Of course, it's the driver I feel sorry for. When you think about it, it's a selfish thing to do, kill yourself like that. That poor driver'll probably never get over it. I mean, if you've got to do it, at least don't involve anybody else. And then all these poor people—' she gestured round her to indicate the paramedics and the BTP – 'have got to clear up the mess.' She shuddered delicately and sipped again. 'Selfish,' she concluded. 'I wonder why he did it. Maybe he left a note.'

She looked hopefully from Atherton to Conroy, but neither of them was interested in satisfying her curiosity. They turned away. Outside, Atherton looked at his watch.

'Keeping you from something?' Conroy enquired ironically.

'You might say. I gave up a perfectly good funeral for this,' said Atherton.

There was thin April sunshine, but a brisk, chilly wind was blowing: not weather for lingering, though the cemetery was delightfully full of spring-green grass and trees just coming into bud, and there were daffodils everywhere, leaning and straightening in the breeze, on the graves and beside the paths.

Porson had a cold, and looked terrible in the sharp wind and acid sunshine, his face raw and bumpy, pale where it was not reddened. But he was never less than a leader, and everyone naturally gravitated towards him as they exited the chapel. The sullen roar of the nearby A40 was the background to the tweeting and twirting of the birds. *Rus in urbe*, Slider thought. When it had first been established, Acton Cemetery had been on the far outskirts of London, and the traffic would have been horse-drawn.

Joanna had her arm through Slider's. She huddled down into her coat against the wind, and pressed close to him for comfort. She had cried during the meagre little service inside. She hadn't known Hollis well, of course, but a quick imagination would always feel sympathy. And Slider couldn't help being aware that this was about the due date for the baby that she had lost in December. If he was remembering it, she must be too. In fact, he hadn't wanted her to come, though it was hard to put her off without mentioning the baby. But she had insisted – as worried about his state of mind, he supposed, as he about hers. She had been giving him covert looks ever since the news of Hollis's suicide had come in. She thought he was a guilt junkie.

Apart from the police contingent there were only about ten people there. They had made an awkward group in the chapel. Slider regretted the old days of the *Book of Common Prayer*, when at least you had always known what to expect. Nowadays at a funeral you were more likely to be ambushed by embarrassment than grief. But there had been no eulogies or 'Fred would have loved this' jokes, or inappropriate music. Slider had felt only sadness that Hollis's life should have ended as it did, and be closed with such a paucity of ceremony.

The clergyman who had officiated had already hurried away to his car, and the undertaker's men had assembled the floral tributes in the porch of the little stone chapel. Hollis's second wife, Debbie, a hard-faced blonde in what looked like a new black skirt suit and coat, and a small feathered black hat that would have been more appropriate for a wedding, was inspecting them along with the man she had thrown Hollis out for, a lean and professionally-coiffed bounder in a tight-waisted M&S suit. He was a technician at the King Edward hospital and a good few years younger than her.

It was the first wife, Brenda, that Slider had known socially. She came towards him now, bareheaded, in a coat that had seen many seasons, her face worn and softened, as if eroded with cares. Beside her were the two children of the marriage, awkward teenagers of fifteen and sixteen, tall like their father, and with an unfortunate combination of their parents' worst features. It was somehow all the more heartbreaking that Hollis's children should be so plain. The boy, besides, had teenage acne and the girl was uncomfortably big-breasted and overweight. They looked so alike with only a year between them, one might have taken them for twins. They stood close together, supporting each other, and Slider had an image of them huddling that way for comfort while the marital split was going on. The girl's nose was red, the boy's lip trembled. They gazed out in bewilderment from behind glasses with NHS frames that did nothing for glamour.

Joanna slipped her arm out of Slider's to free him and hung back to talk to them. Slider took Brenda's hand. 'I'm so very sorry,' he said.

'It was nice of you to come,' she said. 'How are you?'

'More to the point, how are you? Holding up?'

She glanced at the children, and lowered her voice. 'Colin was still supporting us. I don't know how we're going to manage. I suppose . . .' Tears filled her eyes and she bit her lip and breathed out hard to control them. 'I suppose the social services will help us out. Somehow. Eventually.'

Slider felt helpless. 'It's a rotten business,' he said. 'I had no idea – none of us had any idea. I knew he was depressed, but . . .'

Brenda nodded miserably. 'Debbie . . .' she began, but didn't finish. There were no words adequate to the occasion. She looked around in a lost way. 'Well,' she said reluctantly, 'we'd better go.'

Debbie was now holding court, receiving the commiserations of the other guests and hogging Porson's attention. She was the official widow. It was all about her. In the chapel she had passed Brenda and the children on her way to the front row and pointedly not asked them to join her.

'I've taken those two out of school,' Brenda concluded, as though it were not a non-sequitur. The boy was trying desperately not to cry. He had his father's protuberant eyes, and would have his male-pattern baldness too, one day. The chubby girl put her arm clumsily round his shoulders, staring defiance at the world.

Slider, turning his shoulder so they shouldn't see, fumbled out his wallet. Brenda moved a hand to stop him. 'Oh – no. You mustn't.'

'Please,' Slider said urgently, in a low voice. He removed all the notes, folded them in his palm, and pushed them into hers. 'It's not much, but – buy them lunch, or something. *Please.*' He'd taken out cash the day before, so there was about £160 there. 'Please, Brenda. I don't know how we're going to manage without him. He was a good man.'

It probably wasn't exactly the right thing to say to the wife he had left for another, but they had remained on civil terms, and he had always supported the children. And Brenda had come to the funeral, hadn't she?

She nodded, slipping the notes into her pocket, unable to speak, and turned away. She smiled brightly and crookedly to her tall, plain children and they walked off together. Slider wanted to say 'Keep in touch', but he knew they wouldn't – and to what point, anyway?

'Poor things,' Joanna said. 'Those poor children.'

'If only anyone had known how far gone he was,' Slider said. 'I *should* have known.'

'Don't start that again,' Joanna said. 'It wasn't your fault.' She looked at her watch. 'I'd better be getting back.'

'Yes, we ought to go, too.' She had come in her own car, as had Porson. Slider had brought McLaren and Mackay, with Nutty Nicholls representing the uniform side. Nutty and Fergus O'Flaherty had tossed for it. Paxman, the other sergeant, was a strict Christian and would not attend the funeral of a suicide on principle.

Slider gathered his troops, and they walked with Joanna down to the gates. There was no car park, but plenty of roadside parking in the immediate area. At his car, Joanna said, 'See you tonight,' and left him to find hers.

The four of them got in the car, glad to get out of the sharp wind. Porson was still talking to Debbie's remaining group – or rather, being talked at by Debbie. They saw her lay a hand on his forearm, as if to stop him escaping.

'She could have given Brenda some of the flowers,' Mackay said resentfully. 'Cow.'

Nicholls, beside him, said, 'She wouldn't have wanted 'em.'

'Still, it's the thought,' Mackay insisted.

Slider was aware that Debbie was generally blamed for Hollis's suicide. He had said many times in his life that suicides did the deed because of what they felt about themselves, not because of what anyone else did or didn't do. It didn't stop him feeling guilty, though.

'It's a rotten business all round,' said Nutty.

'At least he done it tidy,' said McLaren. 'Didn't make a mess for someone else to clear up.'

Hollis had hanged himself – the favoured option, statistically, for men, and especially for policemen in a force that did not routinely carry arms. He'd taken some rope with him in a backpack and taken the Central line out to Epping Forest where he wouldn't scare anyone, leaving a note at his lodgings and another in his pocket for the avoidance of doubt. Considerate to the last – if you could discount the suicide itself – was Colin Hollis.

'Well, that's something, I suppose,' Nicholls allowed.

They drove in silence for a while, and then Mackay said, 'Guv, are we getting a replacement?'

'Obviously, at some point.'

'No, I mean, soon. Have you heard anything?'

'No, but Mr Porson knows it's urgent.' Even allowing for the cuts the whole of the Met was having to make, Slider's firm was understaffed for the area and the workload. Of course, the new borough commander mightn't agree – Mike Carpenter was reputed to be a bean counter, who had got his promotion for his mastery of spreadsheets rather than operational prowess – but it was self-evident they couldn't manage as they were.

'Mr Porson'll tell 'em,' McLaren concluded. Their boss might be a strange old duck, and use language like a blind man swatting flies, but he was always ready to fight their corner.

'How was it?' Atherton asked.

'Simply divine,' Slider replied sourly.

'I just asked. Don't you want to know how I got on?'

'Well?'

'Nothing suspicious about it. He jumped. Definitely suicide.'

'Good.' Slider busied himself with what was on his desk, and after a brief pause, Atherton went away.

Now he was alone with his thoughts. He felt terrible about Hollis, the goofy-looking Mancunian who was such a good policeman.

Mild, efficient, encyclopaedic of memory, and with a wonderful talent for getting people to open up to him – perhaps *because* he was goofy-looking, so they saw him as unthreatening. Slider had known he had left the marital home – for a time he had surreptitiously camped out in the Department, to which Slider had turned a blind eye – but lately he had found himself lodgings and Slider had thought he was getting on with his life.

The note in his room had said, 'I'm sorry, but I just can't go on. I'm really sorry if this makes trouble for anybody. I don't blame anybody. I'm doing it off my own bat. I'm sorry.' Three 'sorrys' in one suicide note. Well, that was Hollis.

The note in his pocket had said, 'This is a suicide. Nobody else is involved.' And gave his name and address and an instruction to contact Slider. Which the Epping police duly did.

Determined to end it, Slider thought. Like Atherton's 'one under', he jumped. One at each end of the Central Line. But did either of them think about the people they left behind? They were safely out of the way; someone else had to clear up the mess. Including all the feelings, guilt or otherwise.

The phone rang, breaking the unfruitful cycle, and Slider reached for it gratefully.

'This is DCI Remington, from Uxbridge.'

'Oh yes? Hello, Pete. Long time no see. How are things?'

'Oh, you know. Same all over. Cuts. Targets. Initiatives. It's not like the old days.'

'Even the old days weren't like the old days,' Slider suggested.

'Congratulations, by the way. How are you liking your promotion?'

'Doesn't seem to have made much difference,' said Slider. As a new detective chief inspector he was barely fifty pounds a month better off. 'I have more meetings with council officials, that's about all.'

'Ah yes,' said Remington, with a smile in his voice. 'Actively promoting police/community stakeholder engagement going forward.'

'Yes, I had one of those memos,' said Slider. That was the other difference – an increase in the amount of management-speak bollocks that landed on his desk.

'Sorry to hear about your bloke – Hollis, was it? That's a nasty one. You always wonder if you could have done something. But the truth is, you never can.'

'Thanks,' said Slider, accepting the intended comfort. 'What can I do for you, anyway – or is it social?'

'We've got a hit-and-run victim – young girl. One of those country lanes out Harefield way. No ID on her, but her fingerprints have come back to someone on your ground.'

'What's the name?' Slider asked.

'Kaylee Adams – that's Kaylee with a double e. Age 15. Address, 12 Birdwood House, on the White City Estate. You did her a couple of times for shoplifting.'

Slider made a note of it. The name sounded vaguely familiar, though he wouldn't have been involved in a shoplifting arrest. 'What the hell was she doing out in Harefield?'

'That's what we were wondering,' said Remington. 'Anyway, we're still at the scene, if you wanted to send somebody to have a look. Or if you're busy, I can just copy you the reports when we're done.'

They were busy, of course, but not with anything interesting. So much of the Job now was social work, community liaison and general reassuring. Burglary, domestic violence and missing persons were the highlights. Last week a woman had dialled 999 because she couldn't get her ten-year-old son to go to bed and he was screaming and throwing things at her. 'I din't know where to turn to,' she sobbed theatrically to the uniformed officer who attended.

As the PC related it in the canteen afterwards, with much exasperation, 'Scrawny, undersized little kid, and she must have been four times his weight, but she still claimed she couldn't control him.'

'Give him four years and it'll be our job,' another officer had observed sourly.

So the Harefield hit-and-run was a golden opportunity for Slider to get out of his train of thoughts, and out of the office, before some other shower of bumf urged him to do some blue-sky thinking in a real-time facilitation sense.

Besides, it was an odd place to find a girl from the estate.

'Thanks, I'll be along,' he said.

Slider reached into his reserves of compassion and took Atherton with him.

* * *

Harefield was at the far edge of the London Borough of Hillingdon. It was therefore under Metropolitan police jurisdiction, but it was something of an anomaly, a distinctly rural area of muddy fields, cows and horses, narrow winding roads, hedges and barns – though the latter had mostly been converted into garages or desirable residences. But there were still some working farms, sometimes straw on the road and often the tang of manure in the air. A stranger parachuted in would never have guessed it was part of London.

The warren of narrow lanes was mostly unsignposted, but there was a patrol car parked half across the entrance to Thornbrake Lane, which was a bit of a giveaway. The uniformed officer was telling motorists that there was no through road for the present. Slider showed his brief.

'Oh, yes, sir, DCI Remington told me you were coming. Down here and second on the left. That's Dog Rose Lane.'

Thornbrake was wide enough to have a dotted line down the middle, but Dog Rose – 'Charming names they have in these parts,' said Atherton – barely managed a lane in each direction. Middlesex was an area of the Old Enclosures, so all the lanes had sunk to some extent over the centuries. Dog Rose began claustrophobically between low banks topped by high hedges, but after the first bend the hedges dropped lower and jumped back behind a grass verge and ditch, giving a bit of light and air and a glimpse of damp green fields beyond grazed by a few rough-looking horses.

They soon came to a number of cars parked on the verges. Beyond them, blue-and-white tape stretched across the road a little short of a sharp left-hand bend.

'Looks like the crime scene,' said Slider.

'Crime?' Atherton queried. 'Jumping the gun, aren't we?'

'Leaving the scene of an accident is a crime,' Slider reminded him.

Another uniform was standing guard with a clipboard. He checked them off and courteously lifted the tape for them.

It was a nasty, blind sort of bend that the cautious driver would creep round. Beyond it things were well under way, with the Uxbridge detectives, the local SOC team, and the collision scene specialists all busy. A forensic tent had been erected in the middle of the road.

Remington shook their hands. 'You can see what would have happened,' he said. 'She must have been walking along the road here and chummy comes round the corner too fast. It's a nasty bend, as you can see – local black spot – and the natives all drive like maniacs round these lanes.' He gave a little shrug. 'Think they're immortal.'

'Where was she found?' Slider asked.

'Down the ditch, just over there. Must have been sent flying when she was hit. Of course, the driver might not have seen her at all if it was night – felt the bump, thought it was an animal, didn't bother to stop. Or else knew what he'd hit and panicked. No witnesses have come forward, unfortunately.'

'Who found her?'

'Dog walker, this morning. There's been plenty of traffic down this road, but you wouldn't have seen her, where she was, from a passing car. We've moved the body now,' he added, gesturing to the tent, 'but I've got some photographs of the position, if you want to see them.'

Slider and Atherton bent over his screen and scrolled through. There was the general position – they could see exactly where, just up ahead, with an overgrown thorn sprouting from the hedge and throwing arched tendrils over the ditch. Then the girl – lying face down, but with her head slightly turned to the side, one arm under her, the other flung out, one knee bent, just as she might have landed from the brief, violent flight. She was wearing a leather jacket and a miniskirt, and her legs and feet were bare.

'No shoes?' Slider asked.

'We found them further along,' said Remington. 'I don't know if she was knocked out of them, or if maybe she'd taken them off and was carrying them. Has to be said they weren't best suited for walking.' He scrolled on, and showed them a photograph of the shoes lying in the long grass at the far side of the ditch – four-inch-heeled strappy sandals.

'And you say you had no way to ID her? So no handbag?'

'We haven't found one yet. Of course, that may be why she was walking – say it had been nicked, and she had no money for a taxi,' Remington said.

His blue eyes were guileless. It was obviously natural to him to try to make sense of the world by supplying reasonable solutions to questions. And reasonable they were. It was only Slider who wanted there to be a mystery. Oh well, he thought, at least I've got out of the office for a bit, had a ride out into the country.

'D'you want to see the body?' asked Remington hospitably.

TWO

Starbucks Mater

A police surgeon was making a preliminary examination – a woman called Gill Carstairs, whom Slider had met before once or twice. She was around forty, a strong, rather plain woman of whose private life, it seemed, nothing was known; an achievement in itself in a field where women were still numerically weak and the subject of much impertinent curiosity. What Slider remembered best about her from previous encounters were her large red hands, and her straight dark hair, pulled back in a bun or pony-tail, but from which a single strand always slipped annoyingly forward over her face, making Slider long to get at her with a Kirbigrip.

Today the former were hidden by gloves and the latter restrained by the hood as she knelt in the white Noddy-suit over the body. She looked up – a rather pale face and unexpectedly brown eyes – as Slider approached.

'Hello,' she said. 'What are you doing here? Aren't you Hammersmith?'

'She's apparently one of my locals.'

'Oh, I see. So *she*'s the one out of her comfort zone. Is she missing?'

'Not that anyone's reported. So far.'

The body was lying on its back now, decently straightened out, revealing a pudgily young face with a wide nose and a full underlip, pink with hypostasis except around the mouth and nose. The upper lip had been pushed up by her face-down position, giving her a contemptuous sneer. Part of the left ear had been eaten and one of the toes had been nibbled.

'Weasels, probably,' said Carstairs. 'Toothmarks too small for foxes.'

The hair was long, slightly wavy, dark brown with artificial highlights. The jacket was open, under which she was wearing a cropped top in baby pink with a Hello Kitty design on the front, and below it a very abbreviated black leather skirt which movement had rucked up above her thighs to reveal lacy pink panties. The combination of nursery cartoon and hooker-wear was unsettling.

Snugged in the middle of the gap between top and bottom, her belly button looked red and sore.

'Navel piercing,' Slider said, 'with the ring missing. Could it have been torn off in the accident?'

'I don't think so,' said Carstairs. 'If it had happened at the time of death, it would be a completely fresh wound. I'd say from the swelling it was at least some hours earlier.'

'Had a quarrel with her boyfriend maybe,' said Remington. 'He pulled it out in the fight. She stormed off, forgetting her handbag, tried to walk home.'

'When do you think she died?' Slider asked.

'Rigor's almost completely gone,' said Carstairs, her big hand gently feeling the jaw, 'so you'd be looking at – what? – probably Saturday night, early Sunday morning.'

'Makes sense,' Remington said. 'Saturday night, out on a date. Probably a drunken quarrel with the boyfriend, she's trying to walk home, maybe trying to hitch a lift, along comes chummy, going too fast in a dark lane, and – whammo.'

Slider leaned closer. 'I'm no expert,' he said, 'but those knickers look wrong.'

Carstairs gave him an amused glance over her shoulder. '*Knickers*? Girls don't wear knickers any more!'

'Whatever it is, that reinforcing gusset should be on the inside, shouldn't it?'

Carstairs slipped a finger under the elastic and pulled them out to look at the inside of the cloth. Slider couldn't help noticing that the pubic area was quite hairless, which in a girl of her age must mean waxing. Another disturbing image. 'Quite right,' said Carstairs. 'She's got them on inside out.'

'She must've got dressed in a hurry,' said Remington. 'After the fight.'

Carstairs continued with her slow examination, and Slider and Remington moved away a few steps.

'So, seen enough?' Remington asked. 'I never thought you'd come out yourself. You must've been desperate for some fresh air,' he added genially.

'Well, when it's one of your own . . .' Slider said.

'No mystery about it, though,' said Remington. 'Except what she was doing out here. I suppose we'll have to find out who the boyfriend was. And the usual round of the garages and repair shops, try and find if chummy's noticed the damage to his motor yet. It'll be a long job,' he sighed. 'Unless he does the decent and comes forward. They often do, when they've had a chance to stew. Nothing here for you, anyway – unless you want to do the Knock?'

'That would make sense, as it's on our ground. We'll take that off your hands for you,' said Slider.

'Thanks,' said Remington. 'Saturday night, eh? You'd wonder why nobody's missed her yet.' He mused a moment. 'But she looks as though she might have been a bit of a handful. Anyway, I'll let you know if anything interesting comes up.'

'Same here,' said Slider. He shook hands, and walked away to join Atherton, who had been talking to the collision scene officer.

'No skid marks,' Atherton reported. 'No sign of hasty braking or accelerating. Either he didn't know he'd hit her, or he just carried on regardless.' He looked curiously at his boss. 'What *are* we doing here?'

'I was bored with community liaising. Anyway, she comes from our ground. I told DCI Remington we'd do the Knock.'

The breeze was bowling some dark-bellied April clouds across the sky from the northwest.

'It's going to rain on us any minute now,' Atherton observed. 'You know this area, don't you?'

Slider had lived in Ruislip – a village a few miles away – with his first wife. He knew what Atherton was really asking. 'There's a decentish little pub not far from here,' he said, glancing at his watch. 'And a man has to eat.'

The Rose and Crown was wrapped in Monday quiet, but it had a log fire going. A couple of locals and a black Labrador had taken the table closest to it, and the air smelled agreeably of fresh burning wood, old wax jackets and damp dog. Slider and Atherton took a table where they could see the leaping flames, and ordered ham, egg and chips. With the small number of customers, the food arrived quickly.

'There *was* something odd about it,' Atherton said at last, having taken a long pull at his pint. 'The edge of the ditch where the body was found wasn't broken down or the grass flattened at all. You'd expect some sign of passage if she had rolled in. It looks as though she was thrown in a perfect arc.'

'Well, that's possible. If the vehicle was going fast and hit her hard enough, she would have just flown,' said Slider.

'But then, wouldn't she have landed on her back?'

'You think she was hit from the front?'

'She was on the left side of the road, the driver's left, I mean,' Atherton said.

'You're assuming she was walking facing the oncoming traffic like a well-trained country person.'

'No, I'm assuming she was heading *towards* London,' Atherton said. 'Trying to get home. Why would she have been walking further into the alien countryside?'

'She might have been lost and not known where she was or which way was up,' said Slider. 'And people who don't know any better are more likely to walk on the same side as they drive. But there was something odd about it, all the same. Her shoes. If the impact had knocked her right out of them—'

'Which could happen.'

'Right.' They had both seen their share of traffic accidents. Things a layman wouldn't believe could happen were common occurrence when speeding metal met human form. 'But they're not the sort of sandals you can just slip off, yet none of the straps were broken. And the heels, which are the weakest spot, weren't broken either. And why did they end up in the ditch?'

'Well, perhaps she had taken them off and was carrying them, like Mr Remington said,' Atherton offered.

'The soles of her feet weren't dirty enough to have been walking barefoot. And,' Slider continued before Atherton could discount that one, 'her pants were on inside out.'

Atherton looked at him steadily. 'So what are you saying? It wasn't a hit-and-run?'

'I didn't say that. Just that there's something odd about it. Starting with someone from Birdwood House being in Harefield in the first place.'

'So you did have an instinct about it,' Atherton said triumphantly. 'I *thought* there was something going on.'

Slider didn't want to sound fey. 'Instinct is just the subconscious assimilation of evidence.'

'Tell that to the marines,' said Atherton. 'Or rather, to Mr Porson.'

Porson wasn't pleased. 'I don't expect my senior officers to go off on pleasure jaunts. A hit-and-run? What were you thinking? If you haven't got enough to do I can soon find you something.'

Slider's father had said the same thing to him when he was a boy, if he ever complained about being bored. 'I've plenty to do, sir,' he began.

'I should hope so, if I'm going to get a replacement for Hollis. You go taking over cases from other boroughs and you've blown our argument for more personnel right out of the water park.'

'I just said we'd inform the family, sir. Obviously the Harefield enquiries are better handled by the local team.'

'I'm glad you think so.' Porson stopped to cough rackingly and then had to blow his nose. He had a box of man-size tissues on his desk, and his wastepaper basket was already half full.

'You shouldn't be here, sir,' Slider said.

Porson gave him an inflamed and resentful look. 'Had to come in for the funeral. Anyway, my boiler's broken down. Cold as a witch's cucumber at home. I'm better off here.' He seemed to soften. 'Do you think there's something in this RTA, then?'

'No, sir, not really. But I would like to know what she was doing there, and why nobody's missed her. She was only fifteen.'

'Ah. Bastard when they die that young. And I hate hit-and-runs.' He had another blow. 'But don't waste time on it. We've got to watch our productivity these days.'

Slider nodded. Their new Borough Commander, Mike Carpenter, was mustard on the spreadsheets. Rumour had already gone round that he was lettered 'budget' all through, like a stick of rock.

'Here we are,' said DC Kathleen 'Norma' Swilley, elegant in a beige trouser suit, her blonde hair held back with combs. 'Kaylee Adams.

Age fifteen – sixteen in December. Lives with her mother and younger sister on the estate. No father around. Mother's on benefits. Kaylee goes to Richard Towneley school – when she goes. Poor attendance record.'

Richard Towneley – the most misspelled school in the state sector – was the local secondary which had risen all the way from 'sink' to 'special measures' and was now officially described as 'challenging', meaning that the police had all too frequent contact with its inmates. Some might say that truant Kaylee Adams would have benefitted more from staying away.

'Disruptive behaviour, fighting and so on when she is there,' Swilley went on. 'Arrested four times for shoplifting, starting age nine, but let off with a warning and a referral to social services. Social services—' she turned a page – 'had her marked up as at risk. Mother was on drugs, possibly paying for them with prostitution. But after the fourth bust, Mum seems to have cleaned up her act. She went to rehab classes, hasn't come on the radar since. That was eighteen months ago, and apart from truanting, Kaylee hasn't been in trouble either.' She looked up. 'That's all that's on her arrest record. I haven't run her through Crimint yet.'

'Right,' said Slider. 'Do that, just in case. And before the mother hears it from somewhere else, we'd better send someone round to the flat.'

'Uniform, sir?'

Slider thought a moment. He still didn't quite feel easy about this hit-and-run. 'No, I'd like one of us to go. Sniff around without being too obvious. What's Connolly doing?'

'I'll get her,' said Swilley, and departed.

The rain had been swift in passing, and the wet pavements gleamed again in the sunlight from a sky like faded denim. The White City Estate was a vast area of five-storey former council flats, all named after heroes of the Empire. Birdwood House was one of the smaller, older blocks, so it had no lift and number twelve was on the top floor. It would be, Connolly thought, as she paused on the balcony outside the flat to catch her breath and look at the view. It wasn't bad for an inner-city estate – a grassy lawn between the blocks and a big tree waving naked fingers over the top of the roofs. She'd grown up in grimmer surroundings in Dublin.

She rang the bell, and hearing no sound from inside, knocked as well, in case the bell was broken. Eventually, a child's voice said from inside, 'Who is it?'

'It's the police, love,' Connolly said. 'Is your mum in? I'd like to talk to her.'

A pause. 'How do I know you're the police?'

'Just fetch your mum, willya.'

'She's asleep.'

'It's important. Open the door a little bit and I'll show you my warrant card.'

The door opened slowly to halfway, enough to reveal a skinny child of about ten, with thin, slightly sticky fair hair. Her face was so pale that her mouth looked unnaturally pink by contrast, as if she had been sucking a cheap lolly. She was dressed in pink cut-offs with sequins round the cuffs and a grubby T-shirt.

She observed Connolly solemnly. 'You got a funny voice,' she said.

'It's me Irish accent,' said Connolly. 'Have you never met anyone from Ireland?'

She thought about that. 'My friend Abshiro's from Somalia,' she offered.

'What's your name, pet?' Connolly asked.

'Julienne,' the child said proudly. 'That's with an e. There's a Julie Anne in my class but that's, like, two words. I like mine better.'

'It's a nice name,' Connolly said. Name a God, who'd call their child after a method of chopping vegetables, she thought. But then she remembered the mother had been on drugs. 'Can you go and wake your mum up for me? I have to talk to her. It's very important.'

The pink mouth turned down. 'I don't like waking her up. Sometimes she's really ratty.'

'I'll come with you, if you like,' said Connolly. The child backed off and let her in to the narrow passage. The flat smelled stale, of dirty clothes and the ghosts of many meals of fried food and take-aways. Through the door on the left was a small, cramped kitchen awash with pizza boxes, KFC tubs and cardboard coffee containers. The door at the end of the passage was closed. Julienne stopped in front of it and looked back at Connolly. 'That's mum's room.'

'Shouldn't you be at school?' Connolly asked belatedly.

'I stayed home,' she said simply. 'I don't like leaving her when she's like this.'

'Has she taken something?'

'Like, White Lightning an' vodka. Her and Jaffa was partying last night. I think he brought coke and something as well. But he's gone now.'

'Is that her boyfriend?' Connolly asked. The girl shrugged. 'So she's on her own now? Well, let's wake her up, then.'

The bedroom was in gloom from the drawn curtains, and was a frowsty-smelling pit of old clothes, full ashtrays, empty plastic bottles and other litter. The woman face down in the tangle of bed sheets was visible only by her hair. Connolly stepped across the room cautiously to pull the curtains and open the window, letting in a draught of cold clean air. The body in the bed started to stir and mutter. Julienne stood at the door, apparently unwilling to take part, but a cough and a jerk of the head from Connolly induced her to step forward and shake a shoulder.

'Mum, wake up. Mum! The police're here. A lady policeman. She wants to talk to you. Mum!'

The body moaned, thrashed a bit, muttered some profanities, and finally sat up, shoving hair out of its face and rubbing its eyes. 'What you friggin' wakin' me for, you little pest?' she growled at Julienne, who stood her ground expressionlessly, then glanced significantly towards Connolly.

The woman was startled. 'Oh my good Gawd! Who're you? What you doin' in my house?'

'Detective Constable Connolly, Shepherd's Bush police. I have to talk to you, Mrs Adams. Would you get up, please.'

The woman rolled her eyes. 'Now what?' she complained. 'What you always coming round here for, bothering me, frightening my kids? We haven't done nothing. If it's Jaf you're after, he's long gone. And I don't know where he hangs out, so it's no use asking.'

But she was dragging herself out of bed. Connolly was deeply relieved to discover she was wearing an oversized T-shirt for a nightie. She slung her feet over the side, sat on the edge of the bed, rubbing one foot up the back of the other leg, and indulged in a long and phlegmy coughing session. Then she wiped her nose on her hand, rubbed her eyes again, and muttered, 'Got a mouth like a hamster's cage.'

'What about a cup of tea,' Connolly suggested to get things moving along.

'There's no tea,' said the woman. 'Only instant. Jule, make us one, ey?' The child sidled away. 'Here,' Mrs Adams went on, her expression suddenly sharpening, 'what you being nice for? What's going on?' Alarm followed suspicion. 'Something's happened, hasn't it? Tell me.'

'You'd better get up and get dressed first,' said Connolly, not sure she was fully compos mentis yet.

But the woman stared at Connolly, her face hardening. 'If you got something to say, say it. Tell me what you come here for right now, or get the fuck out.'

Connolly sighed inwardly. 'I'm afraid I've got some bad news for you,' she said. 'It's about your daughter.'

'What, Julienne? I don't believe you. She's a good kid.'

'No, your other daughter,' said Connolly. 'Kaylee.'

'Kaylee? She's not in trouble. She's doing all right, now.' Julienne had oozed back again from the kitchen. 'Here, Jule, where's Kaylee?'

'I don't know, Mum.'

'What d'you mean, you don't know? Didn't she go to school this morning?'

'I've not seen her, not since Sat'dy morning.'

'Mrs Adams—'

'Has something happened to her?'

The child was looking at Connolly with eyes very like her mother's, a little pink round the rims and infinitely old. There was no help for it. 'I'm afraid there's been an accident,' she said.

Mrs Adams, dressed in a smart Marks & Sparks dressing gown of chocolate brown with white polka dots, sat on the sofa cradling a mug of poisonous instant coffee that the child had made for her. Connolly knew it was poisonous because she'd been given one, too, made with tepid water (out of the hot tap, she guessed) from the cheapest powder and without milk or sugar.

'I hate this stuff,' Mrs Adams moaned. 'I need my Starbucks. I'm no good till I've had my Frappuccino, am I, Jule?' But she sipped at it anyway. Perhaps anything in the mouth was better than nothing.

She had pulled back her tangled hair – curly, mid-brown with purplish highlights – with a scrunchie, revealing a face so ordinary it would be hard to remember it the moment you turned your back. It was pale and pouchy, and looked mid- to late-forties, which given the drug use probably meant she was mid- to late-thirties. Her eyes and nose were pink, and she sniffed constantly and dabbed hopelessly with a handkerchief, but that could have been the cocaine as much as anything. She had wept a bit when Connolly told her, but it looked more like a performance of what she thought, from an extensive consumption of TV, would be expected of her. Whatever genuine grief and shock she might feel was probably swimming upstream against the drugs and several litres of Russian cider.

Julienne leaned against the arm of the sofa the furthest from her mother. She had made the coffee, fetched cigarettes when her mother demanded them. Otherwise she had taken no part, said nothing, only watched, her eyes moving from one speaker to the other, her face set and mute, with that look of simply enduring that you see on children's faces all over the world when they have witnessed something incomprehensible happening in the adult world.

The room was an oddity, compared with the kitchen and mother's bedroom. The flat had been done out in standard developer's off-white walls and cheap beige carpet, but in the middle of the sitting-room floor there was a square rug of purple swirls on a grey background, and the walls had been papered in a pattern of enormous purple flowers which, while vile, was certainly not cheap. There was a large sofa, nearly new, facing a huge wall-mounted TV, which must have cost a bit. Most different of all, it was tidy, moderately clean, and was suffused with a throat-choking peach air-freshener, an evident attempt at refined living.

Connolly wondered where the money came from. The mother's boyfriend? Meanwhile, she wasn't getting anywhere with her questions. Kaylee went out Saturday lunchtime to visit a friend, saying she wouldn't be back that night. She often stayed over with friends when they went out together. Where did they go? Up the West End. Clubbing. Just like anyone else. Worried about not seeing her on Sunday? Course not. She was a big girl, she could take care of herself. Likely she'd've still been with the friend. Which friend? Couldn't say. Kaylee had so many. She was a very popular girl.

'What might she have been doing in Harefield?' Connolly asked.

'Harefield?' Mrs Adams said. 'Where's that?'

'Out Uxbridge way. Ruislip?'

'Never heard of it. Never been to Uxbridge in me life.'

'Do you have any relatives out that way? Friends. Someone Kaylee might have visited?'

'No,' she said indignantly. 'I tell you, I've never heard of the place.'

'Perhaps Kaylee's got a boyfriend who lives there.' Mrs Adams shrugged. 'Does Kaylee have a boyfriend?'

'Not that I know of. No one special.'

'Really? I find that hard to believe. A lovely girl of fifteen?'

'Lovely' was pushing it a bit, but what mother doesn't think her daughter a beauty? There was a school photograph of Kaylee Adams that the mother had produced on Connolly's request from a drawer stuffed with papers. It had been taken the previous June, when Kaylee was fourteen, and showed a face as ordinary as the mother's, with the round cheeks and full lips of youth and a look of cheeky self-confidence. She had supple skin and thick hair and a certain freshness, so she was attractive in the way all young creatures are, but that was all.

'I'm sure she must have had lots of boyfriends,' Connolly insisted.

'She's hung about with some of the boys at school, I s'pose,' Mrs Adams said indifferently, 'but not anyone like you might call a boyfriend. She's not interested in 'em like that. She wants to better herself – got ambition, my Kaylee. She's doing all right for herself now that bit of trouble's behind her.'

'Doing all right?' Connolly queried, but the mother didn't answer. 'But she's still truanting, isn't she?'

'She's what?'

'Bunking off school.'

Mrs Adams looked indignant. 'Why shouldn't she? What use is school to a girl her age? They never learn her nothing anyway. Shouldn't force fifteen-year-olds to go to school. Making jobs for teachers, that's all it is,' she grumbled. 'My Kaylee can make her own way, thank you very much. Doing all right, like I said. Why, she's . . .' She began to wave a hand, but stopped herself abruptly.

Connolly had a flash of insight. It was Kaylee who had bought the TV, smartened up the room. The dressing gown, too, perhaps – being good to her mother. But where did she get the money from? However, that was not in the scope of her present visit.

She tried a few more questions about boyfriends and Harefield, but couldn't get anything out of Mrs Adams: she seemed genuinely never to have heard of the place, and was probably as genuinely ignorant of her daughter's dating practices – even probably of her whereabouts day to day. Connolly had an idea that Julienne might know more about her sister's comings and goings, but she couldn't question a ten-year-old without good reason. And so far, the good reason did not exist.

And now at last the fact that Kaylee was dead was finally beginning to register, and the mother in Mrs Adams was starting to ask questions of her own, many of them the same as Connolly's, and to which of course Connolly didn't have the answers.

THREE
Coupe and Contrecoup

'You'd want to've seen her. Swear t' God, there's farm cats that are better mothers,' Connolly concluded her report to Slider. 'If we hadn't gone round, I wonder when she *would* have started to miss her own kid.' She gave Slider a bright, curious look. 'So will you be having any follow-up, boss? I mean, we're no closer to why she was in Harefield at all, but . . .'

But there's nothing here for us to investigate – those were the words Connolly didn't need to articulate. Slider was about to speak when Swilley appeared in the doorway.

'The Adams girl, sir. I put the name through Crimint.'

'And?' Slider encouraged.

'She came up in connection with the Tyler Vance business.'

'Ah! That must be where I heard her name before,' said Slider.

'Tyler Vance? Why does that sound familiar?' Connolly asked.

'Tyler Vance was a fourteen-year-old girl from Shepherd's Bush whose body was found in the Thames,' Slider explained. 'When was it?'

'January,' said Swilley.

'Oh, right,' said Connolly. 'But we didn't investigate it, did we?'

'It wasn't our case,' said Slider. 'Don't you remember, the body washed up much further downstream, and Westminster conducted the inquiry. It was determined that she'd probably gone into the water somewhere near Hammersmith Bridge, so there was some local interest from Borough Command, but nothing came out and the case went cold.'

'Anyway, it seems Kaylee Adams and Vance were friends and went to the same school,' said Swilley. 'She was interviewed about it at the time.'

'Was she raped?' Connolly asked.

'Vance? There'd been some rough sex,' Swilley said, 'but it might have been consensual – the evidence was she was sexually experienced.'

'She was only fourteen,' Slider said shortly. 'Which means it was rape.'

'Technically, yes,' Swilley admitted.

'So,' said Connolly, looking from one to the other, 'what does that mean for this other thing, the Kaylee Adams death?'

'Probably nothing,' said Slider. 'Adams is probably just an RTA. Nothing really to suggest otherwise.'

'And we're short-handed anyway.' Swilley concluded the reasoning for him.

On cue, Porson appeared at Slider's other door and beckoned. 'A word,' he said.

In his office, Porson reclaimed his normal zone of restlessness – the strip of floor between his desk and the window – and prowled up and down it as he spoke.

'I've had Detective Superintendent Fox on the blower, about this hit-and-run. He can't account to himself for one of my DCIs tipping up at an RTA. He's asking what our interest is.'

Det Sup Cliff 'Duggie' Fox (he was a large, fleshy man with unexpectedly well-developed mammaries) was the head of Uxbridge CID, a man ferociously territorial, ambitious, and suspicious of any approach he could not immediately recognize as hostile to his interests. His unhelpfulness to fellow officers was legendary. Wouldn't give a glass of water to a drowning man. Or, in the London vernacular, 'he wouldn't give you the drippings off his nose'.

However, the recent cuts had forced a new perspective on the

Foxes of the Met world, and if a case looked like being troublesome, it made more sense to try to shove it off onto some other borough, where it would hit their budget and be their problem.

'He was fishing about, trying to fathom if it was *more* than leaving-the-scene-of-an-accident, in which case the imprecation was we could have it, with a cherry on top. I didn't rightly know what to tell him. As far as I know, we *haven't* got any interest. Have we?'

He gave Slider as much of a look of puppy-dog appeal as a man with a heavy cold could manage. Slider hesitated, and Porson put a hand to his head and moaned. 'Oh my good Gawd. Don't tell me!'

'It could be nothing, sir,' Slider said, 'but it turns out she was connected with Tyler Vance.'

'Vance? What, that body that was fished out of the Thames?'

Trust the old boy to remember the name, Slider thought. 'Yes, sir. Adams was interviewed as Vance's friend.'

'And?'

'She said she didn't know anything.' A snort. 'But of course she would say that. And there are some things about the hit-and-run I don't like. No handbag. Her pants were on inside out. Her navel piercing had been pulled out. And there doesn't seem to be any reason for her to be out there in the first place.'

'All of which could have perfectly reasonable explications.'

'I know, sir, but—'

'But me no buts. We can't waste time and manpower on every little trollop who has a row with her boyfriend and tries to walk home.'

'She was only fifteen, sir.'

'Thanks for reminding me.' He glared at Slider. 'She's not even been reported missing. We can't go making stuff up.'

Slider looked back uncomfortably. After a moment he said, 'We've got nothing major on hand at the moment, sir.'

Porson did another couple of lengths, a walk violent enough to have set fire to the carpet. Then he stopped in the centre, leaned his fists on his desk, and said, 'I suppose you want Cameron to do the PM?'

It was capitulation. 'I'd prefer it, sir.'

'Duggie Fox'll be grinning his tail off,' Porson muttered. 'All right, you can make some preliminary enquiries, but if nothing comes up by the end of the week that's it, understand? And if the driver comes forward meantime, it goes straight back to an RTA.'

'Of course, sir,' said Slider. Having got permission to look into it, he was as unhappy as Porson could have wanted him to be. If there was anything in it, it was likely to be the sort of anything that gave him sleepless nights, worrying about the state of the nation. 'Can I have extra manpower, sir? And overtime?'

'Not until you find something to warrant it,' Porson snapped.

'What about a replacement for Hollis?'

Porson had had enough. 'And a couple of pints of my blood while you're at it?' he bellowed.

Slider tiptoed out.

Atherton had joined the group hanging round his doorway. It was going-home time for the department, but everyone wanted to know where they stood. Was there going to be an investigation, or wasn't there?

'Doc Cameron's going to do the post-mortem,' he told them.

They exchanged looks. 'And?' Atherton asked for them all.

'We'll see what comes up,' Slider said. 'Then we'll know.'

'And if anything does?'

'You'll know when I know.'

They drifted away to their desks to start packing up. Atherton lingered. 'Want to go for a pint?' he offered.

'Haven't you got a date?'

'Yes, but not until later. She's in court today. She's going to ring when they adjourn.'

Slider didn't ask who 'she' was. At the last count Atherton was dating three solicitors. He seemed to have a thing for them. Swilley thought it was unhealthy. She said it was Atherton's equivalent of snake-handling – the thrill of danger plus perversely embracing natural repulsion.

'Thanks, but I'll pass,' Slider said. 'I haven't spent an evening with my wife for a while.'

Joanna was practising when he got home, proof that George had been long enough in bed not to be disturbed by it. And there was, he was glad to note, a warm smell of cooking in the background.

She stopped when he walked over and kissed her. 'What was that?' he asked.

'Smetana's *Buttered Bread*. Lots of tricky bits. And they've put it in a concert with *Don Juan*. What do they want – blood?'

'Difficult?'

'Well, it's not a walk in the park,' she said. 'Want some supper?'

'Please. I'm starving. Smells good – what is it?'

'Neck of lamb stew. It's all ready in the oven.'

There were mashed potatoes and green beans too, and when he sat down at the kitchen table she brought the bottle of Lirac they had started the night before and sat down with him to drink a companionable glass.

'Lovely,' he said.

'You look tired,' she said.

'It's been a full, rough day,' he said.

'The funeral was a bit of a downer,' she said mildly.

Slider started. 'Good Lord, I'd forgotten about that. So much seems to have happened since then.'

'Oh dear, don't tell me!'

'It might be nothing. A fatal hit-and-run, but the victim may be connected to an old case, so it has to be looked into.'

'Oh,' Joanna said, but seemed reassured by his words. A traffic accident was nothing to bother her man.

He roused himself. 'I hope the funeral didn't upset you too much. I couldn't help knowing – well, the date was significant.'

She looked at him across the rim of the glass. 'I didn't think you'd remembered. I hoped you hadn't.'

'Of course I remembered. I'm so sorry, Jo. It must have hurt, thinking about it.'

Her eyes moved away, proving it was still painful, though she said, 'It's all in the past now. Let's not talk about it.'

He chewed a mouthful, and then obliged by saying, 'What's it like being back at work?'

'Hard,' she said. 'Though of course, being further back in the section you can hide a bit more.' She had been Deputy Principal in the Royal London Philharmonic, but after having so much time off she had had to take a rearward desk when she went back. 'And of course, it has to be remembered I'm older than I was. Getting back up to speed takes more out of you when you get past thirty.'

'Oh, past thirty is a tremendous age,' Slider scoffed.

'It is when you've got kids coming out of the colleges these days who can do stuff only virtuosi could manage ten, twenty years ago,' she said. 'It's all us oldies can do to hang on to a place. Dickie Strauss! And Bruckner, my God! Twenty-four minutes of non-stop tremolo!'

'Aren't the modern pieces worse?'

'Well, they aren't heaven. Dutilleux, for instance. Very fast string crossings, playing diminished fifths across three strings, staccato. But you're more exposed in the classical repertoire.' She grinned. 'When the audience can actually tell if you play a wrong note.'

'I thought they were all ignoramuses?'

'Not *all*,' she said generously. 'Top you up?'

'Thanks.'

'Phil Redcliffe was telling a funny story about *Don Juan* today. Apparently a student of his said she was going to play it in her college orchestra and asked what it was like. He said it was hard and she ought to get the part out ahead and practise. She came back and said the music library had never heard of it. Turned out she'd been asking for "Don's First Symphony".'

It took a moment. 'Oh, Don One, I get it,' he said.

She shrugged. 'Well, it was funny at the time. What's this new case of yours?'

'I don't know if it is a case yet.'

'Well, what's the case it might be connected to?'

'Tyler Vance,' he admitted reluctantly.

Joanna looked concerned. 'Oh no. Not that one again. They never got anyone for it, did they?' It was the sort of thing that bothered him most – helpless victims, especially females, who never received even post-mortem justice. She looked at him sternly across the table. 'You're not to let it get to you.'

'No, ma'am.' He had to deflect the attention from himself. 'How's my boy?'

'We had a lovely afternoon finger painting,' she said. 'It's nice to have a bit of time with him. Although the schedule will start heating up soon.'

'You don't have to take every gig that's offered,' he said.

'I know, but if you turn down too many, you slide down the fixer's list. They want someone they know they can rely on. And with all these young hotshots fresh out of college, all competing for the same work, it doesn't do to get picky. You can bet your life *they*'ll be hustling for every date.'

'They may have bionic arms and tungsten fingers,' Slider said, 'but they can't replace experience.' And to her sceptically raised eyebrow he said with a grin, 'At least you've heard of "Don's First Symphony".'

Freddie Cameron was doing the autopsy – or, as he always insisted was more correct, necropsy – the following morning. Slider went in to his office early to reacquaint himself with the Tyler Vance case. Not that there was much of a case to absorb. Tyler was a fourteen-year-old from Mayhew House, a care home in Scott's Road. No one knew who her father was, and her mother had died of a drug overdose when she was twelve. She had been running wild ever since. However, in the last few months of her life she seemed to have calmed down. It was only after her death that other girls in the home admitted she had been getting out of the home at night, not returning until the early hours. No one knew where she had been going, though it was thought she was meeting a boyfriend.

She was reported missing one day and washed up two days later on the beach of the Thames opposite the Southbank complex. She had not drowned: the post mortem said she had been dead when she went into the water, and the cause of death was eventually determined to be heart failure, probably brought on by the quantity of drink and drugs the tox screen discovered in her system. There had also been a previously unrevealed congenital heart defect. Her mother had had a similar weakness.

No one knew where she had been or who she had been with: she had kept her secrets impressively well for a fourteen-year-old. There were, however, signs that she had engaged in a lot of sexual activity shortly before death, and from her physiology she had been far from a virgin. It was assumed that the boyfriend she had been slipping out to see had dumped her in the river in fright when she unexpect-edly dropped dead in the middle of partying; but who the boyfriend was they had never been able to discover, and no witness to the disposing of the body had ever come forward.

Kaylee Adams's name had come up as being Tyler's closest friend in the same class at Robert Towneley. Denise 'Deenie' O'Hare had also been named as being in the same circle, but denied she had ever been a friend of Vance. Kaylee admitted friendship, but said she knew nothing about Vance's nocturnal adventures. Whether she really knew nothing, or rather wouldn't tell, was, of course, impossible to know.

With no leads and no witnesses, and – perhaps it was not too cynical to say – no family with an interest in discovering the truth, Westminster had let the case go cold. Slider had felt bad about it at the time. A fourteen-year-old girl ought to have her life before her, not be thrown out like a sack of rubbish.

Apart from the photograph taken after death, there was one snap in the file with a note that it had been taken some time before, possibly as much as a year earlier. It was one from a photo-booth series, and showed Tyler's face squashed in between two others. The one on her right was tagged as Kaylee; the one on her left as Shannon Bailey, who, it was noted, had been at the same school but had left six months before the incident, and had not been interviewed. She was a mixed-race girl with long corkscrews of gold-lighted brown hair, who was pulling an abominable face, eyes crossed, tongue stuck out and waggling. Kaylee was laughing hugely, her eyes squeezed shut and her mouth was wide open, so not much could be seen of her face.

Tyler, in the middle, was a thin-faced, pixie-ish girl with dead straight, pale blonde hair, and she was staring wide-eyed and straight ahead, with an air of anticipation – though she was probably just waiting for the flash to go off. He'd have liked to see the rest of the series, but only the one snap was on file. Possibly the other girls had them.

Slider stared a long time, and Tyler Vance stared back. She had delicate shadows under her eyes and her cheeks were hollow – attractive perhaps in a catwalk-model way, but possibly hinting at ill health. Or was it the strain of the last few months of her life showing through?

And now her friend Kaylee was dead. Coincidence? Quite possible – but Slider didn't like coincidences. Too often they were God's way of telling you there was something that needed looking at.

Freddie Cameron had enough connections with the Charing Cross Hospital to make use of their state-of-the-art facilities, which now included a remote viewing suite where the various hangers-on – what Freddie had always called 'the football crowd' – could watch without getting in the way. At the table beside him he had only his assistant, a favoured student, and Slider.

'So, what's your interest in this one?' Cameron asked through a miasma of peppermint. He always sucked Trebor's Extra Strong. Slider had besides taken the precaution of smearing Vicks ointment round his nostrils before putting on the mask. Death smells, even to someone without Slider's hypersensitive nose.

'I don't know, really. Just curiosity at first – couldn't think what a girl like this was doing out in carrot country. And then when I got there, it just didn't sit right with me.'

'Ah! Well, I shall do my best to salvage your position,' said Cameron. 'It interests me, just at a first glance, that all the injuries are to the back.'

'That bothered me, too,' said Slider, 'because it suggested she was walking the wrong way, away from London, instead of towards home.'

'Maybe she was running away,' the student suggested.

'But then she surely would have been carrying something,' Slider said. 'Does anyone run away without taking anything at all?'

'Pay attention, Jason,' Cameron said sternly, 'while I educate you. Pedestrians struck by cars generally suffer a well-recognized pattern of injuries. The front bumper usually strikes first, hitting at or just below knee level. Then the thigh or hip may be struck by the radiator or bonnet. With a bigger vehicle, like, say, a Chelsea tractor or a lorry, primary injuries may be at chest level. Then, of course, the body is projected by the momentum and suffers secondary injuries on impact with – whatever it impacts. Such as?'

'The road?' Jason hazarded.

'Yes, resulting in various fractures; and you'll often see "brush abrasions" from skidding along the ground. Or the victim may be rotated up onto the bonnet.'

'Scooping up, we call it,' Slider put in.

'Where he may strike the windscreen or pillars, causing head injuries,' Cameron went on, 'before falling off into the road to gather yet more. I may say that the secondary injuries, caused by hitting the road, are more often the fatal element.'

'From the position of the body,' Slider said, 'it looks as though she flew forwards through the air and landed in a ditch.'

'Soft landing?' Jason asked.

'Well, it was dry,' Slider said, 'but compared with landing on the road, yes.'

'And there are no facial injuries,' Jason said, 'which fits with that.'

'Hm,' said Freddie, and continued with the external examination. The pale body lay prone, vulnerable, but less personal with the face hidden. 'Now, you see, the primary impact seems to have been at the pelvis, shoulder and head. That's not typical of collision with a motor vehicle.'

'Impossible?' Slider asked, unsure now whether he really wanted his doubt to be vindicated.

'Nothing's impossible, especially if the vehicle's travelling at speed. But it's not what I'd expect to see.'

He carried on, whistling as he went. It was his habit to whistle while cutting. Slider didn't think he knew he was doing it. After a moment, Slider recognized the tune as 'Little Deuce Coupe', and shuddered. He would *not* want to examine Freddie's subconscious, he thought.

'Plentiful traces of lubricant in the rectum and vagina,' Freddie said when they came to that bit. 'No semen, unfortunately. It looks like recent sexual activity.'

'Rape?' Slider asked.

'I think probably not,' said Cameron. 'Nothing to suggest it wasn't consensual. There's some bruising of the vaginal wall but no laceration. No defence injuries, no sign that she was tied down or restrained.'

'What about the injury to the navel?'

'Yes, I'd say some kind of piercing was ripped out, but that could happen during consensual sex too. It's a pity the pubic area has been waxed. It's usually a fertile ground for trapping foreign hairs. Ah well, let's have a rummage about inside, shall we?'

Cameron stopped whistling when he came to the examination of the brain. The bit Slider liked least was the whine of the electric saw as it took the top off the skull, like a power tool for a boiled egg. The student was swaying a little on his feet, though whether that was from squeamishness or fatigue Slider couldn't tell. It had been a long session – but informative.

'Well,' Freddie said at last, 'you can take your pick as to the cause of death. 'Transection of the thoracic spine. Crush injuries to the liver. Personally, I'd go with brain damage.'

'From the fractured skull,' Jason said, eager to show he was still awake. 'Impact with a motor vehicle going at speed.'

'The back of the skull is certainly fractured, but it's not the busting of the bone that does the trick, as my friend Chief Inspector Slider here will tell you.'

'Shearing stresses,' Slider said intelligently.

'Quite so,' said Freddie. 'Almost every blow to the head has some rotational component, which causes the layers of brain tissue at different depths to slide over one another, resulting in lesions and ruptured blood vessels.'

'But—' Slider began.

'Quite,' said Cameron, flicking him a look. 'That's not the case here. What caused the fatal damage here is contrecoup. You see, when a head that's free to move is struck a heavy blow, the damage usually occurs directly under the point of impact. However, if a head is falling and strikes a rigid surface, the brain tissue is projected away from the blow, and the damage is found at a point diametrically opposite the point of impact. Clear?'

'Yes sir.'

'Which is what we call contrecoup, from the French. Contra as in opposite—'

'And coup as in ice-cream,' Slider finished for him. Jason gave him a look. 'Just a little tension humour.'

'To help create more tension,' said Freddie. 'Now, in this case, the blow was to the anterior skull, but the frontal poles are contused and the undersurface of the frontal lobes are lacerated. There's your contrecoup. Also the thin bone of the anterior fossa is fractured, which, curiously, is caused by the forward momentum of the brain causing a partial vacuum in the fossa for a fraction of a second.'

Jason nodded intelligently. Slider's knowledge of anatomy was more basic, but he got the idea. 'So you're saying she fell?' he asked.

'Probably from a considerable height, landing on her back and striking her head against a hard surface, causing death. In my opinion, these injuries are not consistent with impact from a moving vehicle.'

Now Jason was looking puzzled. 'So – what does that mean? If she was found face down in a ditch—'

'That's not where she died,' Slider concluded sadly. He had the answer to his question now, and he wasn't glad he had been vindicated. 'Someone took her body out there and dumped it.'

Freddie looked at his old friend and said bracingly, 'She might well have fallen by accident, from a high window or a balcony. She was probably pretty wasted. There was no food in her stomach, but quite a lot of vodka, and who knows what else. I'm going to send off for a tox screen. Partying too hard, drinking, drugging, maybe having rumpy pumpy against the balcony rail and went over. It needn't be murder.'

Jason looked impressed at the word. 'Murder?' he repeated softly.

'I know,' said Slider. 'Thanks, Freddie.'

Probably not murder. But then, Tyler Vance probably wasn't murdered either. Didn't make any difference to their deadness. And the sex-plus-death-plus-dumping-the-body made it a coincidence too far. He knew he was going to have to investigate this one, and that it wouldn't be easy.

FOUR

Adams Family Values

Porson shook his head. 'It's not a murder investigation – and God knows we don't want one. Couldn't afford it. You'll have to make do with what you've got.'

'Falling from a height *could* be an accident,' said Slider, 'but someone tried to get rid of the body, and that looks suspicious.'

Porson was irritated. 'Do you think I don't know that? You know the financial situation. I'm like bloody Canute sticking his finger in the dyke! Borough Command scrupulizes every penny we spend. I can't put in for big biccies for something that's probably nothing. Uxbridge will follow up the Harefield end and ten to one they'll nail the bugger that dumped the body – *if* that's what happened.'

'Doc Cameron's report will say—'

'Yes, yes, not consistent with blah blah blah. That's his opinion. You can look into what she was up to, see if there's any connection with the Vance death, and that's my best offer.' He cocked an eye.

'You're a chief inspector now, Slider. You're on the inside. It's not them and us now, it's us and us. You know the score.'

Like Klemperer, Slider agreed silently. 'Yes, sir,' he said.

Porson softened. 'You've got to work within the restraints,' he said. 'But I'll see what I can do about replacing Hollis.'

Hollis, Slider thought as he trudged away. I keep forgetting and then being reminded.

Connolly went back to the Adams home, along with a woman constable, Lawrence, on the basis that a uniform sometimes helps to concentrate minds. 'But don't make any suggestion that the death was anything other than a traffic accident,' Slider instructed Connolly. 'Officially you're just trying to find out who she might have been with on Saturday night.'

'Gotcha,' Connolly said.

'And be very careful about mentioning Vance. There was nothing in the media at the time, so we don't want to spark anything off now. Make sure Lawrence understands.'

'I'll mind her, boss. Don't worry.'

The scene was very different when they got to Birdwood House, as they could see even from the yard below. 'It looks like open house,' Lawrence said. The front door was ajar and there were people on the balcony, standing around chatting or going in and out.

'Janey, your woman's having a wake,' Connolly said. 'We'd better get up there while there's anything left to see.'

It was clear that Mrs Adams, awake, clean and dressed this time, was taking full advantage of being the centre of attention. Neighbours had come round to share in the drama, and it had spread to the rest of the block, so that there were little knots on most balconies with their arms folded, having a good oul' natter, as Connolly observed to herself. Inside the flat, someone had made an effort at clearing up. All the fast-food containers had gone from the kitchen, and on the counter instead there were packets of biscuits and sausage rolls that visitors had brought, while a small but dedicated team was making relays of tea and handing out mugs.

The festive atmosphere intensified as you got nearer the heart of it, the sitting room where Mrs Adams was enthroned on the sofa, nose and eyes red and tissue in hand, alternately weeping and eulogizing her lost child, while her immediate companions plied her with tea and sympathy.

'Would you look at the carry-on of her,' Connolly muttered to Lawrence. 'Her kid's dead and she's going for an Oscar. Name a' God, it'd sicken you.'

At the sight of Connolly and Lawrence, Mrs Adams's moaning escalated to wailing. 'My baby! I can't stand it! My Kaylee's dead! Oh, who could do such a thing! Oh, I think I'm going out of my mind!'

This was the cue for several of the hangers-on to give the police stern and disapproving looks, and one of them tried to interpose herself between them and the grieving mother and said, 'Can't you leave her alone? You can see the state she's in!'

'We're very sorry for your loss, Mrs Adams,' Connolly said, ignoring the stranger. 'We'd like to take a look at Kaylee's room, if you don't mind. There may be some clue there that will help us find who she was with.'

Increased sobbing. 'They don't know! All this time and they still don't know who killed my baby!'

Connolly took that for permission and backed out. 'You circulate, see what you can get from the visitors,' she told Lawrence. With the prevailing excitement they'd probably be eager to talk. 'I'll find the bedroom.'

It wasn't hard to find in a two-bedroomed flat. It was slightly bigger than the mother's, about fifteen feet by twelve, and had the same cheap beige carpet and off-white walls, both much marked and worn. There were two single divan beds, one down either side, with a dressing table and mirror between the heads. At the foot of one bed was a wicker chair painted mauve by an amateur hand. Against the short wall by the door was a narrow Ikea wardrobe and beside it a matching three-drawer chest. Surprisingly, for such a small space, it was relatively tidy. Both beds had been made – at least, the duvets had been pulled up and straightened – and though there was a heap of clothes on the chair, and belongings cluttered the tops of both dressing table and chest, nothing had been left on the floor, and there were no empty plates or food detritus anywhere.

The bed under the window didn't have much wall space, but it was decorated with Disney princesses and mermaids, so Connolly assumed that was Julienne's. On the opposite wall, above the other bed, was a poster, old and creased and slightly torn at one corner, of One Direction, with a lipstick kiss imprinted on the face of Harry Styles. Long loved, but now forgotten? Or perhaps the love had been bequeathed to the next generation.

On the dressing table there were some half-used, crusty bottles of nail varnish in rather Goth colours, a sticky near-empty tube of foundation, a grubby zipper bag containing a few tired and used-up cosmetics, a brush clogged with hair and a set of eyelash curlers with one handle broken off. There were several well-thumbed copies of *Bliss* magazine (headline stories 'I KISSED BRITNEY SPEARS' and 'I WIPED MY BUM ON A SOCK!' – *o tempora! O mores!*) and some Julienne-sized knickers and socks, clean, that had not been put away. On the top of the chest were more ten-year-old's clothes, a drawing pad covered in princesses and a muddle of felt-tip pens, dolls, much-abused tweenie storybooks, bits of ribbon, hair ties, screwed-up tissues. The wardrobe was crammed with clothes, cheap, shabby, and many clearly Julienne's.

A sense of being watched made Connolly turn. Julienne had oozed quietly up to the door and was leaning against the frame there, her face set in an expression of mixed boredom and misery that said nothing was any good any more and it never would be again. She was wearing the same pink pedal pushers but with an outsize grey jumper pulled down vampishly to expose one bony shoulder, and today she was definitely wearing lipstick, though it didn't seem to have cheered her up.

'Hello,' Connolly said in a friendly way.

Julienne shrugged. Then she said, 'Is that lady policeman with you?'

'That's my friend Jilly,' Connolly said. 'She's all right.'

Julienne said listlessly, 'What you doing?'

'Hoping to find something that'll tell us where your sister was on Saturday night.'

'She don't keep her nice stuff here,' Julienne said. 'Mum keeps nicking it. She sells it to buy coke and stuff.'

Connolly wanted to encourage her. 'So this is your room now?'

'Sort of. It's hers too, but she's not here much, not now.' Evidently the past tense was not registering with the child yet. Kaylee was away, but would come back.

'I expect you miss her.'

'She comes back to see if we're all right,' Julienne said, as if Connolly had criticized her.

'She buys you things? Gives you money?' Connolly asked. A nod. 'I expect it was her bought that nice telly. Ah, she's a good sister, so she is.'

There was a faint lightening of the gloom. 'You don't arf talk funny,' Julienne said.

'If you went to Dublin, they'd think you talked funny,' said Connolly. She could see the idea intrigued the child. While interest was sparked, she went on quickly. 'So where was Kaylee keeping her stuff?'

Julienne opened her mouth to answer, then frowned. 'You're the filth,' she said. 'I'm not s'posed to tell you stuff.'

'Who told you that?'

'Me mum. She said if I told you stuff you'd get the social in and they'd take me away.'

'Ah, that's a different class o' police she's talking about. We're not that sort. We're here to try and help find out what happened to your sister. We're the good guys, see?'

Julienne looked as if she didn't quite buy that, but she was still leaning against the door frame, which proved she was receptive – or perhaps just lonely. Either way, Connolly primed her with a neutral question to keep her moving. 'Is it you doing the tidying up?'

'Yeah. Mum messes everything up. Kaylee said we don't have to live like that, so she started making the lounge nice, an' in here. I try and do a bit. But Mum don't care, and that Jaf just drops stuff everywhere.'

'So where does Kaylee keep her stuff now?' Connolly asked again, but casually.

This time the answer came easily. 'Round Deenie's, I 'spect. She's her best mate. That's where she went Sat'dy. I reckon she sleeps there an' all, when she don't come back here.'

'Isn't it nice to have the bedroom to yourself?'

'I s'pose.' Another shrug, which sent the shoulder of the jumper slipping further towards the elbow. She hauled it up a bit and went on, her lower lip trembling slightly. 'I got no one to talk to. Mum's out all the time, or when she's here, she's out of it. I wish Kaylee'd come back.'

Connolly reined in pity. 'So, this Deenie's her best mate. Where does she live?'

'Round the corner. Kaylee says soon as she's sixteen she's getting out. She's getting a place of her own, and then she says I can go and live with her. Mum wouldn't care.' It was said as a matter of fact, without bitterness. 'She's making good money now, Kaylee, and she says she'll get me in on it when I'm old enough. I wish I was older. I hate being a kid.'

'What's she making good money at?' Connolly asked.

'She never said,' Julienne answered indifferently. 'I think she keeps the money up Deenie's an' all. It's not here, anyway. She used to keep some in a box under the bed but Mum found it and her and Jaz done it all.'

'I thought his name was Jaf?'

'Jaz was the one before. I think they're brothers.' She stopped and yawned hugely, reminding Connolly of a kitten that any moment would simply pass out into sleep.

'So whereabouts does Deenie live?' she asked. Julienne shrugged, her eyes heavy. 'It's important, pet. You said round the corner – d'you mean the flats?'

'Nah, one of them houses, across the road.' She gestured with her head. Then she yawned again.

'You look as though you need a kip,' Connolly said. 'Why don't you get on your bed and read a book – you might drop off.'

'Mum might need me,' Julienne said.

'She's got plenty of people with her just now,' Connolly said.

Lawrence worked the visitors, who were mostly only too happy to talk about the terrible tragedy. But none of them knew anything useful. The general opinion was, not withstanding their current sympathy for her as a bereaved mother, that Mrs Adams was a terrible parent, and her carryings-on were shocking. Kaylee had been a little monster and it had been touch and go whether she'd be taken into care, but they hadn't seen much of her recently. They had always predicted she'd come to a sticky end, and now they were vindicated, though of course you wouldn't wish that end on anyone, knocked down and the bloke didn't even have the decency to stop. Hit-and-runners should be strung up. And, said a minority group – though they might have been articulating a more general opinion – being killed the way she was had probably saved Kaylee from getting into worse trouble. It was Julienne they felt sorry for.

'Not sorry enough to do anything about it,' Lawrence remarked as they walked down the stairs again. 'Did you notice not one of them spoke to the kid, or offered her a cuppa tea. Someone could have taken her into their house while all this is going on. And how come the kid hasn't got any friends? School's been out half an hour and not one kid has shown up at the door.'

'Maybe they feel intimidated by the crowd,' Connolly said. They emerged into the yard, which was empty. In her day, it would have been full of kids playing out, but kids didn't do that any more. They'd be indoors, watching telly or playing computer games. *Would it killya to get out a skippin' rope or a feckin' ball once?* She addressed the missing hordes. *Sure God you've got all your lives to be grown-ups.*

'So,' said Lawrence, 'who's this Deenie person?'

Lawrence went back to the station. Connelly called it in and reported, and Gascoyne got the O'Hares' address for her from the Vance file. They lived in Collingbourne Road, a slip of a terrace parallel with Bloemfontein Road and slotted in between it and Ormiston Grove like a makeweight in a box of chocolates. Connolly decided to go straight round there. There was still an hour before end of shift, and the girl Deenie ought to be home from school by now.

It was a mid-terrace doll's house, typical of the immediate area, and Connolly knew the layout from experience: two rooms and a kitchen downstairs, three bedrooms and a miniature bathroom upstairs. A frayed-looking woman in an apron opened the door to a smell of potatoes cooking and the sound of boy-children quarrelling somewhere within. Connolly instantly recognized the mammy hairdo and the faded eyes behind the glasses. 'Mrs O'Hare?' she asked, and though the boys were arguing in pure Shepherd's Bush, she wasn't surprised when the woman answered in a County Clare accent.

'That's me. And who might you be when the sun shines?'

'Detective Constable Connolly, from Shepherd's Bush Station.'

She frowned, but it seemed less with concern than faint weariness, as though she was about to be bothered with some pointless bureaucracy. 'What's this about, so? I hope you've not come bringing me trouble. Me kids are all home safe, thank God, bar Deenie that's gone round the shops, but she's only been gone five minutes.' Then, belatedly, came alarm. Her hand jumped to her throat. 'Oh, dear Baby Jesus, it's not me husband?'

'No, no, don't worry,' Connolly said hastily, 'it's nothing like that.'

'Thank the Lord. You had me heart going there like the butcher's pony. So what did you want? Only I've the kids' tea to get.'

'We're making enquiries about Kaylee Adams,' Connolly began.

Despite the tea to get, Mrs O'Hare seemed to settle slightly on her feet, as if in for the long chinwag. 'Ah, God rest her, what a terrible thing! Deenie said they gave it out at school today she was run over. And the gouger never stopped, is that right? He should be locked away, and the key tossed.'

'I understand Kaylee was a friend of Deenie's?'

'Ah, they were, worst luck. They were very tight for a time, those two.'

'And that Kaylee was here on Saturday?'

Mrs O'Hare frowned, which made her glasses slip down. She pushed them back up and said, 'Well, now, that I can't tell you. I was at work Saturday. But Deenie'll be back in a bit. D'you want to come in and wait?' The boy-battle within reached a crescendo and she bellowed over her shoulder, 'Keep the head shut, you boys, or I'll be in and give you such a clatter!' The volume dropped a notch, and she seemed to hear something else. 'Oh Mother of Mercy, me potatoes're boiling over! Just come in, close the door.'

She dashed away. Connolly followed more slowly. The narrow passage had stairs straight ahead, and the wall between them and the door was hung with pegs on which a great mass of coats of all sorts and sizes greatly reduced the passing-space. On the floor below them was a jumble of shoes and trainers. A glimpse through its door showed that the front room was the 'best parlour'. The patterned wallpaper was hung with a variety of crucifixes and religious repro-ductions that made her feel quite at home. There was a three-piece suite, a television, a mirror over the fireplace, and framed family photographs on every surface.

The back room was almost entirely full of a table with chairs round it, at which three boys were (or weren't) doing their home-work, overseen by a large, highly coloured print on the wall of the

Sacred Heart of Jesus. The Blessed Saviour had apparently torn open his own chest to reveal the throbbing organ, which was inexplicably wound round with a blackberry runner, and his eyes were rolled upwards in understandable agony. Connolly was glad her mother had favoured The Light of the World over the more visceral representations that haunted Catholic childhoods, but the three boys didn't seem to be bothered by their grim guardian. They were robustly ordinary boys in scruffy school uniforms and looked about nine, eleven and thirteen, and they fell silent and stared openmouthed at Connolly as she came in.

Mrs O'Hare poked her head round the kitchen door. 'Have manners!' she snapped. 'Stand up when a lady comes into the room!'

The boys scrambled to their feet, and Connolly smiled her thanks and said, 'Good afternoon. Carry on with your homework. I've just come to talk to your mammy.'

She progressed to the kitchen doorway, while behind her the boys sat down and got their heads together for an urgent murmur. The room beyond was tiny, being the scullery of the original layout, as she knew from her own home in Clontarf. It had space only for a gas stove, sink, refrigerator, work surface with a cupboard beneath, and a door in the corner which was probably the larder. Two people could have passed each other in there, but not if they were both obese. Opposite her was the back door, but these houses had no gardens, only a slip of a yard behind for hanging out washing. There were two rows of garments out there now, pegged out and waving their arms in the breeze.

The potatoes were simmering in a large pot, and Mrs O'Hare was chopping onions. A shrink-wrapped packet of mince lay on the counter-top. Mince, taties and peas, Connolly thought. The good old stand-by.

Mrs O'Hare looked up. 'Tuesday's my day off, because I work Saturdays. Not that it's much of a day off – what with the washing to do and everything, I'm worn thin be nightfall. But we try and have a meal all together of a Tuesday. Brian'll be home about half past six. The rest of the week Deenie gets the boys something after school so they don't have to wait. They go to St Joseph's, but Robert Towneley's is nearer, so by the time they get home she can have something on the go for them. They get so hungry. Growing boys'll eat you out o' house an' home, so they will.'

'I know,' said Connolly.

'You've brothers?'

'Four sisters. I've boy cousins, but. So Kaylee Adams was Deenie's best friend, I'm told?'

'Used to be,' said Mrs O'Hare shortly. 'I don't think they've been so close lately.'

'What did you think of her?'

'To tell you the truth, I didn't like her much when Deenie first brought her home. A bit of a madam. Too old for her age, you know the sort? Too sure of herself. I thought she'd be getting Deenie into trouble, so I wasn't best pleased at the friendship. But it has to be said, she never misbehaved in this house. A bit cheeky now and then, maybe, but no trouble. And Deenie never had many friends, so I laid low and said nothing. I was glad for her to have someone.'

'Kaylee got into trouble a few times for shoplifting – that must have worried you.'

'Well, I never really knew about that – not until afterwards, when she'd already got a hold and tried to put a shape on herself. And you see, it'd come out that she stood up for Deenie and stopped her gettin' bullied, so I thought a bit better of her.'

'Tell me about that,' Connolly invited.

She pursed her lips, remembering. 'The two of them came home from school one day – well, I was here, so it must a' been a Tuesday – and Deenie's in floods and her shirt's torn and there's dirt an' scratches on her face, and Kaylee's all over blood from a clatter on the nose, and it looks like she's gettin' a black eye. So I was giving out to Deenie about fighting, when Kaylee starts in telling me to leave her alone. Well, I wasn't taking that from no little madam, when it was probably her started the fighting in the first place, because it has to be said Deenie's always been a bit milk-an'-water – but then Deenie says, no, Ma, you've got it wrong. And it turns out some bullies had cornered Deenie outside the school gates, an' Kaylee just wades in and fights the lot of 'em. And it wasn't the first time, either, according to Deenie. So after that I took kinder to her.'

'She sounds as if she was a good friend.'

'Well, there was benefits on both sides. At one time she was round here practically every night after school, and I was having an extra mouth to feed. But it has to be said she didn't have much to go home for, if what I heard was true. Mother's a head case, so they say, and no father in the picture. She used to call for Deenie in the mornings too, at one time, on the way to school. I suppose Deenie'd give her breakfast – I have to leave for work early, so Deenie feeds herself and the boys. There was a time I started thinking we'd adopted her. But then she stopped coming round so often, and her and Deenie weren't so thick any more.'

'When did this happen? I mean, when did the friendship start to fade?'

'Oh, I don't know exactly. Last year some time. You know what girls are. They have their own little lives, and now they're friends and now they're not. I can't keep up. You'd have to ask Deenie. I've enough on me plate taking care of a husband and three sons, without worrying about that one and every little teenage tiff she has. But Kaylee's definitely not cropped up in the conversation so much lately. So really—' she raised faded eyes to Connolly's face – 'I don't know that Deenie'll be able to help you much. Ah, that sounds like her.'

The front door had opened and slammed. Connolly turned and stood back from the kitchen door so that the mother could get a clear view. The girl was shrugging off her anorak, jamming it on top of the pile, and then she stumped heavily down the passage towards them with a plastic carrier in her hand, her body language speaking of unhappiness. She didn't see Connolly until the last minute, and stopped uncertainly, looking from her to her mother questioningly.

She was a plain girl, plump with puppy fat, her nose too big for her face, her skin blotchy, her mousy hair frizzy, long, and tied back carelessly with a scrunchie. Her lack of prettiness was not helped by a look of sullenness and discontent, or the school uniform that seemed to be a size too small for her, so that her burgeoning bosom was packed away bulgingly like washing in a pillow case.

'This is Constable Connolly, who wants to have a word with you about Kaylee,' said Mrs O'Hare with a firmness that allowed no dissent. 'Did you remember the peas?' Deenie passed over the bag, from which Mrs O'Hare unpacked a large bag of frozen peas, a tub of spread, and a frozen strawberry cheesecake – a special extra, Connolly supposed, for the culmination of the togetherness family meal. It had a bright red label on the front, 89p reduced from £1. Connolly knew from experience that the treat inside would be a great deal smaller than the box, and that it would only really divide into four – the male half of the household. She had long experience of the way Irish mammies thought.

Deenie watched her mother as she slouched on the other side of the doorway, her head slightly averted from Connolly. Mrs O'Hare looked up sharply. 'Well, don't just stand there like an ancient ruin! Take the lady into the front room where it's quiet. I don't want the boys listening in,' she added sotto voce to Connolly. 'They mustn't be disturbed when they've their homework to do and exams to be thinking about. Mind and answer her questions properly, Deenie, and don't be all night about it – I need you to get the washing in before it rains again.'

Deenie turned, without meeting her mother's eyes, and began to walk away. Connolly went to follow her, when Mrs O'Hare spoke again, 'Oh, mercy me, haven't I lost me manners entirely! Will I make you a cup o' tea, miss? Deenie, fill the kettle!'

Connolly liked the fact that she didn't know the correct way to address a detective constable. It spoke of a basic innocence – even if she didn't have much tenderness towards her daughter. 'No, thanks all the same,' she said. 'Not for me. I'm fine.'

FIVE

But She Was Too Young to Fall in Love

I n the cramped little parlour, surrounded by religion and kin, Connolly felt the comfort of familiarity. Things were shabby but Sunday-clean, the little bits of decoration hopelessly naff and touchingly cared for. There were starched white antimacassars on the sofa and chair backs, plastic flowers in a vase, china ornaments on the mantelpiece and a lingering smell of furniture polish in the air.

Deenie stood inert just inside the door, looking as if she'd never move again.

'Come and sit down,' Connolly invited. 'Don't worry, Deenie, you're not in trouble. I just want to find out what I can about Kaylee.'

The girl lurched across and slumped into one of the armchairs. Connolly sat on the sofa catty-corner to her and tried an encouraging smile as she examined her. It seemed to be more a general discontent than sharp grief over the death of a beloved friend. She got the impression of a girl no one much cared about. Deenie picked at the cord binding the arm of the chair. Her nails, Connolly noticed, were bitten.

She tried a curve ball on her, to shake her up a bit. 'Are you still getting bullied at school?'

Deenie looked up, surprised. That was not the question she'd expected. 'No,' she said at last. 'That's all finished.'

'Kaylee scared them off for good, did she?'

'I dunno. They sort of lost interest, I s'pose. Some of 'em were older, and they've left.'

She had no vocabulary to describe the disruption of a pattern, but Connolly understood. 'She was a good friend to you,' she suggested. Deenie shrugged. 'You were best mates.'

'We *were*,' Deenie said. 'Till she started going round with that Shannon and Tyler. Then she never had time for me.'

Ah, so that was it. Resentment. Thwarted love. Jealousy. That might give her something to work with.

'What, she dropped you for them?'

'No, not . . . Not exactly. We were still mates, I s'pose. But she was always busy with them. I'd be like, "Are you coming round tonight", and she was like, "No, I'm going out with Shannon and Tyler".'

'That's Tyler Vance, is it?'

'Yeah.' It was said disparagingly.

'You didn't like her?'

'She was all full of herself. She was like, "Oh, I'm so pretty, I'm so lovely, everybody's mad about me."'

'So you weren't one of their gang?'

'It wasn't a gang. It was just them.' She looked up resentfully 'And I *told* that policeman, after Tyler – you know – in the river. I *told* him I was never her friend. Why d'you keep asking?'

'It's all right, I believe you,' Connolly said soothingly. 'What about Shannon? What's her other name? Shannon what?'

'Shannon Bailey. She's left school now. She was the year above us. Soon as she was sixteen, she left.'

'When was that?'

'Last June.'

'Did you like her?'

'She was all right,' Deenie said with another shrug. 'She was a bit of a nutcase, but . . . I never had much to do with her. She was sort of a loner, till she took up with Kaylee. Then they were, like, really tight. With that Tyler.'

'So when did all that happen, then – when did Kaylee get so close to Shannon and Tyler?'

She shrugged, but as Connolly kept waiting for an answer she said, 'I dunno. Last year. Maybe – round Easter? We were gonna do stuff in the Easter holidays, but she was all like busy with them and I hardly saw her.'

So that would be around April, a year ago, Connolly thought. Then Shannon left in June, and probably the remaining two, Kaylee and Tyler, got even closer and Deenie was shut out. And Tyler died in January.

'But Kaylee still came round sometimes?' Connolly suggested.

Deenie shrugged. 'Like, since Tyler died, she started wanting to hang out with me again. A bit.'

She stopped, and there didn't seem to be any more to come. Connolly said, 'She was keeping her stuff here, wasn't she?'

Deenie looked surprised. 'You what?'

'Her sister Julienne said she was keeping her stuff here, to keep it out of her mother's way.'

'Julienne? She's just a kid, what does she know? Anyway, have you seen my room?' Obviously a rhetorical question. 'I get the small bedroom 'cos the boys have to have the big one, and you couldn't swing a cat in it. There's not enough room for my stuff, never mind anyone else's.'

'But she *was* here on Saturday, wasn't she? What time was that?'

'Lunchtime. She come round lunchtime and said we should do something.'

From her voice, Connolly gathered that was unusual. 'You were surprised? You said she wanted to hang out with you.'

'Well, we were still mates at school, sort of. But I never saw her weekends. We'd walk home from school sometimes.'

'So last Saturday she, what, just turned up?'

Deenie shrugged. 'Yeah, sort of. She turned up and said what you doing and I said nuffing. So we went and got pizza from the place at the end of the road, and come back here and eat it, up in my room, and, like, talked.' Her expression softened. 'It was nice, sort of.'

'Your mum was at work.'

'Yeah, and Dad was out with the boys, so I was on my own.'

And lonely, Connolly thought, in a receptive mood for the old friend who wanted to be forgiven.

'So it was like old times?'

She wrinkled her nose in thought. 'Not really. She's different now.'

'Different how?'

'We used to be all laughs and having a good time together. But then she got in with Shannon and Tyler and she was all serious, like pretending to be a grown-up. She never talked about stuff any more.'

'What *did* she talk about?'

'Money, mostly. She's always talking about money. Saying she's saving up to get out of this shithole – that's what she calls it,' she added, defensively. 'Start a new life, sort of. Soon as she's sixteen, she says. Well, that's not until December. She was fifteen just before Christmas. I'm not fifteen till May,' she added sadly.

'Being fifteen's not so great,' Connolly said.

Deenie gave her a sceptical look. 'Better than fourteen.'

'Where was Kaylee getting the money from?'

'I dunno. I reckon her boyfriend was giving it her,' she said indifferently. 'She had this older boyfriend.'

'Did she? What's his name?'

'I don't know. She never said. I mean, I don't *know* it was anyone, but she was always saying she preferred older men, and going on about it, kind of smug, how great they were and everything, so I reckoned there was someone.'

'What else did she talk about on Saturday?'

'I dunno. She was kind of . . .' A long think. 'Funny. Like – depressed. Or worried about something. She kept talking about the good times her and me used to have when she used to come round all the time. Well, it was *her* changed, not me.'

'Did you say that to her?'

'Yeah. She said you got to grow up sooner or later. I said she was the same age as me, practic'ly, and she told me not to be such a baby.' Her face creased a moment with hurt.

'That was unkind.'

'Yeah, well, she always did have a big mouth.'

'So what was she depressed about?'

'I dunno. She never said. I thought maybe it was Tyler. I mean . . .'

'I expect it was a shock when she disappeared like that,' Connolly said helpfully. 'Did she mention her?'

She thought a moment. 'She said the police never really tried to find out what happened to her. She said you lot don't care about girls like her.'

'What else?'

A shrug. 'Nothing.' She seemed to search around, trying to be obliging, as a girl like her was brought up to be. 'She said she was going to a party.'

'What, that evening?'

'Yeah. We were, like, sitting on my bed talking, and she says, "I'm s'posed to be going to this really important party tonight, but I don't know." Said there was going to be loads of really hot blokes there, but she wasn't sure if she wanted to go. Then she gets her mobile out. Showing off,' Deenie added discontentedly, 'cause she knows I've not got one. And she has this conversation. I reckoned she was phoning her boyfriend.'

'Why did you think that?'

''Cause she, like, said, "Will *you* be there?" and I s'pose he must've said yes, because she goes, "Oh, all right, then."'

'Where did she say the party was?'

'In this big house, really swanky, she said. Somewhere in Holland Park. I dunno where. She said she was getting picked up in a car for it.'

A party in Holland Park? What the feck was she doing in Harefield, so? Connolly wondered. 'While she was talking on the phone, did she say the name of who she was talking to?' Shake of the head. 'When she started the conversation, for instance, didn't she say something like, "Hello, Jack, it's Kaylee"?'

Another shake, slow, this one, and thoughtful. 'No, she just started talking, right off. Like, "This party, you *will* be there?" Just like that.'

'Did she say, "Will *you* be there?" or "You *will* be there?"'

The distinction was too subtle for Deenie. She looked bewildered, and said, 'I dunno. Is it different?'

'It may be,' Connolly said. Then, to comfort her: 'It probably doesn't matter.'

Deenie had been thinking meanwhile. 'You asking all these questions – did something happen to Kaylee? I thought she got run over, a hit-and-run driver. That's what they said at school.'

'That's what it looks like,' Connolly said. 'Just an accident. But you see, we don't know where she was on Saturday night, or who she was with, and we like to be able to write a full report about it, when someone dies. So if you remember anything she might have told you about this boyfriend, or where the party was, or anything at all about people she'd been seeing—'

'You want to ask Shannon if you want to know that sort of thing. She's the one she's been spending all her time with,' said Deenie, with hurt.

'Oh, we will, don't worry,' said Connolly. 'Was she still seeing Shannon, so?'

'I s'pose so. She talked about her. Thought the sun shone out of her – eyes.' She changed the word at the last moment – her mother's influence. 'That's where she was going after she left here,' she added. 'She said she was going over Shannon's to get poshed up for the party.' A thought came to her. 'That might be where she was keeping her stuff, if she *was* hiding it from her mum.'

'That's a good thought,' Connolly said encouragingly. 'Where does Shannon live?'

'*I* don't know. Somewhere round here, I think – but I told you, she left school last year, and *I* wasn't thick with her, not like Kaylee.' She tired suddenly of the whole subject. 'Can I go now? Only Mum wants me to get the washing in.'

'That's fine, you've been very helpful,' Connolly said, releasing her. It came to something, so it did, when you were outclassed for entertainment value by an armful of washing.

Deenie jumped up with more energy than she had shown so far, but at the door she stopped abruptly, and turned with a troubled look.

'Yes?' said Connolly.

'About Kaylee,' said Deenie slowly.

She didn't seem to be able to articulate her question, and Connolly could guess it. No need to load any more troubles onto this forgotten girl; and besides, any police doubts were still strictly in house. 'It was just a road accident,' she said kindly.

Deenie stared a moment, doubtfully, and then nodded.

Connolly hoped she couldn't read a thought bubble over the child's head saying, 'Like Tyler??' With two question marks.

'I've seen it before,' Connolly said to Slider, sipping gratefully at a mug of tea. One thing they didn't tell you before you joined the Job – asking all those questions left you thirsty as the divil. 'It's the curse of Irish families – the boys are everything and the girls are nothing. Mammy O'Hare was all "The boys haven't to be disturbed, they've their homework to do, they've careers ahead of them." And it was "Deenie, fetch the washing, go down the shops, make the boys their tea." Because o' course Deenie's future's assured as a drudge and dogsbody. Like Mammy's before her.'

'I'm not sure I should let you do any more interviewing if it leaves you so bitter,' Slider said mildly.

Connolly grinned. 'I got out be the skin of me teeth. I know where the trap lies, that's all. What I'm sayin' is, no wonder Deenie was flattered when Kaylee wanted to be her friend, and depressed when she dropped her.'

'Fascinating though that is . . .' Slider said suggestively.

Connolly became brisk. 'The interesting thing, I think, boss, is the conversation she had on her mobile. Deenie says there was no preliminaries. Just straight in with, "This party, are you going to be there?" Or it may have been, "You *are* going to be there?" Which means there'd been a conversation about it before – maybe he'd even been the one to invite her.'

'Though by the same token, it wasn't *his* party,' said Slider.

'Right,' said Connolly, eagerly. 'So whoever owns the big swanky house, it wasn't the boyfriend.'

Slider lifted a hand slightly. 'Except that she may not have been talking to the boyfriend. It could have been a female friend she was hoping would be there for moral support. Could have been the ineffable Shannon.'

'Oh, right,' said Connolly, deflated. She thought for a moment. 'So what the feck was she doing out in Harefield if the party was in Holland Park?'

'It's a good, reasonably near bit of countryside for dumping a body,' said Slider.

'Which makes it more likely she *was* dumped.' Connolly brightened again.

'If Kaylee was telling Deenie the truth and if Deenie's remembering it right,' said Slider, cautioning again. 'We'd better have a word with Shannon Bailey. She seems to be the one in the know about Kaylee's last days.'

'Good title for a fillum, boss,' Connolly said, getting up. 'Got to find an address first.'

'Not tonight,' said Slider. He hadn't got the say-so for overtime yet. 'I'll put in the request for the Kaylee's mobile phone records.' Lawrence had got the number from her mother. 'You write up your report and get off home. Tomorrow is—'

'Another day?'

'I was going to say, soon enough.'

In the old days, Slider thought as Connolly went out, he could have given both jobs to the night duty officer (latterly all too often Hollis, who hadn't got a home to go to – damn, he'd forgotten about Hollis again) to give him something to do to wile away the hours. But with the cutbacks they no longer had night cover in every CID office. Instead, except in an emergency, they had one team covering the night hours for several boroughs. Crime was down across the board, so it made sense – there had rarely been any external calls on the night officer's time. Hollis had managed to get a good night's sleep – or as good as his restless mind would allow – most nights.

And he was back to Hollis again.

Slider was in early the next morning, but he wasn't the first. Waiting for him in the outer office was a tall black woman in a neat bottle-green trouser suit, her hair a Medusa-head of thin, tight plaits. She started towards him as soon as he appeared, with one of those smiles that should have come with a *ping!* sound effect.

''Ello, guv. S'prised to see me?'

'You could knock me down with an HGV,' Slider assured her. It was Tony Hart (Tony was spelt the boy's way and wasn't short for anything – 'Me mum's a bit of a nutter,' she had explained. 'I'm lucky she didn't call me Bernard.') Hart had been one of Slider's team until she passed her sergeant's exam and moved on to better things.

'How's SW6?' Slider asked.

Hart shrugged. 'How is it everywhere?' she countered. 'The brass are tryna make the Job into just a job, if you get me. Nine to five. Or eight to six, more like, but you know what I mean. I miss the old days. More policin' and less management, that's what we want.' She slapped a hand over her mouth, pretending to be shocked at what she had said. 'Blimey, I forgot for a minute – you're one of 'em now, aren't you, guv? Congratulations, by the way. You ain't gonna stick me on for insubordination, are you, Detective Chief Inspector Slider, sir?'

'I see they haven't knocked the cheek out of you,' Slider said. 'Not that it isn't a pleasure to see you, Detective Sergeant Hart, but is this a social call, or what *are* you doing here?'

'Mission a' mercy,' she said. 'I've come to help out.' Her mobile face fell several inches into a downward arc of sympathy. 'Sorry about Colin Hollis, by the way, guv. Bummer! I was well gutted when I heard – he was a decent bloke. Anyway—' her face rose again – 'they said you was short of a sergeant, and it's quiet back at the old homestead, and I got leave owing, so, what with one thing and another . . .'

'*Who* said we were short of a sergeant?' Slider cut to the heart of it.

'Mr Porson rung up my guv'nor and chucked some 'eavy hints about, and my guv'nor asked for volunteers and – here I am.'

Slider cocked an eye at her. 'Come to save our bacon out of the goodness of your heart?'

Hart looked shocked. 'Blimey, no! I'm gettin' paid,' she assured him. 'I can't stand 'olidays, and I'm saving for a deposit on a house, so it makes sense. It's all about the money, guv, honest! I'd never do anyone a favour, I swear!'

'I believe you,' Slider said solemnly. 'I withdraw any imputation of philanthropy, and apologize for impugning your character.'

Hart grinned. 'I don't understand what you're saying, but I defend to the death your right to say it. So what you got for me?'

'A lot of routine catching-up, but there is one thing that might turn out to be interesting.' He got her up to speed on the Kaylee Adams incident. 'Perhaps you'd like to start on finding out where Shannon Bailey is.'

'Right, guv. Get you a cuppa first?'

'If you're brewing up – thanks.'
'Gotta get me priorities right. Tea first.'

Slider from his room heard a succession of excited greetings as the
rest of the firm came in one by one. By the time Atherton appeared
in his doorway and raised a Vulcan eyebrow, Slider had spoken to
DCI David Century, his opposite number at Fulham, to discuss
the matter, and had got what he thought was a handle on the situation. Century's boss was Detective Superintendent Orvan Palliser,
whose odd Christian name had given rise, naturally enough, to the
sobriquet of 'the Organ', which it was subversively suggested he
deserved. He was efficient but unloved, and was also something of
a snob – it was rumoured that he had been mightily displeased when
he had missed out on Kensington and got Fulham instead, the hippy-
dippy cheap end of Chelsea, entirely the wrong end of the Fulham
Road, which ran from the riches of Egerton Place to the rags of
Fulham High Street.

And the Organ, as it was not exactly stated by Century, didn't
like Hart. He suspected her of derision, and Slider could understand that – she was so in-your-face that even her respectfulness
could come across as insolently chirpy. Palliser, as Century didn't
exactly say, would be glad to get Hart off his hands permanently,
as there was in his firm a very nice young detective constable
from a good home, who was ready for promotion and might leave
Fulham for another borough if there wasn't an opening there for
him soon.

Of course, David Century didn't exactly tell Slider any of this,
so Slider was not at liberty to pass it on to Atherton. He said, 'She's
volunteered to work her leave here – saving up for a house so she
needs the money. We've got her for a month, but . . .' He inserted
a delicate pause.

'She might stay on?' Atherton said. 'Well, Fulham's loss would
be our gain – though why she'd *want* to come back here I can't
imagine.'

'What's wrong with here?' Slider said, wounded.

Atherton grinned. Hart had had a crush on Slider when she'd
worked under him before, though he wouldn't expect his boss to
know that – or approve of it if he did. He said, 'Better shops, pubs
and clubs in Fulham, and Chelsea just down the road. And probably

more interesting cases. We'd better hope something comes of this Kaylee Adams business, to keep her from getting bored.'

Slider got up. 'I'm going to see Mr Porson. If it was his idea to begin with, he's probably got a plan for keeping her.'

Porson was inscrutable, and wouldn't even confirm that he'd rung Det Sup Palliser at all, but each rank had its own rumour mill, so Slider guessed Porson had been both putting out feelers and taking in hints.

Porson did, however, agree that if Hart wanted to stay on permanently, it would probably be arrangeable. 'But she might not want to, so let's not cross our chickens. Meanwhile, I expect to see some of the backlash of casework dealt with. We've got no excuses now.' He paused for Slider to look suitably submissive, and went on: 'What's happening with this Adams business?'

Slider brought him up-to-date.

'I don't like it,' Porson said, with a frown like boulders rushing down from opposing hillsides. 'Something fishy about it. I can smell it.' He tapped his considerable beak. 'And we're going to get stuck with it, thanks to you and your friend Doc Cameron. We should have left it with Uxbridge.'

'They wouldn't have followed it up,' Slider said. 'Westminster didn't.'

'You don't know there's any connection,' Porson snapped.

Slider only looked at him. In the modern world of nine-to-five, by-the-book, tick-box, spreadsheet policing, there was no room for fishy feelings. They hadn't the time. They hadn't the money. And those above them hadn't the patience, not with the door to the corridors of power temptingly ajar for superiors who kept their noses clean. But Slider knew that Porson was in the Job for reasons other than the pay and the career trajectory. It was why he loved him.

At last Porson made an irritable movement. 'All *right*! I've told you you can have to the end of the week. For God's sake get me something that *looks* like something, so I don't have to close you down.'

'Thank you, sir,' said Slider, and went away, satisfied for now.

Who cared for Kaylee Adams? No one, not even her mother. Who had cared for Tyler Vance? Not even social services, who had all too many of them the same. Here, in the space after the full stop, there was only Slider and his team left, to say that someone's death couldn't just be reduced to a budget decision. *He* cared – and thank God Porson did too, for all his crustiness.

SIX

Wake Duncan With Thy Knocking?

Shannon Bailey, it emerged, had been living with her sister Dakota.

'Good Lord!' Slider complained mildly. 'Doesn't anyone call their daughter Jane or Elizabeth any more?'

Hart gave him a stern look. 'Benefit mums, the only thing they've got to give their kids is a weird name.'

Shannon's mother Dee (whose current surname appeared to be Walls) was a skinny white woman, so lavishly tattooed it might have been an attempt to blend in with her black neighbours. She had a hoarse, cigarette voice and a wary, not to say suspicious eye, but once she absorbed that Hart was not after her for anything, she became almost embarrassingly forthcoming.

She volunteered that she eked out her benefits with prostitution – 'Well, you can't live on what the bleedin' state gives you, can you, love?' – and so was known to social services, who kept a sketchy eye on her four younger children, all boys. Dakota was her eldest; at twenty, well past the reach of all guardianship.

'Then there's Tommy, he's eighteen. I dunno where he is. He took off when I started shacking up wiv Griff. Him and Griff never got on. Then Shannon, which you know. She moved out soon as she left school and Dakota said she'd have her. Mind? Why should I? There's not room to swing a cat in this dump, but the council won't give me a bigger place. I've asked till I'm blue in the face, but all they say is there's a waitin' list. Bastards. She's better off out of it, anyway, Shannon. I don't like her in an' out of the bathroom half naked with Leroy around. He's got a wandrin' eye.'

'Leroy?'

'Him what I live with.'

'Oh. Not Griff.'

'He moved on. Him and Leroy had a fight. Knives. Leroy give him a cut down his arm needed twenty stitches,' she added with some pride.

A photograph of Dakota from when she was below age, which Hart acquired from social services, showed that, like Shannon, she was mixed-race, though not as pretty as her younger sister. However, from her address she was doing all right.

'Minford Court,' Hart said to Slider. 'That's private rent, not council or housing association. Her mum says she's a call girl. Right proud of her, an' all. You'd've laughed, guv. "Does it in the comfort of her own home," says mummy. Somefing to aspire to.'

'You'll notice me laughing,' Slider said gravely. 'Better get over there straight away, see if you can get hold of Shannon.'

Hart looked at her watch. 'Yeah, they ought to be awake by now, just about.'

Minford Court was a modern, low-rise block, in a well-kept, tree-lined street just off the Shepherd's Bush Road. Hart had to knock and ring for some time before the door was answered by a slim young woman wrapped in a peach satin dressing gown that went very well with her golden brown skin. Her eyes were gummy and her hair was wild, and she had obviously been woken by the knocking.

Hart showed her brief before any protest could be spoken, and said, 'Dakota, is it? I'm looking for Shannon. Your mum says she lives with you.'

The woman stared for a long moment, presumably catching up with the waking world, before saying, 'You're too late. She's gone.'

'Gone where?'

'Took off. She left a note.'

Hart gave her a kindly look. 'Can I come in? Don't wanna talk like this on the doorstep.'

Dakota shrugged and stepped back. The flat smelled clean and warm. There was a tiny entrance hall, with the sitting room straight ahead, with a kitchenette at one end of it. The walls were all painted white and the flooring throughout was imitation woodstrip laminate, the furniture modern, cheap but not yet shabby. Dakota led the way into the sitting room, then turned to face Hart, hands in pockets, and stopped, as if uncertainly.

'It's not trouble for her,' Hart said. 'We think she can help us, that's all. We're trying to find out about her friend Kaylee.'

'What about Kaylee?' Dakota asked.

'Don't you know?' Hart asked, with a hard look.

Apprehension began to dawn through the twilight of sleep. 'What? Has something happened?'

'Kaylee was found dead on Monday morning,' Hart said.

Dakota stared. 'Oh Christ,' she said. 'What's she got herself into now?' She drew a shaking hand out of her pocket with a pack of cigarettes in it. 'D'you mind?'

Hart made an equivocal gesture, and Dakota walked to the end of the sitting room where a glass door gave onto a tiny balcony, just about big enough to hold two upright chairs. She opened the door and stood in the doorway, leaning against the frame, as she lit the cigarette and blew the smoke outwards. Hart observed the routine and Dakota said, as if answering a question, 'I can't have the smell of fag smoke in here. My *friends* wouldn't like it.' *Friends* was obviously a substitute noun.

'S'all right, girl,' Hart said. 'I know you're on the game. That's not what I'm here about.'

Dakota looked annoyed. 'Who told you that? It's a lie!'

'Your mum,' said Hart. 'Ease off, babe. You're not in trouble. I just wanna talk to Shannon about Kaylee. When did she leave?'

'Sunday morning, some time. She was gone when I woke up.'

'When was that?'

'Around eleven, eleven thirty? She left a note on the kitchen counter.'

'Can I see it?' She half expected to be told it was destroyed, but after a hesitation Dakota jerked her head towards the kitchen counter.

'Under the phone.'

The note had obviously come from a square block that stood beside the phone. In a round, childish scrawl was written: 'Dear Dakota, I got to go away for a bit. Don't worry Ill be all right. I done nothing wrong babes honest. Ill call you if I can. Love you, Shannon.'

Hart turned from the note towards Dakota, smoking hard and not looking at her. 'Where's she gone?'

'*I* don't know.'

'Come on, love. You must have some idea.'

'I don't!' Dakota said, calling on a little annoyance to bolster her. 'Look, she just crashes here, that's all. She's my sister, I had to give her a bed when she wanted to get out. I mean, I love my mum and everything, but you wouldn't want to live in that place, not if you didn't have to. And once she started shacking up with that Leroy – well, he's not nice to know. And Shan's not a kid any more. You know what I mean . . .'

'Yeah, I can guess,' said Hart. 'But come on, love, two sisters living together, havin' heart-to-hearts, chattin' over the cornflakes – you must know what she gets up to.'

'I *don't*. She don't tell me an' I don't want to know. Look, she's a good kid. She wouldn't get mixed up in anything dodgy.'

'But she is mixed up in *something*?' No answer. 'We reckon Kaylee died some time Saturday night, Sunday morning. And Sunday morning Shannon takes off. Looks like she knows somefing, dunnit?'

Dakota was smoking too hard, and the glowing end of the cigarette fell off onto the laminate floor, so she had to scuff it out with the toe of her slipper, cursing under her breath. 'That bloody Kaylee. I knew she was trouble. Stupid little cow.'

'So you knew something'd happened to her.'

'*No*! I never heard anything, not till you told me. I mean, why should I? She's not *my* friend, she's just a kid. Someone Shannon knows from school, that's all.'

'But she was round here quite a lot, wasn't she?'

She turned now to face Hart, her hands clasping and unclasping nervously in front of her. 'Look . . .' she began, but seemed at a loss how to go on.

'If Shannon's in trouble, your best bet is to tell me everything you know, so's we can help her.'

'But I don't know anything,' Dakota said, and this time it was not defensive but a wail of frustration.

Hart softened. 'All right, girl. Put the kettle on, let's 'ave a cup a coffee, an' we'll have a natter. Just friendly, orright? And you can tell me what you *do* know, cos it might turn out to be important.'

'Shan's my sister and all that, and I love her, but, you know, I'm not responsible for her,' Dakota said over the coffee. 'I don't see all that much of her, tell you the truth.'

The mugs were rather nice, bone china with a dainty pattern of pink wild roses, and they took them outside onto the balcony so that Dakota could continue to smoke. The rate she was going through them, Hart thought, she'd soon have a voice like her mother's. For now it was pleasant enough.

Kaylee had come over on Saturday afternoon. It wasn't unusual. 'She was often here weekends.'

'Staying over?'

'No, just popping in and out. Mostly of a Saturday. I didn't like her much. I thought she was a sly piece. I was worried she might get Shan into trouble.'

'What sort of trouble?'

Dakota frowned into the distance. 'I dunno. Just something . . . shoplifting, maybe. She looked the sort. You wouldn't put anything past her, know what I mean? And I can't have any trouble of that sort, not here.'

'What time did she arrive?'

'She was here when I got home about six. I'd been shopping up the West End. Her and Shannon were in the bedroom talking. Shan come out and I said, "What's *she* doing here?" Because I had people coming.'

'Customers?'

'Clients,' she corrected firmly. 'And I couldn't have a kid here. But Shannon said, "It's all right, she's going to a party. She's just come here to get dressed."'

'Was Shannon going to the party?'

'I dunno. She said she was going to meet a friend, so maybe not.'

So it wasn't Shannon that Kaylee had phoned from Deenie's house, Hart thought. 'Was Kaylee keeping some of her stuff here?'

'I dunno about that. There's loads of clothes and shoes and things, but I thought they were Shannon's. Maybe they shared them. They were about the same size.'

'What time did Kaylee leave on Saturday?'

'Shan said she was being picked up at half eight from the end of the road. I didn't see her go – I was busy. I told 'em to keep out of sight, and they did. I think Shannon went out the same time, but I couldn't swear to it.'

'Do you know where the party was? Did she mention an address, or a name? Did Shannon?'

'No,' said Dakota. 'No idea.'

'What time did Shannon come home?'

'I don't know. I was busy. I never heard anything. Her room door was shut when I went to bed at around three. Then in the morning when I got up, I found the note.'

'Did she pack a bag?'

'I s'pose so. There's some of her stuff missing.'

'She must have made some noise, moving around, open and shutting drawers – you must have heard something,' said Hart.

'I didn't! I sleep heavy, nothing wakes me. Look, when you say Kaylee was found dead – I mean, what, like, happened to her?'

'Looks as though she was knocked down, hit-and-run,' Hart said, watching her carefully.

Dakota looked relieved. 'Thank Christ for that. I mean, I'm sorry and everything, but I thought you meant something worse.'

'Why would you think that?'

'Well . . .' A long pause. 'I thought maybe she'd got mixed up in something, and she'd got Shannon involved.'

'What sort of something?'

'*I* don't know. I gotta have another fag.' She lit up, with shaky hands.

Hart observed her with narrowed eyes. 'You *do* know,' Hart said.

'I don't. I swear. I don't know what that Kaylee was into. She was a bad lot, that one.'

Hart knew a brick wall when she saw one and let it go. 'Have you tried ringing Shannon?'

''Course. It just goes to voicemail. I'll have to wait till she calls me.'

'You'd better give me the number,' said Hart, and Dakota gave it with obvious reluctance. 'I'd like to see her room, please.'

There was a bedroom on the left side of the passage as you came in, and another plus a bathroom on the right. Hart, walking ahead of Dakota, went into the former. It was about twelve feet square, and contained a double bed covered with a quilted satin counterpane. There was a wardrobe with a full-length mirror on it, a dressing table with a mirror behind it, and a small basin in the corner with a wrapped cake of soap and a neatly folded clean towel hanging below it. The giveaway was that there was no overhead light, just lamps dotted about the room with dark pink tasselled shades. It was the work room.

Hart gave a quick glance round and turned back to Dakota, who was looking miffed. 'That's *my* room. You got no right to go in there.'

'No worries, girl,' Hart said cheerfully. 'We all got to make a living.'

She crossed the passage to the other room, which was smaller and contained a single bed, a wardrobe and a chest of drawers.

The wardrobe was crammed with trollopy clothes and shoes and handbags, the chest with 'sexy' underwear, cheap jewellery, and in other drawers more serviceable jeans, cut-offs, sweaters and T-shirts. Hair brushes and products and tubes and sticks of make-up crowded the top of the chest. 'How do you know anything's gone?' Hart asked in some amazement.

'There's usually a lot more than this,' Dakota said.

The *serviceable* drawers did look less bulging than the others, Hart thought. She crouched down and looked under the bed. There was a box under there, pushed right back into the darkest corner, which she pulled out. It was a biscuit tin of the sort that was sold at Christmas containing a teatime variety of old favourites; the lid and sides were patterned with snow scenes, lamp-lit inns and coach-and-sixes.

'Is this Shannon's?' she asked.

'I dunno. I've never seen it before,' Dakota said.

'Maybe it's Kaylee's, then.'

'Might be.'

Inside were some packets of condoms and several blister packs of birth control pills; a small tin box containing three foil-wrapped spliffs; and cash – bundles of notes held together with rubber bands and packed in tightly.

Hart began drawing them out, making a rough calculation as she did so. Nearly seven hundred pounds. 'You still say it's not Shannon's?' she asked.

'She'd've took it with her if it was,' Dakota said, missing an opportunity in her surprise. 'She mustn't've known it was there.'

So what was Kaylee doing with all this money? Hart mused to herself. No wonder she hadn't wanted to keep it at home within reach of the druggy mother.

'That girl,' Dakota said, 'was up to something.'

If she was, it turned round and bit her, Hart thought.

'But if Shannon ran away because Kaylee was dead, she must have known about it on Sunday morning,' said Atherton. 'Which presents the question, *how* did she know?'

'Maybe she was at the party too,' said Connolly. 'Her sister didn't really know.'

'We don't know that whatever happened, *happened* at the party,' Atherton said. 'It's much more likely to have been afterwards, otherwise too many people would have known. Kaylee probably met someone there and left with them.'

'But we still need to know where the party was and who was there, so we can find out who she *did* leave with,' Connolly pointed out.

'If she left the party with someone,' Slider said slowly, 'it makes it all the more strange that Shannon heard about the death on Sunday morning, when the body hadn't even been found. She'd have had to have been told by someone who was involved, and why would they do that? *If* that's why she's run away,' he added discontentedly. They all looked at him. 'It's a mess,' he said. 'It certainly looks, because of the money, as though Kaylee was mixed up in something. And given that she and Shannon were friends to the exclusion of Deenie, and she kept the money under Shannon's bed, it looks as though Shannon knew something about it. But further than that we can't go.'

'And we've no link between Kaylee and Tyler other than that they were friends at one time,' Atherton added.

'Thanks for pointing that out,' said Slider. 'Well, we'll have to get a monitor put on Shannon's phone so that we can find her when she does make a call.'

'*If* she makes a call,' Atherton said.

'Have sense,' said Connolly. 'She's a sixteen-year-old girl. If they go more than six hours without texting someone, they get the bends.'

'If she don't use her phone,' Hart said, 'it'll tell us somefing – that either she's dead or scared shitless.'

'Don't let's prance to conclusions,' Slider said. 'Until we can find Shannon, we've nothing to go on to keep this case open. These girls must have had other friends – we must start tracking them down and pumping them. Hart, you've got the right sort of street cred. You go after Kaylee and Shannon. Try the school, social services, Shannon's mother, the neighbours even. Connolly, you get on to Tyler. The home, social services again, and the Westminster team that fielded the inquiry. Get to it.'

They left. Atherton said, 'What else?'

'There isn't much else,' said Slider discontentedly. 'Except that parties can be noisy. Check with our uniform chums in Holland Park if there were any complaints.'

'*If* there was a party, and *if* she was at it,' Atherton said. 'That's a bit thin.'

'Thin's what we've got. And get McLaren to check if there are any cameras that cover the end of the road where Kaylee was picked up. If we can get an index number for the car . . .'

'Would that we could ever be that lucky,' Atherton said.

They got lucky shortly afterwards. Swilley came to Slider's door with a printout in her hand. 'We've got Kaylee's call list, boss,' she said.

'That was quick,' said Slider. 'Anything interesting on it?'

'As a matter of fact, there is,' she said. 'She didn't make any calls on Saturday night after five thirty. OK, she was with Shannon, her best friend, until eight thirty, so she didn't need to call her. But afterwards? In my experience, girls at parties are always calling or texting their friends to tell them what a great time they're having, sending selfies and so on. What's the point of being at a really great party unless your friends all envy you for it?'

'I'll take your word,' said Slider. 'But what does that mean?'

'I don't know,' said Swilley. 'It's odd, that's all. Then, moving backwards in time, there's lunchtime with Deenie. She rang Deenie, presumably to say she was coming over. She rang the pizza place, presumably to order their lunch. And then there's the call Deenie told us she made, when she rang someone to ask if they would be at the party. The same number rang her at eight o'clock that morning. The number goes to a George Peloponnos.'

'Why does that name sound familiar?' Slider asked.

'It's the name of Atherton's "one under" on Monday,' said Swilley.

'Now *that's* what I call interesting,' said Slider.

SEVEN

From the House of the Dead

The sun was shining bleakly, but the wind was so bitter, you got no benefit from it. It was the sort of wind that blew straight at you, no matter which direction you were walking. Just crossing the yard, Slider could feel surgically thin slivers of skin being flayed from his face.

Atherton was quiet for the first few minutes, brooding. 'So was Peloponnos the older boyfriend?' he wondered at last. 'He rang her at eight in the morning to invite her to the party?'

'But then why would she call him back later the same day to ask if he'd be there?' Slider said, trying to filter right through the late-morning traffic. Addison Way was not far, but one-way systems demanded a circuitous route.

'Deenie thought she was just showing off,' Atherton reminded him. '"I've got a boyfriend who takes me to parties and you haven't."'

'It's still an odd question, "Will you be there?".'

'Didn't she say, "You *will* be there?"?'

'Either way, if he's picking her up in his car to take her there, why does she need to ask?'

'Point,' said Atherton.

'And then there's the fact that there's no telephone contact between them before Saturday,' Slider added discontentedly. Peloponnos's number did not occur in either sent or received logs.

'That also is odd,' Atherton conceded.

Or as Connolly had put it, 'How in the name of *arse* did he even get to know her without exchanging phone numbers?'

'Well, let's not get ahead of ourselves,' Slider said. 'She said she had an older boyfriend. That doesn't mean it was Peloponnos.'

'He rings her up Saturday morning, she rings him Saturday lunchtime, she gets killed Saturday night and he kills himself Monday morning,' said Atherton. 'Don't tell me there's not a connection.'

'I won't,' Slider promised.

Addison Way was a narrow cul-de-sac in which an original small number of late-Victorian villas had been pulled down and replaced by terraces of depressingly meagre modern dwellings in yellow brick, with the high flat face and backward-sloping roof oddly beloved of developers. They looked like wedges of cheap cheddar jammed together on a too-small plate.

The British Transport Police – to be specific, Sergeant Conroy – had done the Knock, but there had been no investigation at that time, given that it was an undoubted suicide. In answer to Atherton's enquiry, Conroy reported that Peloponnos had lived with his mother, Mrs Agalia Peloponnos, aged seventy-eight. He was not married, had no children, and apparently no other relatives, or at least not in the UK. Mrs S had said something about cousins in Greece. Naturally Conroy had asked her if there was anyone he could call for her, but she had said no.

'She seems to have been completely dependent on her son. I was a bit worried if she'd be all right for money in the short term, but she said Peloponnos owned the house outright, so there's no mortgage to pay, and she had plenty of cash in hand until things could be sorted out. So I gave her the number of a solicitor we trust and left it at that.' Even over the phone Atherton had heard the shrug. 'There's only so much you can do.'

Space in the redeveloped street was too limited to allow garages or even off-road car standings. It was residents' parking only, and there was only one empty space, at the far end. Slider took it gratefully, put the 'police business' card on the dashboard, and he and Atherton walked back to number 4.

'So what are we going to say to this old dame?' Atherton asked. 'Not that we think her son's a murderer?'

'We don't think it yet,' Slider said sternly.

'Some of us might.'

'Haven't I taught you anything? I hope she speaks English,' Slider added.

'Conroy said a bit fractured, but OK.'

'Then we can fudge it a bit. Say he may have connections to another case we're investigating and we'd like to ask a few questions. That sort of thing. We don't want to scare her into clamming up.'

They stopped in front of the house. In common with its neighbours it had a small unfenced area in front of it, about the same width as the pavement, which was cobbled except for the slabbed path to the front door. The door was shiny and red, with a lion's head knocker and a security light in the form of a pretend-antique carriage lamp, hallmarks of the 'desirable residence' – a.k.a. over-priced Ritz-cracker box. It was depressing to think that even this miniature living space would cost three quarters of a million in today's Shepherd's Bush.

The venetian blind in the single ground-floor window was closed and the upstairs curtains were drawn, which might have been a traditional response to bereavement or a sign that Mrs S had gone away – possibly back to Greece, which would be a serious bummer.

'OK,' said Atherton summoning cheerfulness, 'let's nail this puppy.'

Slider boggled. 'You want to *nail* a *puppy*?'

'Figuratively speaking,' said Atherton, and rang the bell.

The answer was a long time coming, but at last there were scuffing, snuffling sounds behind the door, and it was opened a crack, just wide enough for Slider to hold up his warrant card in front of the eyes behind it. The door opened fully, to reveal what could only be Mrs Peloponnos: small, brown-faced, wrinkled, with sorrowful dark eyes, grizzled hair drawn back in a bun, and clad all in black. She needed only a headscarf to stand in for any down-trodden peasant woman in rural Greece, Spain or Italy.

'May we come in?' Slider asked, after introducing themselves. 'We'd like to talk to you about your son.'

She stared for a moment, and then shrugged and shuffled back-wards as if accepting the inevitable. Even her heel-trodden carpet slippers were black. Perhaps, if she had a large family, she kept a pair specifically for bereavements.

Inside, apart from a closed-off room immediately on the right, the downstairs was all open-plan, with a staircase on the left, and a living and kitchen space taking up the rest. It was small, but the fittings were top-spec. The floors were uncarpeted woodstrip and the walls white, and the back wall was mostly window and French doors. It meant there was plenty of light, but also made the place seem empty and echoing. Behind was a tiny garden with a square of lawn, raw-looking new fencing, and two concrete urns containing pansies that were the worse for winter wear.

Slider did his best to put Mrs S at ease – sorry for your loss, and so on – but she didn't respond much. She seemed listless, and perhaps a little wary, which was not too surprising. He primed the pump with some general questions about her son, which she answered easily enough.

George was forty-eight, unmarried – had never been married. Mr and Mrs Peloponnos had come to England when Greece acceded to the EU in 1981, when George, their only surviving son, was fourteen. George was a bright boy and had got into Holland Park School's sixth form, and had gone on to get a degree in architecture at Cambridge, plus a master's in urban design. For most of his career he had worked for the local borough, rising to be chief planning officer, but two years ago had got a 'fine, new job' with the North Kensington Regeneration Trust.

Her husband had died eighteen years ago and George had come back to live with her in the rented flat in North Kensington. Eight years ago he had bought this house for them, but he had paid off the mortgage – this was evidently a matter of intense pride to her – two years ago, so now it was his entirely. It was a lovely, clean, modern place, not like the flat they had lived in before, which was in an old, old house in Ladbroke Grove. Victorian, she thought it was. She did not like old things. Old things were dirty. This house was almost brand new when he bought it.

George's office was in Notting Hill. He had been on his way to work when the 'terrible accident' had happened.

'How did he seem that morning?' Slider asked. 'Was he different in any way?'

'No, all was same. He left at ten to nine, his usual time. He was very regular, very dependable. Always the same time to go to work, always ring at lunchtime to see how I was, ask if I want anything bringing home.'

'So you had no idea that he might take his own life?'

She looked at them with angry eyes and set jaw. There was no way she was going to agree that it was suicide. 'My Yorkos would not do such a thing. He was a good boy, a good Christian, he would never do such a sinful thing. Also,' she added triumphantly, 'he left no note, and never, never would he leave without a word to his mother.'

'Had he been depressed lately?' Slider asked.

'No, not depressed. He was worried, maybe – he had a lot of responsibility. His job was very important, he was responsible for large amounts of money. He was an important man, my Yorkos. Naturally such a man would have worries.'

'Did he seem to have more worries than usual recently?'

She seemed to think, and conceded reluctantly, 'Maybe a little. Maybe he was more serious just lately. He was a lot of time in his study, on the computer. And sometimes at night, he walks about the house. I hear him always, for a mother does not sleep when her son does not sleep. But I do not go down, because it would upset him to think he had disturbed me.'

'How was he on Sunday? What was his mood?'

'Quiet. He was thinking. In his study most of the day. I said Yorkos, you must eat, you must rest, have a little fun. Even President of America must have his leisure time. You are not President of America. And he say, yes, Mama, I come soon, Mama, and he does not come.' She shrugged. 'I tell him job is job, it is not the whole of life. But he had – something on his mind.'

'Do you know what he was working on, when he was in his study?'

'No,' she said, as though it was a silly question. 'It was his work. I don't ask about his work.'

'But perhaps you might see papers in there, on his desk, or something on his computer screen?'

Her mouth set hard. 'I don't see anything.' Slider looked into her eyes unwaveringly, and heat came into them as she stared back. 'I go in there only to clean. I don't look what he is doing.'

There was something here, he thought; but she would not yield it to him – at least, not yet. She was defending her son, and he would not break through that without having some idea of what it was she was defending him for.

He changed tack. 'Did he have a girlfriend?'

'No,' she said, definitively.

'A boyfriend, then?' Atherton slipped the question in.

She looked angry. 'What are you saying? My Yorkos was not like that. He was normal, healthy man. Very handsome, very clever. Any woman would be lucky to get him. But he was not interested in marrying. His work was everything to him.'

'But I expect he had a normal social life,' Slider suggested. 'He went out in the evenings, saw friends?'

'Of course,' she conceded graciously. 'He is very popular man. Everyone likes him.'

'And some of his friends were women, naturally.'

'He never brought a woman here,' she said, again with the stubborn set of her mouth. She was shifting position, like a skilled warrior. 'Never speak of a woman. What he does when he is out in the evening, I do not know. He is grown man, he does not ask my permission. But never, never did he bring a woman here. That, I swear.' She folded her hands in her lap and closed her lips tight. End of subject.

Slider asked if they could see his office and examine his papers. He had his reason ready, but she didn't seem to require it. She shrugged resignedly and got up at once, led them with the same shuffling, bent walk to the closed-off room by the front door. It was tiny, about six feet square, and dark with the venetian blinds closed. She went over and opened them. The hard April sunlight streamed in over an office-type desk with a swivel chair, a two-drawer filing cabinet, and some IKEA bookshelves packed with what looked like reference books.

'While my colleague looks around here, may I see his room?' Slider asked.

She dug in a little. 'Why? What you want to see? My son was good man. He was not criminal. What you accuse him of?'

'I'm not accusing him of anything, Mrs Peloponnos. But there's a possibility that he might have known somebody who was mixed up in something else we're investigating. It would be very useful if I could just look and see if there's anything that will help us.'

It was deliberately evasive language. The alternative was: 'We think he might have murdered a teenage girl.'

Her eyes narrowed, her English became more fractured. 'How I know you real police? Maybe you bad people, robbers. How I know you really from police?'

'You're very wise to be cautious,' he said. He showed her his brief again, and told Atherton with a glance to do the same. As she examined them rather hopelessly, he said, 'If you would like to telephone the police station, they will confirm who we are, and that we are here on official police business.'

She gave back the warrant cards with a sigh. 'I show you room,' she said. 'Yorkos has nothing to hide. Why not show?'

She led the way up the open-tread, echoing stairs – slippery and dangerous, he would have thought, for an elderly woman in trodden-down slippers, but it wasn't his business. Atherton remained below to search the office.

There was a tiny upper landing with three doors. One stood open to show a small bathroom. She opened one of the others onto a bedroom cloaked in gloom from the drawn curtains.

When they were pulled back, he saw a double bed, neatly made with a white woven cotton counterpane, a Wedgewood blue carpet, a wardrobe, chest of drawers, and a white cane chair by the windows. On the wall were several enlarged and framed photographs of Greek village scenes, the houses very white in a blinding sun, the sky very blue, the geraniums very red. The bedside cabinets were white laminate, and the lamps had blue shades. On one rested a much-thumbed paperback copy of *War and Peace* – ongoing bedtime reading – and a glasses case. On the other was a framed studio photograph of George Peloponnos with his arm round his mother, in front of which stood a tiny blue glass vase containing a single white rose. On the windowsill was a glass ornament in the shape of a leaping dolphin and a small, heavy glass ashtray. It was all very tidy, smelt of furniture polish, and the carpet showed the rake-marks of recent hoovering.

'Have you cleaned the room since – since Monday?' he asked.

She looked at him. 'Of course,' she said.

Of course. When someone died, you made the house decent and closed the curtains. And put a tribute of flowers in front of their photograph.

There was nothing here of great luxury, but the carpet was newish and of good quality, and the decorating had been done by a good professional. He looked into the wardrobe, saw good quality suits and shirts, and expensive shoes on individual trees lined up below. In the chest-of-drawers were woollens and underwear, likewise of good quality and neatly folded. Either he had been a neatness freak, or Mummy was organising his drawers. By the eagle way she was watching him, he suspected the latter.

He tried the bedside cabinets, without hope. If she was in and out all the time, he would hardly keep anything incriminating where she could find it. There was the usual man-rubble of loose change, spare batteries, an empty and unused wallet, several combs, some handkerchiefs, a decongestant spray, another pair of glasses in a case, and a small photo album containing old black-and-whites of, presumably, his parents and other family members back in Greece, and childhood snaps of George in childhood. A lonely childhood, it seemed – he was always alone in the frame, barelegged with a net on a stick in a rock pool, windswept on a cliff top, backdropped by a temple ruin on the Acropolis, rather embarrassed sitting astride a pony. No friend, companion or dog shared these iconic moments. A lone little boy with rather elderly parents, who had ended up in a strange country, living with his mother, and ultimately under a tube train. What had he done in between? Where did Kaylee Adams come into it?

Slider shut the disturbing album away in its drawer. Between the wardrobe and the window was another door, ajar, to an ensuite shower room. Every two-bed development now had to have two bathrooms, even if fitting them in made the bedrooms unliveably small. George's bedroom – and Slider was much mistaken if it weren't the larger of the two – was about eleven by twelve. The shower room was small, but again, the fittings were high-spec.

Mrs Peloponnos didn't follow him, so he was able to go straight to the medicine cabinet. Everything else had obviously been cleaned and tidied, but it seemed unlikely that she would have turned it out yet. And indeed, he found an impressive haul of medicaments, over-the-counter nostrums for headaches, backaches, indigestion, constipation and haemorrhoids (oh, what an attractive fellow he now seemed!), together with prescription tranquilizers and sleeping pills. Slider made a mental note of the doctor's name. Running a hand along the top of the cabinet, where Mrs S would have difficulty reaching, he found some dust, two packets of cigarette papers, five loose, foil-wrapped condoms, and a small key. You couldn't see any of them from ground level. The key looked as though it would fit a desk drawer or a filing cabinet.

He went back into the bedroom, and saw her still standing at the bedroom door, her face blank and lost. Remembering.

'Do you know what this key is for?' Slider asked.

She barely looked. 'No,' she said. 'I don't know it.'

'May I take it?' She shrugged consent. 'Did your son smoke?' he asked.

She snapped back to life. 'No,' she said. 'Never. In Greece everyone smokes, but in Greece life is out of doors. You cannot smoke in a cold, damp country. It makes houses smell bad.'

'You're very right,' Slider said, and she seemed to warm at the praise.

'Would you like I make you a cup of tea?' she asked.

While she was putting on the kettle, Slider went back to Atherton. He was examining something spread out on the desk.

'I had a quick look in the drawers, but there's nothing unusual. On the computer there's a couple of files that are password protected, otherwise nothing interesting. But I found this tucked in between two books up there,' he said, nodding towards the shelves.

It was a blueprint-sized architectural drawing of what seemed to be an alteration or addition to a large, square, Georgian-looking house. Front and side elevations showed the roof removed and replaced with a roof terrace, including a glass structure in which modern sofas, chairs and a bar had been sketched. The terrace area had been given planters and outside space heaters, and figures – thin, rich people – were disporting themselves with champagne flutes in their long, elegant hands.

'What do you suppose it is?' Atherton said. 'There's no address or technical details on it. A fantasy, d'you suppose? His dream house?'

'But then why would it need altering. If he was designing his dream home, he'd design it from scratch. And it would be a modern building. Trained architects all hate pastiche.'

'Well, maybe he saw this house, fell in love with it, and thought it would be perfect if only it had a sheila-trap on the roof. Did you find anything?'

'Only Rizla papers, condoms and a key.' He showed it.

'Well, the desk and filing cabinet here aren't locked. Maybe it's from his work office.'

Mrs S reappeared at the door, and Slider turned to her. 'Do you know what this drawing is?'

She glanced at it. 'I don't know. I never ask about his work. Tea is made.'

In the kitchen, over tea, they showed her photographs of Kaylee and Shannon, and even Tyler Vance, but she said she didn't recognize them, and did not know their names. She said again, as if it was important, that her son had never brought any woman to the house. 'These too young for him,' she said, with a dismissive gesture at the photographs. 'He would not be interested anyway in young girls like that.' She peered more closely. 'They don't look like good girls,' she added, and gave Slider an angry look. 'Why you think he would mix with girls like that?'

Slider soothed her feathers, and asked about his social life, but as to who his friends might be, or where he went in the evenings for his socialising, she could not say. But she did confirm that he had gone out on Saturday night – not to a party, but to the opera. 'Katya Kabanova, at Covent Garden. He loves opera, my Yorkos. He goes often.'

'I can't see him taking Kaylee Adams to a Janáček opera,' Atherton said as they walked back to the car.

'Hmm,' said Slider, deep in thought.

'What?' Atherton asked.

'Don't you think,' Slider said slowly, 'that she ought to have been less forthcoming?'

'The bereaved often want to talk about the beloved,' Atherton offered.

'That's true. But she didn't really, did she? She didn't volunteer anything, share her memories of him, get out the photograph album. She just answered our questions – and *why* did she? As far as she knows, he committed suicide. Why wasn't she more curious about why we were there at all?'

'I don't know, guv,' Atherton said patiently. 'Why do *you* think?'

'Because she knows he was up to something. Maybe she doesn't know what, but she knows it was bad and doesn't want to hear about it. She wants to remember her good son the way he was to her. So she answers up and tries to get us out of her hair with as little trouble as possible.'

'The bad things he was up to could be no worse than just drugs and girls,' Atherton said.

'Oh, I know,' said Slider.

EIGHT
The Wife of Bach

'There *was* a ticket bought with a credit card in the name of George Peloponnos,' Swilley reported the result of her enquiry of the Royal Opera House, 'and the seat *was* occupied, but we don't know who by.'

'Security cameras?' Porson asked. He was perched on the end of her desk and holding a mug of tea, which was standing on a saucer, whose purpose was solely for the transportation of two custard creams and a Bourbon. Slider looked at them enviously. He hadn't had any lunch.

'They have them, of course,' said Swilley, 'but they don't keep the tapes longer than seventy-two hours, unless there's an incident.' This was quite common. Some commercial concerns only kept them forty-eight hours. 'We could interview the people who were on duty that night, show them his photograph, see if they remember him.'

But that was laborious. 'And if he was at the opera,' McLaren said, 'he wasn't at this party, so he's not our man anyway.' He had a Cornish pasty cooling on a plate on his desk, but didn't like to eat it in front of Mr Porson, who had recently been extremely sharp about greasy fingermarks on a document.

'Just because Kaylee said she was going to a party, doesn't mean she went,' Mackay pointed out.

'By the same token, telling his mother he was going to the opera doesn't mean Georgie was the one in the seat,' Atherton added.

'When was the ticket purchased?' Slider asked.

'On Friday, five forty-five. By phone with a credit card.'

'Bit of a last-minute purchase,' Slider said.

'It was an expensive seat, too,' Swilley said. 'Orchestra stalls – the best.'

'Probably all that was left by then,' said Slider. 'Just the one?'

'Yes, sir.'

'So it could have been bought as an alibi,' Atherton said.

'But alibi for what?' Porson barked restlessly.

'If he bought the ticket *before* inviting Kaylee to the party, does that mean he was planning to kill her?' Mackay wondered.

'We don't know that he *did* invite her to the party,' Slider said. 'Only that he phoned her that morning. And,' he added, against the looks of resistance from his crew, 'if she was being picked up in a car at the end of the street, we have to take into consideration that Mrs Peloponnos says her son didn't own a car and couldn't drive.'

'Anyone can *say* they can't drive,' McLaren grumbled sotto voce.

'So all you've got to connect him with Adams,' said Porson, 'is the two phone calls on the day. And nothing to connect him or Adams with the Vance case.' Slider recognized this for a rhetorical question and said nothing. 'You've got the square root of sod all, pardon my French. They'll have my testimonials on a plate if I go upstairs with that.'

'I'd really like to bring in his computer,' Slider said.

'Can't do that,' said Porson, chomping his last custard cream and spraying crumbs. 'Not without more to go on.' He fielded their protesting looks. 'Oh, it's a mystery, all right. What it's not is a case.'

'So – we pull it?' Slider said. Over the years he had learned, like a good dog, to read his master's body language and recognize his tones of voice, so he knew the answer would not be a flat 'yes'.

'I don't like it,' Porson said. 'Something stinks, and it's not just one dead sprat. You can stay on it, as long as you get your other work done at the same time. But you'll have to be quick, get me something solid. What are you following up?'

'Fathom's out now, looking for a camera that might have caught Kaylee being picked up on Saturday night. We're waiting for Peloponnos's phone records. I want to look into this trust he was working for and have a sniff around his office. We're monitoring Shannon's phone – a sixteen-year-old can't go for long without using it. And Hart and Connolly are out looking for other girls in Kaylee's and Tyler's circles who might have something to tell.'

'Is that it?' Porson said, wounded.

'And, of course, something might be forthcoming from Harefield about the motor,' Slider added unhappily.

'*Forth*coming? You'll need the *second* coming to get you out of this. Well—' he stood up, apparently done with punishing them – 'do what you can.' He swilled back the last of his tea, stood up and gave them a final, sharp look to share between them. 'It's all cisterns go on this one, because by the end of the week you've got to show up, or shut up.'

Connolly was back late. She had gone to social services first. The case worker supervisor said that Tyler was flagged up by the care home because of her nocturnal absences; but she had presented well on interviewing – quiet, polite, not aggressive. 'We look out for signs of self-harming and anorexia,' she said. 'They're usually the big signs that something serious is wrong. But Tyler came across as a confident girl, not likely to be bullied. And not depressed. She wouldn't tell us where she went when she broke out at night – just said she wanted a bit of fun. We supposed she had a boyfriend. Well, you can't really stop them by that age. Frankly, there are so many girls really on the edge that we can't follow up on the less critical cases.'

And then Connolly had gone to the care home. 'Jesus Mary an' Joseph, you'd want to see that place,' she said. 'Rough as a badger's arse. But the superintendent let me talk to the girls. The older ones are hard as a bunch o' crack whores, and the younger ones are just pathetic. The one lot givin' me the dog's abuse for bein' the filth, the other lot streelin' round in a fog o' depression, and between them never an answer to a straight question. More stone-wallin' than the Yorkshire Dales.'

'So you got nothing?' Slider asked.

'Well, there was one girl seemed a bit more on the ball than the others. Said she reckoned Tyler was doing a line with an older feller, used to get out Saturday nights and come back in the early hours. Well, we knew that anyway. But,' she added, 'she said Tyler used to hang around with another girl, called Jessica Bale, only she's left now. So I asked the superintendent. This Jessica was older than Tyler, and they chuck 'em out when they get to sixteen. She gave me the address of this hostel they send them to. So I went there.'

'And?'

'She wasn't there. She'd moved on. Apparently they generally do. They didn't know where she'd gone. But wait'll I tell ya,' she went on quickly. 'I showed the warden Kaylee's an' Shannon's pix,

and she didn't recognize Kaylee, but she reckoned she'd seen
Shannon before, thought she was a friend of this Jessica's. So it
occurred to me that if we can find Jessica, she might know where
Shannon is. She might even be stayin' with her.'

'If you can find her,' Slider said. 'She might be anywhere.'

'Yeah, but these girls rarely move far away,' Connolly said. 'They
stick around the streets they know. And I got a photo of her. If we
put it out on circulation, there's a good chance one of our guys'll
spot her.'

'Well, it's a long shot,' Slider said, 'but we haven't got any short
ones. Go for it.'

Hart came back even later. The school said Kaylee had been in
trouble for getting into fights, stealing, and damaging school property, until about a year ago when she had quietened down. After
that her misbehaviour was mainly absenteeism. She had brought
forged notes from her mother, and frequently used the excuse that
her mother was ill and needed caring for, or that she had had to
take her to A&E after a fall or domestic mishap. Her absences were
usually on a Friday or Monday, which had triggered the suspicion
that she was truanting to extend the weekend.

Social services were still monitoring the family because of the
mother's drug habit, but they were more worried about Julienne
than Kaylee, who had seemed to be 'coping'.

'And o' course I couldn't talk to the kids because they're
underage,' she concluded. 'I could 'ave anuvver go at Julienne wiv
her mum present. She might know a bit more about where big sis
went at night.'

'I can't authorize that at the moment,' Slider said, 'given that it
isn't even officially a case. Write up your notes and go on home.
We'll hope for better luck tomorrow.'

Peloponnos's doctor, Bhatia, worked out of a surgery on Brook
Green, and Slider caught him before he finished for the day. He
was a lean and handsome GP of the modern sort, well-dressed,
friendly, and energetic. His room was neat and tidy, with a framed
photograph of a smiling wife and two children on the side of his
desk. He put Slider in mind of a successful young executive – which
he supposed, with the current fund-holding NHS arrangements, he
was.

'Oh yes, I've been treating Mr Peloponnos and his mother for four years,' he said. There was no trace of the Punjab in his accent. Slider had looked him up, and he had been in England since he was two and had studied medicine at Barts. 'Ever since I took over the list from Dr Camden when he retired. They've been with this surgery about eight years, I believe.' He accessed the computer record with a rapid jabber of fingers. 'Yes, they came over from Ladbroke Grove, Dr Odessa. What did you want to know?'

Slider mentioned the drugs he had found in the medicine cabinet. 'Was that a usual prescription for him? Had he been on them long?'

'No,' said Bhatia. 'In fact, he hasn't come on our radar much over the years. It was his mother I saw more of – just the usual pains of age. Mr Peloponnos was pretty healthy. There was a scare a few years ago when he came in thinking he had bowel cancer, but I sent him for tests and there was nothing there. A touch of constipation – plus hypochondria. I expect he'd read something in the Sunday supps. I'd class him as a rather nervous, imaginative person. Of course, we always take anything like that seriously, but he was as clean as a whistle inside.'

Which Slider found an odd simile, in the circumstances. He shied away from the mental image and said, 'So what gave rise to these sleeping pills?'

'Well, he came in on January the 15th, complaining of insomnia. He seemed nervous and depressed, and he looked as though he hadn't slept. I asked him if there was any reason for it, and he said he had a lot on at work, and it was preying on his mind at night and stopping him sleeping. So I gave him a benzodiazepine compound. A couple of weeks later he came back wanting something he could take in the daytime that wouldn't make him sleepy. I prescribed a fluoxetine.'

'That's the Prozac, is it?'

'That's right.' He smiled. 'The so-called "Happy Pills".'

'Was he still taking the sleeping pills?'

'Yes. He said they were working. He came back for a repeat prescription—' he scrolled again – 'at the beginning of March. I didn't see him that time – one of my colleagues did. And he's had repeats of the Prozac, taking him up-to-date.'

'When did you last see him?'

'Let me see – on March the 18th.'

'And how was he then?'

Bhatia consulted his notes, then sat back, crossed his legs, steepled his fingers, and frowned in thought. 'Nervous and depressed,' he said. 'Not to a non-functioning level, but he was definitely not in his normal state of mind, as far as I remembered it. He seemed to be brooding about something and – yes, I remember someone dropped something in the corridor outside, made rather a crash, and he jumped. Nerves on edge.'

'But he never told you what he was worried about?'

'Only that he was busy at work, as I said.' Bhatia seemed to take it as a criticism. 'We have ten minutes per patient, and that's *maximum*. We don't have time any more for the chat.'

Slider took *that* as a hint, and rose. 'It's good of you to give me your time.'

'Not at all,' said Bhatia, rising too and offering his hand. 'Is there anything else I can help you with? Well, do give me a ring if there is.'

Slider had reached the door when he heard Bhatia draw a preparatory breath, and he turned back to see him gestating of a confidence. He smiled receptively.

'There is just one thing,' Bhatia said. He gave a troubled smile and a little shrug. 'I suppose it doesn't matter now, in the circumstances. But I have a suspicion that he might have been using cocaine.'

'What makes you think that?'

'Oh, one knows the signs, you know. It's comparatively common these days, especially with your high-powered executives. I saw him a couple of times last year with minor ailments and thought that might be the case. It obviously wasn't giving him problems, so I didn't raise it with him – it doesn't do to lose their trust. But you know, cocaine can cause depression. And cocaine users often smoke cannabis as well, and the combination can lead to the sort of anxious, fearful unhappiness that can drive a person to suicide.'

'Did you consider that when you prescribed him sedatives?' Slider asked.

Bhatia bristled. 'As I've said, he was high-functioning. And we don't have time to go into all the nooks and crannies. We have to examine, prescribe and get on to the next patient. It's inevitable that sometimes people will slip through the cracks. I'm sorry Mr

Peloponnos did away with himself. But he didn't kill himself with
the pills, did he?'

'No,' said Slider. 'He didn't.'

Joanna had had sessions all day, and was home when he got back.
He went up and changed and looked in at his son, peacefully sleeping
under his Pooh 'n' Piglet duvet, and went back down to share a
kitchen supper with his beloved. It was macaroni cheese.

'You made this,' he discovered with pleasure. 'When did you
have the time?'

'While your dad did George's bath and story,' she said. Slider's
father lived with his new wife in the attached granny flat. In fact,
it was his investment – from selling the farm cottage, where Slider
had been born, to a developer – that had allowed them to buy the
present house. 'How did you know I made it?'

'Bits of crisp pancetta. Dad never puts bacon in his. And, if I'm
not mistaken, a bay leaf in the cheese sauce.'

Joanna was impressed. 'That's amazing, Monsieur Escoffier. You
must have the delicate palate of a gourmet.'

'No, I have a bay leaf,' Slider said fishing it up. 'You forgot to
take it out.'

'And your dad would never do that. But may I remind you, he
can't play the violin.'

'It wasn't a criticism. How was your day?'

'Not too bad. A bit tedious this afternoon – too many stops. The
engineers kept getting extraneous noises so we had to retake.'

'At least you got a rest.'

'And it's a good time to pass round jokes,' Joanna said. 'Jason
told me a good one.' Jason was her desk partner. 'How many second
violins does it take to change a lightbulb?'

'I don't know.'

'None – they can't get up that high.'

Slider laughed dutifully. He understood musician jokes now, but
he supposed you had to be a musician really to find them funny.

They had just finished the macaroni cheese when the phone rang.
Joanna jumped up to answer it, and it was evidently one of her
sisters, because she went into one of those long meandering conversations that men find baffling. How can women find so much to say
on the telephone? And to someone they've spoken to recently –

perhaps even the day before? Joanna liked to move about while on the phone, and cleared the table as she spoke, then wandered out into the hall. When she reached the bit of the conversation where her contribution was mostly, 'Yes. Mm-hm. Oh yes. Really? Mmm,' Slider got up and made coffee.

It was ready just as she said goodbye. 'Perfect timing,' she told him, taking her cup from him and heading for the sitting room. She put on a disc, turned down low – she didn't approve of using music as background wallpaper, but made exceptions for him if she thought he'd had a hard day – and patted the sofa beside her. 'Come and tell me about it,' she said.

He sat. 'That's nice – what is it? Bach?'

'Well spotted. Darling Rosty playing the "Cello Suite number one in G Major". Many have followed, but there's only one Rostropovich.'

He listened for a bit in silence, thinking that if more people had wives to come home to who made them supper and played them the cello suites, there would be less unhappiness in the world. Peloponnos might not have committed suicide if he'd had Joanna, macaroni cheese and Bach.

'You look tired,' Joanna said after a bit. 'What's happening with your case?'

He roused himself. 'If it were a case, we could pursue it properly,' he complained. 'So far all we've got is Freddie Cameron's opinion that it wasn't an RTA.'

'But isn't Freddie always right?'

'I think so. But if it came to court, the prosecution would be able to disagree. And we haven't really got anything else.' He told her about the day's developments.

'So your thinking is that he killed her, then committed suicide out of remorse. Or fear, perhaps – fear of being caught, going to prison, shaming his dear old mother?'

'That seems the most likely. And buying the opera ticket looks like an attempt to establish an alibi. But there are odd things about it. How did he get Kaylee's body out to Harefield when he didn't have a car and couldn't drive?'

'Maybe he just said he couldn't drive,' Joanna offered.

'There's no record of his ever having had a licence. Then there's the question of why and how he suddenly got hold of Kaylee's number. They didn't ring each other before that day.'

'Maybe she had another mobile.'

'It's not impossible, but I think it's unlikely. A girl from that background. And why would she?'

'Because she was mixed up in something criminal. Like in *The Wire* – throw-away pay-as-you-goes?'

'That was fiction, and it was really big league stuff, anyway. Kaylee was just a fairly dopy ordinary teenager.'

Joanna examined his features. 'So what do you think is behind it?'

'I've no idea,' he said glumly. 'And I can't investigate properly because we haven't established there even was a crime. It's like losing your glasses – you can't look for them till you've found them.'

'If Peloponnos didn't know Kaylee,' Joanna said, thinking it out, 'then maybe someone else gave him her number just for that occasion. He wanted a date to take to the party.'

'If he went to the party. And if he did, why did he buy an expensive ticket to the opera?'

'He bought that the day before. Maybe he didn't know about the party then, and when he did hear about it, decided he preferred it. Especially if it meant taking Kaylee.'

'You haven't seen her. She was no great catch.'

'Or he had a really shy friend who hadn't got the nerve to ask her himself, so he did it for him.'

'He was forty-eight,' Slider pointed out.

'Even forty-eight-year-olds can be shy. In fact, rejection can be worse when you get to that age. Not that you'd know, Mr Confidence.'

'I'll have you know I'm very shy and sensitive.'

'You asked me out the minute you saw me. *And* whisked me off to bed.'

'As I remember, you did the whisking. Anyway,' he said, taking the cup from her hand and putting it down, 'it's different when it's True Love.'

'Oh, is that what it is?' she murmured, kissing him back.

Was it his curse that at this very tender moment, the memory of their dead baby popped into his mind? He didn't want their intimate life to be conducted hesitantly, and in the shadow of the miscarriage, but somehow lately he seemed to have lost his nerve. He had enough courage with regard to his own safety, but he was terribly afraid on her behalf. He didn't want to do or say anything that would increase her pain.

And hard on the heels of the Lost Child came the Hanged Man, aka Hollis. But whereas the Tarot card could mean awakening or renewal, Hollis only meant sadness and guilt, the passion-killer to beat all.

She drew back and looked at him. 'What is it?' she asked.

He didn't want to put it into words, because that would give it substance; and he wasn't sure he could, anyway.

But she knew him very well. 'I'm all right now,' she said. 'Have been for months. But if you're still worried, we can just cuddle. Cuddling's good.'

'It is,' he said, shadows fleeing, dispelled by her smile. She was so very good at cuddling, that in all probability nature would take its course quite effortlessly. As, of course, she very well knew. 'Oh wise young judge,' he said.

'Hang on,' she objected. 'Isn't the next bit "How much more elder art thou than thy looks"?'

'But that's a compliment,' Slider said, and started kissing her again.

The bright sunshine of the day before had gone, and clouds carpeted Thursday's sky with the translucent white of Tupperware. From time to time it darkened to grey and a thin drizzle fell. But at least the wind had dropped.

Fathom, a big meaty lad, who gelled his hair into Keanu Reeves spikes, perhaps in an attempt to appear more interesting, came jauntily into Slider's office, preceded by the smell of his aftershave. It was apparently called Fella. Atherton said that was short for Ox-Feller.

'I struck lucky with the motor, guv,' he announced.

'I hope Lucky wasn't a dog,' Slider returned.

'Come again?'

'Never mind.' Slider waved it away. 'Tell me what you've got.'

'It was a bit of a trawl,' Fathom said, back on safe ground, 'because a lot of shops on Shepherd's Bush Road have cameras, but mostly they don't keep the tapes long enough. But there's a bank across the road and they had an incident last month and it's made 'em nervous so they're keeping stuff a week now. Wanna see?'

Slider followed him back to his desk.

'Course, it's night time, under street lamps, so the definition's not good, but you can see the girl waiting at the kerb at the end of the side road.'

'It could be Kaylee,' said Slider.

Fathom enlarged the image but it became too grainy to identify the features absolutely. However, the clothes looked right – the leather jacket, short skirt and strappy high-heeled sandals. And the hair looked right – though most teenagers these days wore the hair long and straggly like that. Slider noted she had a small handbag on a long strap over her shoulder and was smoking a cigarette.

'I reckon it has to be her, guv,' said Fathom, 'given the place and the time. And here comes the motor.'

A black SUV drew up alongside her. When it moved on, Kaylee was no longer at the kerbside. Fathom enlarged the image again, but the windows were blacked out and it was not possible to see who was driving.

'Well, that's a help,' Slider said. 'At least we know she was picked up in a car at the time she said. But there must be a lot of black SUVs in London.'

McLaren, still breakfast grazing – in the closing stages with a chocolate fudge pop tart – wandered over, attracted by any words that had to do with cars. 'Show us it again, Jezza,' he commanded. Slider made room for him – one always gives way before the expert. 'That's not just any SUV,' he pronounced. 'That's a Mercedes GL550.' He could recognize any vehicle, as a mother can tell her newborn baby from all the others in the nursery. 'Top of the range. All the bells and whistles. Cost you upstairs of sixty k. Bastard of a fuel consumption, but if you got that sort of money to spend on your wheels, who cares?'

'So there won't be too many of them around?' Slider asked, with hope.

'Well,' McLaren said doubtfully, 'they're popular in the Diplomatic. And the rich Arabs buy them for their wives. Same with the Russian oligarchs. But,' he added comfortingly, 'it's not like looking for a Corsa, or a Ford Asbo. Didn't you get the index, Jez?'

'I was coming to that,' Fathom said defensively. 'There was a TfL bus camera. The angle's not right, but I got a partial.' He cued up the shot, where the car was coming round the corner from Shepherd's Bush Green, and for a moment the camera caught it in three-quarter profile.

'You can see it's a Merc all right,' McLaren said, pointing to the badge on the radiator for Slider's sake.

'But you can't read the index,' Fathom said regretfully. 'I've tried everything. You can see it begins with A, then it looks like F, or it might be E. But that's all.'

'Is that what you call a partial. One letter? You don't even know what year it is.'

'It's better than nothing,' said Fathom.

'All right,' Slider stepped in. 'You'd better get a list of all of that model, with tinted windows, sold in this country, and start running them down.'

NINE

Coffee and Donors

Swilley came to the door. 'Peloponnos's mobile record,' she said. Then: 'It's a tricky name,' she complained. 'Can't we refer to him as George, boss?'

'George is my son's name.'

'I think you'll be able to tell when I'm talking about your son.'

'All right, if it helps. Anything interesting?'

'Yes, boss. There's the call to Kaylee's mobile all right, and right after it, he calls another number. Very short call, only fifteen seconds, but the number goes to Gideon Marler.'

'The MP?' said Slider.

'MP for Kensington North, and chair of the Parliamentary Select Committee on police matters,' Swilley elaborated. 'It's a sub-committee of the Home Office Select Committee, so he's got some pretty high-up connections.'

'So I imagine,' said Slider.

It was a position of influence. The chairman of a select committee had the power to demand attendance of anyone and put them under scrutiny. Even luminaries of the Association of Chief Police Officers had to respect him.

'I wonder how George knew him?' Swilley mused.

'Peloponnos worked for the local council. No reason he shouldn't know a local MP.'

'But the timing, boss – it's interesting, don't you think?'

'I do think. We should have a word with Mr Marler.'

'He's got a constituency office in Notting Hill, and I found out from his secretary that he's there this morning, doing a surgery. Shall I go?'

Slider thought. 'No, I think I'll go myself,' he said. With someone so important and well-connected, it was as well to let them think they were getting the full organ grinder and not the monkey.

Atherton had also gone to Notting Hill, to the office of the North Kensington Regeneration Trust, which was in a converted Regency house on the Campden Hill side of the main street.

He had looked up the trust on the internet beforehand and found that it was an NGO and a registered charity. It had been set up in partnership with the local authority with a starting grant of £50,000, but was now a self-sustaining and not-for-profit organisation, handling millions every year. The mission statement said it was 'working alongside the public and voluntary sectors to improve the environmental well-being' of a run-down part of the borough.

'What does that mean?' Atherton asked Virginia ('Call me Ginnie') Lamy, Peloponnos's smart middle-aged PA.

'The trust was started by ordinary people from the neighbour-hood, who wanted to see real change and improvement. Now we promote arts and culture, host events, and provide space and devel-opment opportunities to individuals, businesses and charities, using our resources to realize the full potential of the community.'

'And what does *that* mean?' Atherton asked.

She frowned. 'Are you being deliberately obtuse?'

'No,' he said with his most disarming smile. 'I'd just like to have it in simpler terms. I've never managed to get on top of office-speak.'

'All right,' she said, slightly shortly. 'We have fundraisers, help worthwhile organisations find premises, advise on community projects. We give out a certain number of grants to artists and so on. And we buy land and develop it for the benefit of the local community.'

'You do the development yourselves?'

'Sometimes. More often we facilitate the work of developers who share our aims.'

'I see. So having a former chief planning officer on the staff must be a great help,' said Atherton.

'George is wonderful,' she said warmly; then her expression drooped. 'I mean, he *was* wonderful. I can't believe he's gone.'

'Were you with him when he worked for the borough?'

'No, I was recruited as his PA when he came here. We started at the same time.'

'And he was the CEO here, was he?'

'No, Chief Development Director. Betty Geeson is the CEO.'

'But as Chief Development Director, I expect he had a lot of responsibility.'

'Gosh, yes, massive,' she said. 'Really, he was the final authority on whether anything went ahead. Betty's more day-to-day management. Her background's in charity and government lobbying. George was the real technical expert.'

'Had you noticed lately that all this responsibility was getting him down?'

She coloured. 'No, not at all. What are you saying? He was superb at his job.'

'I'm sure he was. But didn't you think he was rather worried lately? A little out of sorts, as though something was preying on his mind?'

'You're just saying that because he committed suicide. But I promise you, if anyone here had had any idea that he was likely to . . . well, we'd have done anything to help him, anything at all.'

Atherton spread his hands. 'I assure you, I meant no criticism. I'm just trying to establish whether he seemed any different recently.'

'No,' she said. And then her eyes dropped. 'Well,' she began.

'Yes?' Atherton encouraged.

'He had been a bit – preoccupied. Sometimes you'd speak to him three or four times before he'd answer. Sometimes he didn't pick up his phone, and you'd come in and he'd be standing staring out of the window, not hearing it.'

'Was it more a worried preoccupation, do you think, or a sad one?'

She considered. 'Worried, I think.'

'And how long had it been going on?'

'Oh, I don't know. A while. Several weeks – maybe a couple of months. But I don't want you to think he wasn't doing his work. He was. But he was . . .' A long pause. 'Brooding, I suppose is the word. Absent, maybe.' She looked down at her hands. 'But I suppose it was his own death he was thinking about. It's still hard to believe he would do that – throw himself in front of a train. He must have been really so unhappy. And we didn't know.'

Atherton gave her a beat of sympathy, then said, 'I'd like to have a look at his office, if you don't mind.'

'I don't mind – but why? Are you trying to find out why he killed himself? Is that usual?'

She was too sharp for him to pretend it was. 'We think he may have known someone who was mixed up in something we're investigating. Nothing to be alarmed about, though.'

She looked worried. 'I think I ought to ask Betty if it's all right. Trouble is, she's in an important meeting in Westminster at the moment and I can't reach her.'

'There's no need to bother her,' Atherton said soothingly. 'I won't take anything away. I just want to look around, in case I spot anything that could help us.'

'Who is this other person? What's the thing he was mixed up in? Maybe I can help.'

'I'm afraid I can't tell you anything about it at the moment. But you can help by showing me his office.'

She seemed puzzled; but reassured, perhaps, by her conviction of her former boss's innocence, she led him to the door and opened it for him, and then hovered in the doorway, watching. It was quite a handsomely-appointed office: nice paint job, good quality carpet, solid wood desk. A couple of leather easy chairs flanked the fire-place under whose Adam surround a gas coal-effect fire had been installed. There was a glazed mahogany bookcase with cupboard under, and a trolley in the corner bearing bottles of drinks and Waterford glasses.

'Did he entertain a lot of visitors here?' Atherton asked.

'Oh, yes. Developers, charity heads, councillors, politicians, advisers of all sorts. Donors, too. He was very good with the donors.'

'People give you money to regenerate the neighbourhood?'

She gave him a stiff look. 'It's an important project. A worthy cause.' His steady gaze got through the defence. 'And it's very good publicity for them. And we're a registered charity so it can be written off against tax.'

'Ah. So a lot of wealthy and important people come through these doors.'

'Yes, they do. I told you, it's a major project.'

The telephone outside on her desk rang, and she went away to answer it. Atherton took the opportunity to try the computer, which, like office computers everywhere, had been left on. Its folders seemed to be labelled with addresses and the names of projects, as one might expect. There was one labelled 'Letters', one 'Planning applications'. He noticed one called 'Cope', but when he tried to call that one up, it was password protected.

He listened and heard her voice, still on the phone. He looked quickly in the desk drawers, but saw nothing out of the usual. The bottom one was locked. He tried the key from Peloponnos's bathroom, and it worked. Inside there was a metal cash box, locked, and under it a single pink wallet file. He picked up the file. It contained a handwritten sheet, a list of names, some with dates beside them. He recognized some of them – the names of people of influence and importance. On the spur of the moment, he laid it flat on the desk and took a photograph of it with his mobile. Hearing what sounded like winding-up conversation from outside, he returned the paper to the file, put the file back and closed and locked the drawer.

She looked at him sharply as she came in, faithful watchdog that she was. Under her eye, he went through the drawers of the filing cabinet, but saw nothing he wouldn't have expected.

'Well, have you found anything?' she asked as he closed the bottom drawer. From the tone of her voice it was evidently a *num* question.

He turned. 'There's a password-protected folder on the computer,' he said. 'Can you open it for me?'

She looked annoyed. 'I didn't say you could look in his computer.'

'I *am* a police officer,' he said, going for a little authority, 'and this is an important investigation.'

She yielded, just a bit. 'Well, I can't help you with that. I don't know the password.' To his raised eyebrow, she said, 'Really. He had one or two protected files that only he could access.'

'Why? What was in them?'

'*I* don't know. If I knew that, there'd have been no point in protecting them, would there?'

'Surely as his PA, you needed access to every part of his work.'

'If I had needed what was in those files, he'd have given it to me. Really, I don't know what you're accusing him of.'

She was getting irritable and he needed to redirect her. 'Could you give me a list of your principal donors? If they're using the donations for PR and tax purposes, I assume the information must be in the public domain.'

'I can give you a printout,' she said. She used Peloponnos's computer to call up a document, and sent the information to the printer outside on her desk. 'Anything else?' she asked, as the whine and zip of the printer began.

'Yes,' he said. 'Did he ever mention someone called Kaylee to you? Kaylee Adams?'

'No,' she said. 'I don't think so. Who is she?' He showed her a photograph and she shook her head at once, and convincingly.

'What about Shannon Bailey? Tyler Vance? Did you ever, for instance, put through a call from any of them?'

She shook her head again. 'Who are all these people?'

'I know George wasn't married, but did he have a girlfriend?'

'*Girlfriend*?' she said scornfully. 'You're not thinking he'd have taken an interest in a girl like that?'

'Any girl or woman. Lady friend. Significant other, however you like to put it. Was there a female acquaintance of more than usual importance to him?'

She blushed again, and it seemed part embarrassment, part anger. 'I never heard him speak of anyone. But really,' she added with dignity, 'I didn't inquire into his personal life.'

'I'm sure not, but sometimes things just come out in the course of conversation. And a good-looking chap like him, with such an important job – well, he'd be something of a catch, one would think.'

She lowered her eyes. 'I never heard him talk about anyone. If there was someone, he kept it to himself.'

Pique, Atherton thought. She had been a little bit in love with Peloponnos – and Georgie hadn't responded.

'Why are you asking, anyway? What's it got to do with anything?'

'It probably hasn't,' he said soothingly. 'I think the printer's finished.'

She stalked out before him, retrieved the printout and thrust it into his hand. 'And now,' she said loftily, 'I must get on with my work.'

Gideon Marler's constituency office was in what had been an empty shop, and now resembled a doctor's waiting room. Venetian blinds and cheap carpeting had introduced a less commercial, more domestic atmosphere. There were moulded chairs around the walls for supplicants to wait on, a table covered in battered magazines and rather more pristine Party material, and screens had been erected in one corner around the desk at which the MP exposed himself to the concerns of his constituents.

The people waiting looked to Slider like the normal mixture of the obsessed, the indignant and the pathetic. It was perhaps a sign of the times that Marler's assistant, who stood, arms folded, in the entrance to the cubicle, looked more like a bouncer than a Parliamentary researcher or intern – though there was one of those as well, in the waiting-room area, clutching a clipboard and being harangued by someone who couldn't wait for the MP's ear.

Slider walked straight over to the bouncer-type, who ominously freed his arms at his approach, and gave him a swift and efficient G-man once over. He was tall, with thick dark hair and sharp grey eyes, and, unlike most bouncers, a suit expensive enough to fit properly over his muscles, which Slider judged to be adequate but not excessive. This was no steroid-pumped goon, but a quick thinker, who probably knew martial arts. He obviously made Slider as a policeman before he reached him, because he received the warrant card without surprise, gestured to Slider to wait, and went in to speak to his boss. The murmur of conversation ceased, and a moment later an elderly woman walked out, shrugging her coat on and fiddling with her handbag, and a cheerful voice said, 'Right, David, send him in.'

Gideon Marler got to his feet as Slider stepped past the bouncer, and came round his desk with his hand out and a welcoming smile. 'How are you? I don't think we've met before, have we? This is David Easter, by the way, my assistant. Right-hand man, really – I couldn't do without David.'

Easter gave Slider a cool nod and resumed his position in the opening. With his back to his boss, it was like shutting a door and giving them privacy – except, of course, that it wasn't. But if Marler didn't want Easter to know his business, it was up to him to say so.

'Please, sit down,' Marler said, 'and tell me how I can help you.'

Marler was an attractive man, about five foot nine, lightly built, with brown hair so artfully highlighted it might have been natural sun-streaks. His eyes were extremely blue (tinted contacts?), and often crinkled in a smile, his features pleasant, his teeth excellent. He had that indefinable something that generations have called 'charm', hopeless of defining it any more closely. It was that thing that made you want to like him without knowing anything more about him. Invaluable, Slider thought, in a politician – and wasn't it odd that more of them didn't have it? Even odder that people were still willing to vote for candidates with repulsive personalities.

'I don't want to take up too much of your time,' Slider began. 'I can see you've got a full waiting room.'

'Oh, don't worry about that,' Marler said, and lowering his voice, added with a smile, 'most of them are repeat offenders. They come in every week with the same complaint – and always something I can't do anything about. Potholes, blocked drains – it's usually something the local government's responsible for. I make a note and pass it on to the councillors.' He gestured to the laptop open on the desk. 'But it doesn't satisfy them. They'll never be happy until I turn up in person and fix it while they watch.' The smile widened. 'Patience is something you need a lot of in this game. Probably the same for you, I wouldn't wonder?'

'That's true,' Slider said.

'Sorry, I'm talking too much.' The smile widened. 'Must be the relief that you haven't come to complain to me about the neighbour's cat. What *can* I help you with?'

'I wanted to talk to you about George Peloponnos,' Slider said, to give him a chance to send Easter out of earshot.

Marler's smile didn't waver, but his eyebrows looked puzzled. 'I'm sorry, who? I don't think I know that name.'

'I think you must do, because he telephoned you on Saturday morning, a little after eight o'clock.'

Marler shook his head. 'I'm sorry,' he said again. 'There must be a mistake. I don't know anyone of that name.'

'There's no mistake. We have his mobile phone records. He rang a mobile on Saturday morning, and the number is registered to you.' He observed Marler's face closely, but saw no flinching or apprehension, only a genuine puzzlement.

'Well,' he said, 'I really have no idea – oh, wait a minute!' He lifted a finger. 'I think I know what must have happened. There *was* a call on Saturday morning, I remember now, but it was a wrong number. Somebody – a man – rang and when I answered he said, "Is that you, John?" or something of the sort, and I said, "I think you've got the wrong number," and that was that. He rang off, and I forgot all about it. But if it was this chap you're talking about, I suppose it was on his record.'

'I see,' said Slider. 'You say he asked for John?'

Marler made a gesture with his hands. 'I just made that up. I can't really remember. It could have been John. Or Brian. Or anything, really. I was in the middle of getting dressed, I was in a hurry, so I didn't really pay attention. What's this chap done, anyway?'

'He committed suicide,' Slider said.

'Oh, I'm sorry to hear that.' Marler frowned. 'I didn't think the police investigated suicides.'

'We think he was mixed up in something else that we're looking into.' Slider stood up. 'Well, I'm sorry to have troubled you.'

Marler stood too, and offered another handshake across the desk. 'It's no trouble at all. Always ready to help our friends in the Met. You know I'm on the Police Select Committee, don't you?'

'Yes, sir, I did know that,' said Slider.

'Well, anything you want, any time,' he said, 'just let me know.' He pointed at his head with a comical smile. 'You see – two ears, no waiting!'

'Um,' said Slider, hesitating. Perhaps it was worth the question, anyway, on the no-stone-unturned principle. Marler raised a receptive eyebrow. 'Do you know a girl called Kaylee Adams?'

He thought. 'No, I don't believe so.' Slider showed him the picture, and he shook his head. 'Is she one of my constituents?'

'No,' said Slider. 'It doesn't matter. Thank you for your time.'

*   *   *

Several people were gathered round Connolly's computer when he got back. There was a smell of coffee in the air, and someone had gone out for doughnuts.

'I'm glad you're all usefully employed,' he said.

'I'll get you some coffee, guv,' Hart said quickly. 'It's fresh brewed.'

'No, it's all right. I don't want to spoil my dinner. What's going on?'

Atherton answered. 'We've accessed the accounts on the charity's website,' he said. 'Georgie's trust. He was earning a hundred and thirteen thousand a year.'

'And the CEO was on a hundred and twenty,' Swilley added over his shoulder.

'What was he on before, at the local council?'

'Sixty-five,' Atherton said.

'We're in the wrong business,' Connolly mourned. 'What'd it be like to have that sort o' jingle?'

'I'm sure none of us will ever know,' Atherton said.

'A hundred large is a lot o' dosh,' Hart said. 'I wonder what he spent it on.'

'If he'd nice suits and a coke habit,' Connolly said, 'he'd've seen the tail lights of it in no time.'

'How did you get on with Gideon Marler?' Atherton asked Slider.

'He says he's never heard of Peloponnos. There was a wrong number called his phone that morning.'

'Well, it *was* a very short call,' Atherton said. 'Fifteen seconds. That's just enough time to establish it was a wrong number and ring off.'

'And according to the log, George didn't ring that number any other time,' Swilley said. 'Or not in the three months we've got records of, anyway.'

'I don't get this geezer,' Connolly complained. 'Did he spend his life ringing up people he didn't know? He only rang Kaylee the once, so maybe that was a wrong number too.'

'Ah, but Kaylee rang him back,' said Atherton.

'How did *you* get on?' Slider asked him.

'Well, I've got something that's a bit interesting,' he said. 'Come and see.'

On his desk he had the printout that Virginia Lamy had given him, and the handwritten list, which he had printed from the photograph.

'Now, look, these are the official donors for the current financial year so far. All the usual suspects: businessmen, bankers, property developers, a Russian oligarch, Arab oilmen, a football club owner, and so on. Now, the handwritten list – which I remind you was from a file labelled "Donors", and it's not the same. There are one or two of the same names on it, but the bulk are people of wealth and prominence, but probably not the sort who would have millions to give to charity. There's a high court judge, a newspaper editor, a society photographer, a top solicitor, a DJ, a couple of lords, a TV personality, a surgeon, the borough CEO, several politicians—'

'Including,' Swilley said, leaning closer, 'Gideon Marler. And he just said he'd never heard of George!'

'Peloponnos can write his name on a list without actually knowing him,' Slider reminded them. 'What are the dates?'

'I thought it might be the date they gave donations,' Atherton said, 'but if you look at this name, a property developer who appears on both lists, the handwritten date doesn't match the date on the printout.'

'And why have some of the names got question marks after them?' Swilley asked.

'I don't know,' Atherton said. 'Maybe these were all people he was intending to stick for a donation, and the dates were when he asked them and the question marks meaning they were going to get back to him. But that's pure speculation. And as I said, you wouldn't think they were fabulously wealthy, like those on the printout.'

'Maybe he'd gone through the A list,' Connolly said, 'and now he was down to the B list.'

'Look at this,' Slider said, pointing to one handwritten name. 'Derek Millichip. Otherwise known as Assistant Commissioner Millichip.'

'The top dog for our area,' said Atherton. 'Our ultimate boss, under God and the commissioner.'

Swilley said, 'Now, excuse me for talking about our betters, but, I wouldn't have thought AC pay was high enough to be giving big money to charity.'

'A hundred and eighty k, give or take,' Atherton said.

'He *has* got a question mark after him,' Connolly said.

'North Kensington is in his bailiwick,' Atherton said. 'Maybe he's just a caring person.'

'Well, whatever, George cared enough about this list to lock it away in his bottom drawer,' Swilley said, 'so it must be important.'

'Not unless we can find out what it's for,' said Slider. 'And you say the password-protected file on his PC was labelled "Cope".'

'Yes. Cope with what, I wonder?' said Atherton.

'Could be someone's name,' said Hart.

'Maybe he had a thing for bishops,' Connolly suggested.

'If only Mr Porson would get us a proper search warrant so we could bring the PC in,' Atherton said discontentedly. 'How can we work this with one hand tied behind our backs?'

'I'll run the word "cope" through Google,' Connolly offered, 'and see if anything comes up. Sure it sounds like one o' those wanky renames of fine old institutions.'

'Like calling the Marriage Guidance Council "Relate",' Atherton agreed. '"Cope" could be giving help to single mothers.'

'Or something to do with mental health,' Swilley suggested.

'Yeah, given that George was a terminal looper,' Connolly said, fingers busy. 'Or it might be an acronym.'

'Like ACPO,' Slider said, mostly to himself.

Porson moved restlessly back and forth, winding and unwinding a treasury tag round one finger. 'I can't see where all this is taking you,' he said. 'You seem to be getting further away from Adams all the time. *That*'s what you were supposed to be looking into. You're getting your nipples in a twist over this Ploppy-whosis suicide and its ramplications. He was only interesting if he killed Adams and did himself out of remorse. I don't see what this list of donors has got to do with that.'

'I don't either, sir,' Slider admitted unhappily.

'Time's running out,' Porson reminded him. 'We've got the crime figures to get out next week, and the Borough Leaders Conference to prepare for. I need you to be concentrating on those, not chasing your trail over what was probably an RTA anyway.'

'I'm sure there's a link between Adams and Peloponnos. If we could just have a look at the two computers—'

'I can't get you a warrant for them unless you get *me* something,' Porson snapped. 'Look, I'm as frustrated as you are about this, but sometimes there's nothing you can do. Sometimes you just have to let it go.'

He stopped abruptly, and their eyes met. Not letting things go had always been what got Slider into trouble, and Porson had always supported him. The death of a no-count girl from the estate versus the Borough Leaders conference and an attaboy from upstairs for improved crime figures? It was no contest.

Was it?

'You've got till Monday,' Porson said. 'Make it count.'

TEN

Reading Between the Lies

He left his minions toiling over getting backgrounds on the people on both donor lists, plus the phone records, plus the check and elimination of the Mercedes GL550s. Connolly was trying to find out if COPE meant anything, and Atherton was trawling the internet to try and find a house that resembled the one in the drawing.

'I can't help feeling it's important,' he said. 'Why else would he hide it like that?'

'Maybe he didn't,' Slider said. 'Maybe he stuck it there at random one day – when he was answering the phone, for instance – and then forgot about it.'

'Well, there weren't any other architectural drawings in his office, so unless he was using this one as a bookmark . . .' Atherton objected.

Slider went off to the borough planning office to interview one Mrs Avril Parling, who had been Peloponnos's PA when he was chief planning officer.

She was a comely woman in her late fifties, with a neat figure, thick healthy hair that had been allowed to go naturally grey, and patient brown eyes behind gold half-glasses that perched perilously on the end of her nose like mountain climbers, with only a pearly rope around her neck to stop them plummeting to their doom.

She was now the PA to Peloponnos's successor, but he was, fortunately, out of the office, so Slider was able to have a relaxed chat with her. She seemed quite ready to abandon her work for conversation, and quickly got tea on the brew and the biscuit tin out.

'Yes, I did know he'd gone,' she said, to Slider's enquiry. 'I saw it in the paper. Poor soul.' It sounded more perfunctory than heartbroken.

'Were you surprised?' Slider asked.

She pursed her lips. 'We-ell,' she said. 'I mean, you're always surprised, aren't you? But perhaps not as much with George as someone else. I can't say I ever would have expected it, but he was always what I'd call a nervy character. He thought about things too much. Always pointing out what could go wrong, if you know what I mean. Sometimes too much introspection can be as bad for you as too little.'

'You got on with him all right?'

'Oh yes, he was a very nice person to work for. Never bad-tempered or anything like that. Quite considerate; and polite – you'd be surprised how many aren't. Throw work at you without a please or thank you, some people – mentioning no names.' She glared for an instant at the door to her new boss's office. 'George always had manners – a real gentleman. And he took me with him when he was made chief planning officer, which was nice.' She gave him a smile. 'The pay increase was welcome, I can tell you.'

'He wasn't married?' Slider tried.

'No.' She gave him a narrow look. 'If you're wondering whether there was anything between him and me, you can put that idea right out of your mind. I'm happily married, and it was never a relationship like that. And I don't think he was the other way, either – though there has been speculation round the offices. Well, when a man never brings a woman to socials, and never talks about any woman, people are bound to wonder. But I always got the feeling he was quite normal in that department, but too shy to do anything about it.' She looked at him. 'He lived with his mother, you know?'

'Yes, I know.'

'He did talk about *her*. Very good to his mother – isn't that what they say? She probably put the kybosh on him having a romance, poor chap. There are a lot of mothers like that – can't let go. He was very nice, you know, but perhaps a bit *too* gentle, *too* easy-going. Except . . .'

'Yes?' Slider encouraged.

'I was going to say, except in his work. That was why he got made chief, because he was dedicated. Very serious about it. Always took every application on its merits. You couldn't sway him with appeals to sentiment or anything like that. He was impartial – and quite firm. I suppose it was just social situations that made him nervous.'

'So if someone said he had a very young girlfriend – a teenager – would that surprise you?'

'Yes, it would. I never heard he had. Why? Is someone saying that?'

'There's been a suggestion.'

'I can't see George managing to ask a teenager out. Knowing what teenagers are like today – so bold and up to everything, spit in your eye as soon as look at you. You should see them at the bus stop when the schools let out. I suppose if it was a really shy, gentle girl – but where would he ever meet someone like that?' She pondered. 'I know young girls often do go for an older man, but . . . Who is she? This girl you're asking about.'

'Her name's Kaylee Adams.'

Mrs Parling shook her head. 'Never heard that name before. And you say George was going out with her?'

'We don't know that. There was some suggestion of a connection between them, but it was very tenuous. Really, I'm just trying to get a sense of the man. I suppose he mixed with a lot of high-up people?' He changed direction to stop her asking any more questions.

'Well, yes, I suppose so. There's a lot of rich people in the borough, and they're the ones most likely to put in planning applications – the big controversial ones, anyway, the ones that don't get nodded through. We've had a spate of people wanting to dig out their basements to make an extra floor below ground. Those have got to be looked into very carefully. Of course, they can't build upwards in most cases, so down's the only option if they want to live in the posh bit of the borough.'

On the spur of the moment, Slider got out the copy of the architectural drawing, and handed it to her. 'Do you recognize this?' he
asked.

'Oh, that looks like George's work,' she said at once.

'Can you tell?'

'I've worked with architects before. They all have their own style.
You get to know the way they draw their little trees and people and
so on. Of course, him being an architect before he came to planning
was a great help. Where did you get this?'

He avoided that one. 'Do you know what house it is?'

'Oh yes.' She tapped the drawing with a finger. 'Now that *was*
a bit of a surprise. You could usually guess which way George
would jump over a decision, that was one of the joys, but this one
I got completely wrong. You see, it's a Grade II listed house, so
they should never have been allowed to put that terrace on. There
were other alterations to the inside, which weren't really problematic
– I mean, it was only a matter of making sure they used the right
materials and didn't jeopardize the safety of the structure and so on
– but this roof terrace . . . I was sure right to the end he was going
to turn it down, but then suddenly he said yes. Of course, that was
after he'd suggested some alterations. I suppose that's when he made
this drawing. But even so . . . I wondered,' she added uncomfortably, 'whether there wasn't some pressure brought to bear.' She
raised her eyes to Slider's. 'I mean, I wouldn't say anything, except
that he's dead now, so it can't hurt him, can it? But I do know the
borough CEO went in and had a long meeting with him, and when
I went in afterwards, the plans were on his desk – not this drawing,
the proper plans, the blueprints. So I think they were discussing it.
And the same day he said he was allowing it to go through. So I
wonder if Arnold leaned on him. But don't quote me on that – it's
just my own speculation.'

Slider remembered that Arnold Fulleylove, the borough CEO,
had been one of the names on the handwritten list. 'When you say
"leaned", do you mean bribed? Or blackmailed?'

She looked alarmed, 'Oh, I wouldn't accuse anybody of anything
like that. And as a matter of fact, I never would have thought George
was the kind of person to be swayed from something he thought
right – not in the area of his work, anyway. But I suppose we all
have a weakness somewhere. And it's a fact,' she added, staring

into her teacup uncomfortably, 'that he got that new job soon afterwards, and *that* seemed to come out of the blue.'

'Who did this house belong to?' Slider asked, tapping the drawing.

'Gideon Marler,' she said. 'The MP?'

'Yes, I know who you mean,' said Slider. His nerves were tingling. 'I suppose,' he said casually, 'there would have been meetings between Mr Peloponnos and Mr Marler in the course of the application?'

'Well, I know there was one,' she said, 'when George went over to meet him at the house to discuss it with him. I don't know if there were others. But they used to talk on the phone quite often.'

'You're sure of that?'

'I put his calls through,' she said simply.

'Did they talk about anything else, apart from the house?'

She looked at him oddly. 'Well, I never listened in to his conversations. Why do you ask?' She seemed to come to some conclusion. 'Look, was there anything odd about George's death? I mean, it *was* suicide, wasn't it? Only you read things about suicides being faked, and here you are, asking all these strange questions—'

'Oh no,' Slider said, his mind busy elsewhere. 'It was suicide all right. Set your mind at rest about that.'

'Well, what's it all about then?' she asked, with a hint of impatience.

'I really can't tell you,' Slider said. And added in a low voice, 'I wish I knew.'

'So you're suggesting that Georgie rigged the planning application,' said Atherton, 'and in return Marler got him the spiffy new job on the trust?'

'I'm not suggesting anything,' Slider said, but he got no takers.

'Not just the bigger salary,' Swilley said, 'but probably more congenial work, and the chance to meet some high rollers who might be useful to him in other ways. I *wish* I could get a look at his financial accounts.'

'You think he was making more money than his salary?' Connolly asked.

'That's what I'd like to find out. He did pay off his mortgage two years ago, after only a year in the new job.'

Atherton nodded. 'A venial man could really cream it off.

Developers fight over those contracts like foxes over a KFC box, and a sweetener to the right person can get your name to the top of the list.' He met Slider's look. 'What? Don't tell me you've never heard of it happening. Government contracts, council contracts, NGO contracts – where two or three are gathered together, spending someone else's money, there shall ye find the potential for corruption.'

'If he was rolling in it,' said Connolly, 'why'd he keep living in that mingy little cheesebox? He was an architect. Janey Mac, it musta given him a pain in the arse every time he came home.'

'Maybe his mother liked it,' said Atherton.

'Maybe he got rewarded uvver ways,' said Hart quietly. 'Not everyfing's about money.'

'Well, what then?'

'*I* don't know. I'm not his muvver,' she retorted.

Slider thought of Mrs Peloponnos, and his conviction that she knew something about her son, something she didn't want to face. Was that it? Did she know he was on the take, in one way or another?

'The one thing we do know,' he said, 'was that Gideon Marler knew Peloponnos, though he told me he'd never heard of him. Now, it's not as if it was a casual and unimportant contact. And it's not as if he was called John Smith. If you can't remember a name like Peloponnos . . .'

'True, boss,' said Swilley, 'but what then? And what's it got to do with Kaylee?'

'Probably nothing,' he said. 'We've no suggestion of a connection between Marler and Kaylee. We're barking up two entirely unconnected trees here.'

'Each of them containing a mare's nest,' said Atherton. 'You know, I'm sorry to say it, but I'm starting to think maybe it *was* just a hit-and-run. Doc Cameron *could* be wrong.' He looked at Slider. 'It's a possibility. I'm just saying.'

'Yes, I know,' said Slider. It was just that instinct – and Porson obviously shared it – told him it wasn't a possibility, not this time. Kaylee's death had not been an accident. But he had nothing to show that Peloponnos was involved in it. Apart from one phone call.

He came to a decision. 'Get the telephone log for Peloponnos's landline, at his office,' he said to Swilley. 'He didn't use his mobile

for anything interesting, but maybe he'd think the office phone was
safe.'

'Right boss.'

'If Marler did get him the spiffy new job – and we've no evidence
to say he did – they might still have been talking to each other.'

'What will that prove?' Atherton asked impatiently.

'It's just a little more evidence that *something* was going on,'
said Slider. 'God knows we need all we can get.'

McLaren came in with a list, an ominously long one. 'The Merc
GL550s, guv,' he said. 'Even with a first index letter, it doesn't cut
it down much. I haven't had a chance to go through them all yet,
but I have come across one interesting one. Starts with AH. Well,
we thought it was an E, but that could've been a bolt instead of a
top stroke.'

'True,' said Slider.

'And it goes to Gideon Marler.'

'Marler again!' Slider sat up. Now, at last, the possibility of a
connection between the three protagonists.

'Yeah. I checked with DVLA, and he's got four motors. There's
a BMW, a Mazda with his wife as co-driver, a Vauxhall Astra which
looks like his daughter's, and the Merc. I reckon the BMW's his
personal wheels and the Merc's his business wheels. See, the Merc's
the only one registered to his London address.'

'That'd be his constituency home, I suppose,' Slider said.

'Yeah, and where the other three are registered'll be his private
home. It's in Rickmansworth.' He looked up. 'Rickmansworth, that's
about four miles from Harefield.'

'A lot of MPs live out that way,' Slider said.

'Yeah, guv,' said McLaren. 'I'm just saying.'

'Of course. Well, get Fathom on it, tell him start looking for it
on Saturday night or Sunday morning, anywhere between the London
house and Harefield. ANPR, traffic cameras, everything. And give
the full number to Uxbridge – they're in a better position to look
for witnesses, anyone who saw the car go through on Saturday night
or Sunday morning.'

'Right, guv.'

'You'd better keep going through the other Mercedes – we don't
want to miss anything obvious while looking at Marler.'

'Right, guv. But if it was Marler picked her up Saturday night, surely it'll be him that dumped her Sunday morning.'

'*If* it was him. Get on with it.'

Gideon Marler, MP, was at a meeting with the chairmen of several residents' associations, for which purpose he was using a room at the town hall. He came out in his shirtsleeves into the corridor where Slider was waiting. Through the open door, Slider caught a glimpse of half a dozen elderly, well-dressed folk sitting round a table covered in papers and water bottles, and David Easter standing behind the empty chair at the head.

'Oh, it's you again,' Marler said, closing the door behind him. He grinned self-deprecatingly. 'Well, I did say contact me any time . . . Or are you just mesmerized by my charm?'

'I'm sorry to bother you again,' Slider said, 'but I do have another question.'

'All right, spit it out,' Marler said smilingly. 'Anything to help our chums in blue.'

'You had a large alteration done to your house three years ago, for which you had to get planning permission. That involved at least one meeting, plus several phone calls and considerable correspondence with the chief planning officer.'

'Yes?' said Marler.

'Whose name was George Peloponnos. Someone you said you had never heard of.'

Marler's smile seemed to stiffen a little. 'Is that it? What's your question?'

'Why did you deny knowing him?' Slider asked.

'I didn't *deny* anything. Can we not use loaded language, please? I couldn't remember ever having heard of him. Why should I?'

'You had a lot of dealings with him. Your building work must have been important to you – that's a lovely house.'

'The house is important to me; the name of every petty official in the local council who happens to send me a piece of bumf is not. Why on earth should I remember the name of a planning officer?'

'Quite an unusual name,' Slider said.

The smile was fading fast – indeed, it was only hanging on with its fingertips to the corners of the mouth, and had lost the eyes altogether.

'I don't remember him. All right? You seem to be making a big thing out of this, for reasons I cannot fathom. What, exactly, are you accusing me of?'

Slider lifted his hands. 'I'm not accusing you of anything, sir.'

'I'm glad to hear it.'

'I was just puzzled. It didn't seem to me the sort of thing you would forget.'

'Well, I did. *Mea culpa* and all that, but I meet hundreds of people a week, in the course of my work, and I can't remember the name of every person I've ever come into contact with. It was years ago, for God's sake. And now, if you've no other questions, I must get back to my meeting.'

'Of course, sir. Thank you for your time.'

Marler managed a tight, PR sort of smile before he disappeared, and Slider walked away, down the corridor and out to his car. It was, he thought, a perfectly reasonable explanation. Why *should* he remember Peloponnos? Except that it was not the sort of name you wouldn't remember having heard before, once it was mentioned to you, though you might not remember the context.

And Peloponnos had rung his mobile on Saturday morning. Now, of course, it was perfectly possible that Peloponnos had misdialled, and hearing Marler's voice had been too embarrassed to admit it and had pretended it was a wrong number.

Perfectly possible. But along with the Mercedes, it was a co-incidence, and he didn't like coincidences.

Retribution was swift. When Slider got back to the station and went in through the back from the yard, the custody sergeant, O'Flaherty, looked up from his desk and said, 'Ah, dere he is. Hail to thee, blithe spirit. Bird thou never wert, or so it says here.'

'What's up, Fergus?'

'You'd know that better than me, Billy boy. Mr Porson wants you, chop chop. I think it could be the crack o' doom. I know he always sounds like a nerthquake, but this time . . . I'd be puttin' the kevlar on if I was you, darlin'.'

'My conscience is clear,' Slider said sturdily.

Porson's door was open, as always, and as he arrived Slider could see the great man standing behind his desk facing it. Not pacing up and down, but standing still, which was bad.

'Come in,' he said. 'Shut the door.'

Slider obeyed, and approached. Porson's granite features wouldn't have looked amiss on Mount Rushmore, and at the best of times a scowl came more easily to him than a smile. On a good day he could be snappier than a crocodile handbag. Today his glare could have put the Gorgon out of business.

'What the bloody hell have you been up to?'

The fact that he didn't bellow somehow made it worse. Slider was suddenly glad to have the desk between them. 'Sir?' he said.

'Don't "sir" me! I've just had Mr Carpenter on the blower, our new borough commander that we're all trying so hard to make friends with.'

Ooh, satire, Slider thought. You could put someone's eye out with that.

'Mr Carpenter is not happy. He's especially not happy to be rung up by an AC in a temper and put on the carpet for something he's not done. And what does an unhappy borough commander do? *Makes other peoples' lives a bloody misery!*' Now he bellowed.

'Sir,' Slider began.

'You went and bothered the chairman of the Police Select Committee! *Twice!*'

'If I could explain—'

'The man that holds all our fates in his clammy little paw – including the AC's. Apparently, you accused him of lying and consorting with criminals.'

'I certainly didn't accuse him of consorting with criminals.'

'Well, I'm very glad to hear it!' Porson's voice had risen, like the wind before the storm. 'I'm glad there's *some* groundless accusation you didn't throw at him! What the blue, blistering blazes have you got against the man? The man, may I remind you, who is trying to stop our budgets being cut again in the next round and is probably the only person with any chance of doing it!'

'He told me he'd never heard of George Peloponnos. But he'd met him, spoken to him on the telephone several times, had letters from him.' He explained about the planning application, while Porson steamed gently.

'You're supposed to be looking into Adams,' he burst out at the end. 'In fact, you're *not* supposed to be looking into Adams, but anyway. Then it was Ploppy-whosis, now you're wandering off into rarefied pastures on the basis that someone can't remember the name of the man who signed his *bloody planning permit!*'

This was not the moment to bring up other bits of evidence, as far as they *were* evidence. It was all too tenuous – Porson's resistance made him realize just *how* tenuous it was. And Porson was undergoing some industrial strength leaning from leaders in the field. He hadn't mentioned which AC it was that had pressured Mr Carpenter, but wouldn't it be interesting if it was Derek Millichip, who appeared on the same list as Gideon Marler, in Peloponnos's handwriting? He waited for the right moment to ask the question, expecting more explosions.

But Porson's shoulders suddenly dropped, he swivelled on the spot and began pacing, his eyebrow writhing like two caterpillars in a headlock. At last he said, 'You're not thinking like a chief inspector, Slider. The game's changed, you've got to realize that. It's all very well running about being a boy scout, but there are bigger things at stake.'

'Things like the budget, sir?'

Porson fixed him with a gimlet eye. 'If you know a way to run a police force without money, start talking. And the boys who hold the purse strings are our masters. They can cut us off without a thought. They all live in nice big safe houses with electronic gates, their own private copper on guard, and SO19 on fast-dial, so cuts don't bother them. The rest of us have to live in the real world. And in the real world you do not piss off the *chairman* of the *Police Select Committee!*'

'I understand, sir,' said Slider.

'*Do* you?' Porson sounded frustrated. 'I know you, Slider. You think playing politics is beneath you. You think the life of one pathetic schoolgirl is more important than all the MPs and ACs in the book.'

'Sir, I can't let—'

'Let it go! You don't even know what you think the crime was, or if there was a crime at all, or who was mixed up in it.'

This was uncomfortably true. Slider dug in defensively. 'If someone's broken the law, no matter who he is, he has to be called to account.'

'But it doesn't have to be by you, and it doesn't have to be now,' Porson countered. 'If he's done something, it'll come out in the wash. Sooner or later his chickens'll come home to roast. When they do, it'd be nice if we still had enough personnel to do something about it.'

'So are you telling me to stand down, sir?'

Porson ran a hand over his bald head as if looking for hair to rake. 'You don't have any evidence of any connection with Adams.'

'I can't get the evidence if I'm not allowed to look for it,' Slider said.

'Oh, for God's sake!' Porson cried in frustration. 'It's like talking to Jimmy Cricket.' He did another few laps, and Slider remained silent, seeing the yeast at work. Porson stopped in the middle and turned. 'I've said you can have until Monday on Adams. But leave Marler out of it. Don't annoy him, don't bother him, don't ring his doorbell and run away. Don't even think about him, got it? Concentrate on Adams, whatever it is you're doing to follow that up. What *are* you doing, as a matter of fact?'

'Trying to find out who she was with on Saturday night. We've got a partial index on the car that picked her up,' he offered as a sop.

Porson looked happier. 'Well, follow that up. That's a proper lead. Leave all this hairy-fairy speculative stuff out of it. I'm telling you, we're facing a potential budget settlement that would set your hair on edge. We can't afford to rock any boats.'

ELEVEN

The Micawber Approach

'Let's go through what we know,' Slider said. The firm had made itself comfortable, behind their desks or perched on someone else's, with tea and coffee mugs in hand. 'Kaylee Adams died some time on Saturday night or Sunday morning as the result of a fall from height, and her body was subsequently dumped in a country lane to make it look as though she was the victim of a hit-and-run.'

'But she may *actually* have been the victim of a hit-and-run,' Atherton put in.

'Leaving that aside for the moment,' Slider said, glaring at him.

'She told Deenie, Shannon and Dakota that she was going to a party on Saturday night, and she was actually picked up by a car at the time mentioned. She rang up George Peloponnos at lunchtime on Saturday to ask, according to Deenie, "Will you be there?" We also know that he rang her on Saturday morning, perhaps to invite her to the party.'

'But in that case, why would she ask him if he'd be there?' Swilley objected.

'Immediately after ringing Kaylee, he rang Gideon Marler, though Marler claims it was a wrong number.'

'And it could have been,' said Atherton. 'It was a very short call.'

'Peloponnos committed suicide on Monday morning by throwing himself under a tube train when apparently on his way to work. His mother and his PA both say he had been worried or depressed for some time. And his doctor had been prescribing him sleeping tablets and anti-depressants since January.'

'Boss,' said Connolly tentatively. Slider turned to her. 'You've not mentioned Tyler Vance yet.'

'What's the relevance of Tyler?' Atherton objected. 'Just that she and Kaylee were friends?'

'Tyler also died and was dumped,' Connolly said. 'It goes to pattern. And I was just thinking – sure, maybe it's nothing, but Tyler died on the 10th of Jan, and your man George goes to his quack depressed on the 15th.'

'So you think Peloponnos killed and dumped them both, getting more and more depressed until he killed himself?' said Atherton.

Connolly shrugged. 'I'm just sayin' there could be a connection.'

'Going back a step,' Slider resumed. 'We know the car that picked Kaylee up was a black Mercedes GL550 with tinted windows, with an index beginning with A followed by something that looked like an E or an F. Gideon Marler has a black Mercedes GL550 with tinted windows and an index beginning AH.'

'But there's a lot of other candidate cars in London – aren't there, Maurice?' Atherton asked.

'I'm narrowing it down,' McLaren said. 'Prob'ly gonna be about half a dozen with A something on the index.'

''Scuse me, but I'm not getting any big picture here,' Hart intervened. 'If George took her to a party, done her and dumped her –

wiv or wivout previous in the form of Tyler – what's Gideon Marler got to do wiv anything? Apart from the motor – and we don't even know it's the same one – there's nothing on him.' She looked around and received no dissent.

'I reckon Kaylee probably did get offed, and given nobody that knew her seems to care, we gotter. Georgie looks our best bet, but we've not got much on him. And even if he had something dodgy goin' on wiv Marler – which we don't know he did – it don't mean Marler had anything to do with Kaylee.'

'Thanks for the summary,' Slider said. 'Anyone else got a view?'

'It's hard to have a view when you're not allowed to look into anything properly,' said Swilley. 'This trust, for instance. Anything with a lot of developers' money swilling around it has got to be interesting. But I don't know why you're hung up on Mr Marler, boss. He's supposed to be one of the good guys. I had a peek at his record in Hansard, and he argued just last week for our budget *not* to be cut. He's on our side.'

Connolly said, 'I wouldn't go that far. *Nobody*'s on our side. But even if Mr Marler's as crooked as a pig's hind leg, it doesn't mean anything. I wouldn't trust an MP as far as I could spit him, but I wouldn't expect him to murder me.'

There was a general murmur of agreement.

'What about Georgie's alibi?' Hart said. 'Didn't we oughter check that? If he was at the opera, he didn't kill Kaylee.'

'Unless he met her later,' Swilley said.

'All right,' Slider said to her. 'We'd better do everything by the book. Find out who was in the surrounding seats and try them with a photo of Peloponnos, that's probably the quickest way. Keep checking the cars. We're still waiting for Peloponnos's office phone records. Something will turn up.'

'Thank you, Mr Micawber,' Atherton murmured.

'Who?' Fathom asked, but nobody bothered to enlighten him.

Connolly came into his office a while later. 'Nothing so far on Cope, boss,' she said. 'There's an ethics committee that monitors medical publications, and a charity to do with prosthetic limbs, and a lot of individuals with the surname, but I can't see any connection with any of our gals an' fellers.'

'All right,' Slider said.

'I'll keep at it,' she said.

'Don't waste time on it. You've your other work to do,' Slider said. It sounded gloomier on the air than it had inside his head.

Connolly hesitated, examining him. 'Boss,' she said, 'I saw the home Tyler came from. And I saw Kaylee's ma. These are throwaway girls. Nobody cares what happened to them. I think we should keep on trying to find out what happened. Whatever Upstairs says.'

'Thanks,' Slider said.

'If it means anything,' she went on, 'I think there's somethin' goin' on that we haven't figured yet. But it's just a feelin' I got.'

'I've got the same one,' Slider said.

He tried to convince himself that it was coincidence that the same afternoon he had a call from Pete Remington at Uxbridge to say that they were dropping the Kaylee Adams enquiry.

'We've had no luck so far locating any witnesses to the girl or the accident,' he said, 'and Mr Fox is pulling the plug. It's taking up too much time and manpower. You know how it is.' He sounded apologetic. 'Too few people chasing too much work.'

'Yes, I know how it is.'

'This sort of thing is very labour intensive, and for uncertain results. We have to be more efficient in our man-management these days. We have to account for effective use of all our resources.'

Slider had read the same sort of thing on a recent circular from the new borough commander. The Job was turning into a business, with managers, HR, PR, spreadsheets, and all the blue-sky-thinking, stakeholder-involvement, Way Ahead Task Force jargon a company man could want.

'Anyway,' Remington concluded, 'I thought I'd just let you know. Oh, one other thing.'

'Yes?' said Slider. Remington's voice had changed. It sounded as though this last-minute, I-just-remembered clause was actually the whole purpose of the exercise.

'That index you sent over. We haven't looked into it. Won't be doing so. If I were you, I'd forget about it. Really. No point flogging a dead dobbin, eh?' He gave a nervous laugh.

'No, of course not,' Slider said. 'Thanks for the warning.'

'Warning? I just said—'

'Yes, I know. Thanks anyway.'

He had counted as far as ten before his internal phone rang and the summons to Porson's office came.

'What the dicky doodah are you playing at? Sending Marler's index to Uxbridge and asking them to find out if anyone saw it on Saturday night? After I pacifically told you to leave him out of it?'

'You said I could follow up the car,' Slider pointed out.

'Not *Marler's* car! For crying out loud, I'm starting to wonder about your mental stabilitude!' Porson's eyes bulged. 'What part of "leave him alone" do you need translated?'

'Sir, she was picked up on the night by—'

'Don't you realize,' Porson said, leaning heavily on his fists on the desk, 'that he lives out that way? He's a local resident. An eniment one, come to that. Even if anyone saw him, what the bloody hell good would that do you? He's got every right to be there!'

'Yes, sir,' said Slider. No point in speaking when the gale was blowing in your face.

'Oh, go away!' Porson cried in exasperation. 'Go and do something useful. I've already kissed goodbye to making chief super before I retire, thanks to you. I hope you can live with yourself.'

Slider retreated, followed, as he reached the door, by the last injunction, 'And leave Marler alone! We're talking disciplinary measures from this point onwards.'

Connolly seemed to be his natural ally out there. He called her in and gave her a task. Meanwhile, he called up Marler's CV and studied it. It all seemed straightforward. Like most MPs he'd gone straight from university into party politics, as a party intern and then Parliamentary researcher. Did a stint as a PR officer for an MP and then got his own seat. Held several directorships. Married the daughter of a business mogul who was also an hereditary baron – rich and posh in one fell swoop. One daughter at university. Two large houses. The address of the London one was Holland Lodge, Abbotsbury Walk. He looked it up on Streetmap. Abbotsbury Walk was a short cul-de-sac off Abbotsbury Road. The house was at the end, backing onto Holland Park itself – a most desirable situation. It must have cost a bob or two. Abbotsbury Road led at the top end to Holland Park Road and thence to the A40, the fast route west-wards out of London to leafy Herts and Bucks – where so many MPs lived, for the very reason that the transport links were good.

Or perhaps the transport links were good because so many MPs lived out that way. Who knew?

Gideon Marler had wanted work done on his house and had – possibly – leaned on or otherwise encouraged the chief planning officer to put the permission through. Why not? A lot of people did it. If you had either the money or the influence, or in ideal cases both, it would take a person of real integrity *not* to use the leverage for your advantage, especially when, after all, it probably didn't do anyone any harm. So a Grade II house was altered? It wasn't a war crime.

And what, if anything, did it have to do with Kaylee Adams, the girl from the estate? Slider put his head in his hands and felt his thoughts grind together like boulders in a glacier, painful and about as slow.

He was very far away when the hospital rang.

Connolly volunteered to go out of concern for the kid. Mrs Adams had been pumped out and was now sleeping, she was told. Fortunately, a neighbour had called round and found her, otherwise it would probably have been Julienne, coming home from school, who discovered her mother. The friend had knocked and, getting no reply, looked through the kitchen window and saw her lying on the kitchen floor. She'd called for an ambulance, and the paramedics had broken in.

'Is it suicide or an accident?' Connolly asked the doctor.

He shrugged. 'Who knows? There's a fine line in any case, when you get to users like her. The friend who found her thought it was suicide. She said she'd been very depressed since her daughter died?' He added a querying look to the question mark.

'Yeah. She was killed in a road accident last Saturday. Hit-and-run, so it looks.'

'Oh. That's tough,' said the doctor. He was young, tall, and glossily black, with the long features of an Ethiopian. 'So she might have meant it, then.'

'How serious was it?' Connolly asked.

'Touch and go. If she hadn't been found when she was, she'd have been dead in another hour. As it is, we won't know if she's suffered any permanent damage until she wakes up.'

'Brain damage, you mean?'

'Yes, that first of all. But if she escapes that, there may still be organ failure later.' He shook his head, to indicate the outlook wasn't good.

In either case, Connolly thought as she headed for the waiting room, they'd surely take the kid away now. Social services had been called in, of course, and Julienne would be going into care on a temporary basis, until the state of her mother was determined; but it'd be a long time before she'd be allowed to go back home.

Connolly remembered the party atmosphere of the day after the Knock, how Mrs Adams had seemed to be putting on the show she thought was expected of her. There had been no real feeling there. But often such a deep shock takes its time arriving. Such a reversal of the normal way of things can be hard to recognize as reality at first, especially when you were accustomed to altering your perceptions on a regular basis anyway. But when the realisation finally kicks in . . . Even the most careless mother can have maternal feelings. Howling about 'her baby' had probably turned into a real discovery of loss.

But if she'd tried to kill herself over Kaylee, what did that say about her care for Julienne? Connolly shrugged. Thinking ahead was rarely a drug user's prime strength. Perhaps she'd banked subconsciously on being found in time. Perhaps it had only been a cry for help.

It was a private waiting room, reserved for the bereaved or likely-to-be, and had a brown weave sofa and two armchairs, a green carpet, cream walls, and framed prints of botanical drawings of roses and peonies on the walls, which were probably supposed to be soothing. Or at least not irritating. Julienne, in pink jeans and a mauve T-shirt printed with a Disney princess, turned a pale, pinched face towards the door as Connolly came in. For a moment she looked blank. Then her face creased with distress and she cried, 'You! You told the social on us! Now they're gonna take me away!'

'Take it easy, kid,' Connolly said. 'Someone's got to look after you till your ma gets better.'

'You told! You're the filth. You said you were the good guys, but you're not!' Tears of anger squeezed from her eyes. 'I hate you!'

Connolly looked across at the social worker, an overweight young woman in bulging black trousers and a green wool jacket, with a leather haversack for a handbag. Beside her on a chair was a small overnight case – presumably packed with things for Julienne. 'Detective Constable Connolly,' she introduced herself. 'I'd like a word with your wan, here.' She jerked a head at Julienne.

The social worker stood up. 'I'm Karen. But I don't think you can—'

But it was to Connolly that Julienne ran, grinding her fists in her eye sockets. She flung herself at Connolly's legs and tied her arms tightly round her waist. 'I hate you,' she wailed, burrowing into Connolly's midriff. 'I want my mum!'

'Easy there, scout,' Connolly murmured, stroking the tangled head. 'Take it easy. Your mum's being looked after. She's gettin' the best care. You have to let them help her.'

Julienne pulled back and raised her face. It was white and red, but there weren't many tears. 'What's gonna happen to me?'

'This lady'll take you somewhere, just till your mum gets better.'

'Why can't I go home?'

'Cos there's no one there to look after you.'

'I can look after myself. I do anyway,' she added with chilling realism.

'I know, pet,' Connolly said soothingly. 'I bet you're grand at it. But it's the law. The law says you can't be left on your own at home until you're fourteen.'

'I've told her that,' Karen muttered.

Julienne continued to study Connolly's face. 'Did you tell on us?'

'No, I didn't. I told you, I'm not that class o' police. We're still trying to find out where your sister went on Saturday.'

'I don't think this is the right time to be talking about that,' Karen said.

Connolly looked at her. 'I won't upset her.' And to Julienne: 'You don't mind talking to me, do you?'

'No,' she said promptly. 'I like you. You dress smart. And I like your perfume.' She lowered her voice, though not enough. '*She* smells funny. Like school dinners.'

'Come and sit down,' Connolly said hastily, hoping to cover the comment.

'What's it called?' Julienne asked, sitting beside her.

'What?'

'Your perfume.'

'Paco Rabanne. Lady Million,' said Connolly.

'I like it. I wanna look like you when I grow up. Nice clothes and nice perfume and everything. I like your boots. I like your handbag. I wanna have money like Kaylee. I don't wanna live on benefits like Mum.'

'You'll have to work hard at school, so,' said Connolly.

Julienne gave an eye-roll. 'Everyone always says that. But Kaylee never went to school, and she was doing all right.'

'Yeah, that's what I wanted t'ask you. Where was Kaylee getting all that money?'

'She had this boyfriend. He was a lot older, and he had loads of money.'

'Was his name George?' Connolly asked. 'George Peloponnos?'

Julienne wrinkled her nose. 'That's a stupid name. Ploppyloss! What sort of a name's that? She never said what his name was, anyway. He had this nickname – Golden Eagle. It was really cool.'

'Golden Eagle?' Connolly said, baffled.

'Yeah. They all had nicknames. Have you got anything to eat?'

'No, I'm sorry. I might have a Polo mint.'

'Have *you* got anything?' Julienne asked Karen in a demanding tone. 'I'm starving.'

'We can go along to the canteen and get something, if you like,' Karen said. 'I think this lady has finished talking to you.'

'Just another minute,' Connolly said.

'It's not appropriate—'

'Ah, sure, you're here to see fair play. And she doesn't mind – do you, pet?'

'I'd sooner talk to you,' Julienne affirmed. 'You're cool.'

'Nevertheless—' Karen began firmly.

'OK, OK. I'm outta here. Just tell me—' she turned back to Julienne – 'who was it had nicknames? You said they all had nicknames.'

'His friends,' said Julienne. 'He had all these, like, rich friends, but Kaylee said they all had nicknames, like animals and stuff.' Suddenly she flagged. Connolly could see her pale face whiten. 'I'm hungry. I wanna see my mum. I'm tiyered.'

Karen bustled forward. 'You come with me, love, and I'll get you something to eat. This lady's going now.'

'Can I have chocolate milk?' Julienne asked, as if that was the clincher.

'Course you can,' said Karen, holding out her hand. 'Come on.'

Julienne declined to take it, but she walked with her to the door. 'And chips?' she asked. 'And a Boost? And then can I see my mum?'

'We'll see,' said Karen, as they turned into the corridor and disappeared.

'Little chancer,' Connolly said to herself, but with affection.

'Golden Eagle?' Atherton said. 'Peloponnos? Anyone less like the king of birds . . .'

'Ah, but isn't that the whole point?' said Connolly. 'If you're goin' to give yourself a nickname, you'd make it a good one. Sure you're not goin' to call yourself Gerbil or Stick Insect, just because it's more appropriate. The more pathetic you are, the more you'd want to be called Panther.'

'I suppose so,' Atherton allowed. 'But why—'

'Why a nickname at all?' Connolly anticipated. 'God knows.'

'And she said "they all" had nicknames?' Slider puzzled.

'All his friends.'

'Which must mean she met them, at least on one occasion,' said Slider.

'Was he running some sort of creepy club?' Swilley wondered.

'Not at his own home,' said Atherton. 'His mother was quite specific that he never brought anyone home.'

'Wouldn't she say that?' said Connolly. 'Her blue-eyed boy?'

'He could have done it while she was out. Sent her to the pictures, or something,' said Swilley.

'Let's not get carried away with speculation,' said Slider. He turned back to Connolly. 'She said his friends were really wealthy?'

'Yeah,' said Connolly, 'but she's just a little kid. Anyone with ten quid'd be rich to her. And she's only repeating what Kaylee said.'

'Georgie was pretty rich,' said Hart. 'If I had a hundred big ones a year, I'd feel pretty rich, I can tell ya.'

'Well,' said Slider, 'I'm not sure this gets us any further forward. I think we'd better go home and start fresh tomorrow.'

They drifted away to their desks. Slider called Atherton back. 'Fancy going for a pint? Joanna's going to be late tonight.'

'OK, I'll come for a quick one,' he said. 'I'm seeing Eva.'

'Eva Tavistock?'

'Of Arbuthnot, Yorke and Cornish,' Atherton agreed. 'Are you keeping a record?'

'No, but I think you should.'

'I have started keeping a diary,' Atherton admitted. 'It wouldn't do to double-book myself.'

'I don't know how you have the stamina,' Slider said.

'It's what *gives* me stamina,' said Atherton. 'Exercise makes muscles stronger. You have to keep pushing through the pain barrier.'

'I'm sure there's pain in it,' Slider said. 'I'm just not sure whose.'

Joanna got home around eight thirty, and was sitting in the kitchen with him while he cooked her bacon and eggs – frequently their standby meal when their jobs left them eating at odd times – when Atherton rang the doorbell.

'Not that you're not always welcome,' Slider said, as Joanna ushered him into the kitchen, 'but I thought you were going out with Eva Tavistock.'

'Did she stand you up?' Joanna guessed.

'She did not,' Atherton said with dignity. 'We . . . had a difference of opinion.'

'And she gave you the elbow? Eva brick at you?'

'Please feel free to make fun of my suffering.'

'You're not suffering,' Joanna said, examining him. 'Gin and tonic?'

'I am, but that'll cure it. Thanks.'

'I can stick another egg in for you?' Slider offered.

Atherton shuddered. 'No, thanks. I had humble pie on the train.'

Joanna came back in with the drink just as Slider was dishing up, and they all sat round the kitchen table. Atherton took an appreciative gulp, sighed, and said, 'I miss Emily.'

Slider glanced at Joanna. Women were better at knowing what to say in these circumstances.

She said, briskly, 'Write to her. Email. Or give her a ring.' She gestured to the telephone, in its holster on the counter. 'Be our guest. You can take it into the other room.'

'She's in New York,' said Atherton.

'I know that, Dumbo. Telephone lines reach all the way across the Atlantic these days.'

'You can't call me Dumbo. I have an IQ of 140,' Atherton objected.

'Elephants are very clever. Give her a ring. A trunk call.'

'The wit in this house flows like molasses.' He took another swig. 'Actually, she's coming back for a visit next week,' he admitted. 'But she wouldn't want me back now. Things have gone too far.'

'Not if she loves you. Not if you work at it. Win her back,' Joanna instructed. 'Make it your tusk for today.'

'No more elephant jokes,' Slider decreed.

'Ring her,' Joanna insisted.

'Maybe tomorrow,' said Atherton, and turned the subject. 'Was that another warning from Mr Porson this afternoon?'

'Warning,' Joanna asked, knife and fork pausing.

'To leave Gideon Marler out of it,' Slider said, and told her about the day's developments.

'I don't know what you've got against him,' Atherton said. 'Apart from the fact that he's rich, successful, good-looking and charming.'

'He lied about knowing Peloponnos,' said Slider.

'He could just as easily have forgotten. Think how many people he must meet in his daily life.'

'And he's used his influence to put a stop to our investigating him. Why would an innocent man object to being asked questions?'

Atherton snorted with laughter. 'He's an MP! You haven't taken into account the sense of entitlement that comes with the job and the fame and the influence. *Anyone* in his position would be indignant at the invasion of his privacy. It doesn't necessarily indicate guilt.'

'Sense of entitlement or not,' Slider said, 'he's making a very large fuss about some very small questions. In his position, I wouldn't behave that way.'

'But you're a policeman,' Joanna said. 'You're organically predisposed to answer questions and try to find solutions to problems. You're no template.'

'Neither of you would do it either,' Slider asserted.

'Jim's a policeman too,' Joanna said. 'And I'm married to one. I'd object to questions from a journalist, but I wouldn't try to stop the police asking me things.'

'Unless you were innocent and felt you were being victimized?' Atherton suggested slyly.

She grinned at him. 'You think Gideon Marler feels victimized? Well, boo hoo! Now, to a topic of much greater interest, which I know you're trying to avoid – are you going to ring Emily?'

'Now *I* feel victimized,' said Atherton.

TWELVE

Elephant's Child

On Friday the Tupperware sky was back, with a chilly breeze and the threat of showers. Connolly came into Slider's office in a roll-neck cable jumper so chunky it looked as though it was consuming her. Feral knitwear alert!

'I've asked around on Mr Marler,' she said, 'but there's not much goss about him. O 'course, I don't have the inside contacts.' She cocked a curious eye. 'Wouldn't Jim Atherton be the better person to do it? He's the head for politics – always knows who's who. I'd have a job naming a single minister.'

'Just give me what you've got,' Slider said.

'Well, boss, he seems to be pretty straight,' she said. 'There's no suggestion of drugs, and he's never been in a sex scandal – doing the nasty with the interns or any o' that class o' caper. His wife's reckoned to be rolling in it, so he wouldn't be robbin' the till – what need? However, there might be some rupture in the happy home. It's said he lives mostly in the London house, and his wife never leaves the country.'

'Rickmansworth is hardly country,' said Slider, who was born in a farm cottage.

'Country to the likes o' me,' Connolly said. 'I get narky if I can't see a red bus. Anyway, what I read is they're virtually separated, but keepin' it together for the sake of his career, and the kid.'

'Is there another woman?'

'No report of one,' Connolly said. 'And the wife still goes to functions with him. Amicable separation. No heavin' the china about.'

'I see,' said Slider.

'Sorry it's not much.'

'Well, keep your eyes and ears open.'

'I will,' said Connolly. 'But it does look as if he's the real deal,' she added apologetically.

She passed Swilley in the doorway. 'Boss,' said Swilley, her face heralding something of interest, 'I've got George's office phone record, and guess what? Quite a few phone calls to and from Mr Marler.'

If Slider had been the hand-rubbing sort, he'd have rubbed his hands.

Connolly swung back at the sound of the name. 'And him saying he'd never heard of the feller,' she said indignantly. 'The big lyin' liar!'

'At a quick glance, there doesn't seem to be anything out of the ordinary,' Swilley said, spreading the sheets out on Slider's desk. 'They pretty well all seem to be pukka business, apart from a surprising number of calls to his home landline.'

'Keeping his mammy happy,' said Connolly. 'As a good boy should.'

'A lot of calls to Shand Account Cabs – well, that makes sense if he didn't have a motor. And there are several calls from a pay-as-you-go mobile with an unregistered holder,' Swilley went on, 'which might or might not be suspicious.'

'But is certainly no help, if it's unregistered,' said Slider.

'Right. But Mr Marler rings him just about every week, sometimes several times. And listen to this, boss – he rang George on Friday just before half past five. A five-minute call. Finished at five thirty-three. And we know that at five forty-five he bought the opera ticket.'

'Alibi,' said Connolly, excited.

'Let's not get carried away,' said Slider. 'There could just as easily be no connection. Or maybe he was booking the ticket *for* Marler.'

'I'll get on to the Opera House this morning, get the names of the people in the adjacent seats,' said Swilley.

'No, let Connolly do that,' said Slider. 'I'd like you to go and have another word with Virginia Lamy, find out what she knows about Mr Marler and his connection to Peloponnos and the trust.'

'Why didn't Jim ask her when he interviewed her?'

'We didn't know then that there was anything to ask,' said Slider.

'I could do it, boss,' Connolly offered.

'No, I want Swilley to go,' said Slider. 'She's taller.'

'You'll get me into trouble,' Atherton grumbled, as Slider drove towards the West Cross roundabout.

'You don't usually mind getting out of the office for a bit,' said Slider. 'Don't you want to see some nice houses?'

'You're the one who's mad about architecture. I'm more interested in keeping my job.'

'You're no fun any more,' Slider complained. 'Don't you have any curiosity at all?'

'Not about putting my nose between a crocodile's teeth. So Marler rang Georgie's office. So what? Maybe he was having a fling with the PA. She wasn't bad-looking. I wouldn't throw her out of bed for eating toast. Actually, I would, but I have super-sensitive skin. And you can eat caviar with a spoon straight from the pot.'

'You're drivelling. Even if he was ringing Mrs Lamy, he'd have known whose secretary she was.'

'But you're not supposed to go asking him *questions*.'

'Provoking people's the best way to get the inadvertent truth out of them.'

'It's also the way to get inadvertently disciplined.'

'Pooh! He doesn't scare me,' Slider said loftily.

'That's what this is about, isn't it?' Atherton said glumly. 'A pissing contest.'

'No, it's on a "need to know" basis. I need to know what's going on.'

Abbotsbury Walk was a short cul-de-sac with only two houses on either side – but what houses! Atherton blew a soundless whistle as they parked and got out. 'You're into the super league here,' he said.

The houses were detached, though not by much – you couldn't have built a garage between them. They were smooth-stuccoed to look like Portland stone, each with a porch over the front door supported by grand pillars, and a parapet partly hiding the pitch of the roof. There were three storeys plus the semi-basement, the top floor having originally been the servants' rooms, as revealed by the smallness of the windows.

'1840s,' Slider said. 'The first Victorian westward expansion.'

'But they don't have much garden,' Atherton said, as if to comfort Slider, who was like a cat watching the birds feeding on the other side of the window. 'You can see if you look through the gap. About eight or ten feet and then that's the next road.'

The road ended in a high wall with tall iron gates, behind which was a glimpse of Holland Lodge, the object of Slider's curiosity – or rather, the home of the object of his curiosity. Behind Holland Lodge were the green spaces of Holland Park, grass and trees and birds and all the *rus in urbe* you could want.

'There's desirable,' said Atherton, 'and then there's *desirable*. How rich does this man's wife have to be? I mean, the house in Rickmansworth's probably one and a half, two mill, but this one . . . Where's he getting the money from?'

'Wouldn't *we* like to know,' said Slider. It was a bit of a shaker. He hadn't imagined anything this grand.

There was no sign of movement or occupation – not in any of the houses. It was the quietest London street he'd ever been in.

'Let's try the doorbell,' Slider said.

'I'll say you made me do it,' Atherton warned.

There was an intercom box on the gates, which were solidly, electronically closed, with heavy mesh on the back side of them and razor wire wound round the spikes. It seemed a lot of security even for an MP, but perhaps, he added to himself with his innate desire to be fair, being chair of the Police Select Committee made him more of a target.

Beyond the gates was a gravel area, which would provide parking for an impressive number of cars. Slider pressed the bell and waited. A camera was mounted on the gatepost looking down at them, and there was a second one on the other gatepost pointing down the road. In case of invasion or civil disorder? Slider wondered. He rang again, but there was no response.

'Nobody in,' Atherton said, with a hint of relief in his voice.

'Don't want to talk to us, more like,' said Slider.

'Or they think we're selling encyclopaedias,' Atherton said. 'What now?'

'Try the neighbours,' said Slider.

The two houses on the right had the internal shutters closed on the ground floor and basement, and Slider was not surprised, therefore, when they got no response. They crossed to the other side. The first house looked unoccupied, except for the basement which, to judge by the separate gate and doorbell, was probably a self-contained flat. But there was no reply from that, either.

'What is this, Marie Celeste Row?' Atherton complained. 'Three down and one to go.'

There were curtains drawn in the basement of the last house, and the gate to the steps leading down was padlocked. They mounted the steps over the basement to the front door, and rang the bell, noting the security camera mounted high under the porch. Slider was about to admit defeat when the grille above the bell crackled and a woman's voice said, 'Who are you?'

Slider pulled out his warrant card and held it up to the camera. 'Detective Chief Inspector Slider, from Shepherd's Bush. This is Detective Sergeant Atherton.'

'Shepherd's Bush?' said the voice. 'I wasn't expecting *you*.'

'Could we have a word with you?' Slider said, but the intercom had clicked off.

However, a few moments later the door swung open, to reveal a woman with a haughty, suspicious face. Slider guessed her to be in her late fifties, but she was so well-preserved and beautifully presented, she could have been quite a lot older. She was wearing a lavender tweed suit with a double row of pearls around her neck and pearl studs in her ears. Her hair was ash blonde and exquisitely coiffed, her make-up looked professional. She had once obviously been quite a looker. She was very slim, her figure almost girlish, and only the knobbliness of her knees peeking out from under her too-short skirt gave her age away.

Two dogs had appeared with her, a miniature poodle and a Jack Russell-type crossbreed. The terrier was barking, but when Slider looked at him, he stopped, stuck his nose up and scented instead.

'Shepherd's Bush!' the woman exclaimed, examining Slider with an interest equal to the dog's. 'After all the complaints I've made to Notting Hill!' Her voice was clipped and her accent cut glass. Slider found himself automatically thinking *colonial* – an outdated classification, but useful shorthand. 'I even tried the Parks Police,' she went on. 'Their headquarters is in Holland Park, you know.'

'I know,' said Slider.

'But nothing ever happened. I thought as it backs onto a park, they might be interested. And now you come here, from completely the wrong place. Better late than never, I suppose. Well, you'd better come in. I hope you don't mind dogs?'

'I love them,' said Slider. As she walked away and he followed across the threshold, the terrier came to smell his shoes thoroughly, and the poodle hopped backwards on its hind legs, seeking attention. Their hostess started up the stairs, and both dogs abandoned Slider and shot past her, zooming to the top and disappearing. The doors on the ground floor were all closed and gave the house a cramped and gloomy air, but as they mounted to the first floor they progressed into light and space. There was an enormous, high-ceilinged kitchen across the back, made from one of the original reception rooms. Through the open door Slider caught a glimpse of polished wood floors, panelled cupboards painted in that National Trust shade of grey-green, a brushed-steel range, a central island with a granite top and inset sink, copper pots hanging from a ceiling rack – a nice mixture of the antique and the high-tech modern. The dogs had shot in there, but shot out again, claws skidding, as the woman went past and towards the front of the house, where she led them into a sitting room. It had an elaborate marble fireplace, bookshelves with cupboards to either side filling the alcoves, a Persian carpet on the polished floor, antique chairs and tables elegantly placed, and long windows onto the street.

The woman turned, waved them to a settle in the middle of the room, disposed herself on the edge of an eighteenth-century armchair, and said, 'Now, then, inspector – I'm sorry, I didn't catch your name.'

Slider re-introduced them, and said, 'May I ask your name, ma'am?'

'I'm Mrs Havelock Symonds,' she said. Then her eyes widened. 'But if you're here about my complaint, you must know my name.' She rose to her feet, and Slider and Atherton rose too, automatically; the dogs, who had just settled on the carpet before the hearth, jumped up, and the terrier started barking. 'Who *are* you?'

Slider got out his warrant card again. 'We *are* police officers, ma'am. But I'm afraid we don't know anything about your complaint. We wanted to talk to you about the house at the end of the road – Holland Lodge.'

Now she only looked puzzled. 'But that's what my complaint is *about*,' she said. She looked from one to the other uncertainly.

'If you'd like to ring Shepherd's Bush police station, they will vouch for us,' Slider said.

She seemed to make up her mind. 'Oh no – I've seen enough of those—' she nodded at the warrant card – 'to know a genuine one. Sit down. We've obviously been talking at cross purposes.'

'Possibly not,' said Slider, 'if we're both interested in the same house.'

She didn't need much prompting to start talking. Despite her obvious wealth, education and composure, she was obviously a lonely woman. It was explained quite early in her monologue by the revelation that her husband worked for an international finance company and travelled a great deal. 'He could have retired, of course, years ago – he's sixty-eight – but it's what he loves. The world of finance, the affairs of men – even the travel. I couldn't care if I never stepped on another aeroplane or slept in another hotel, but he seems to be fulfilled by it all.' She sighed. 'And this road is so quiet nowadays.'

'Are the other houses empty?' Slider asked.

'The two across the road are. They were bought as an investment, I believe. *Russians*.' She mouthed the word as though they might be listening. 'I've never seen anyone going in or out, though I believe they are furnished. And next door is owned by a South African, a banker. His bank's headquarters is in Switzerland and he's there a lot, and he travels all over the world, so he's hardly ever here. I don't think he's married. Or perhaps he's divorced. I've never seen him with anyone, on the few occasions I *have* seen him.' It sounded as though the South African banker was denying her the solace of a female neighbour quite deliberately. 'There used to be someone in the basement flat – that's separate – but he's gone now. So you see, as it is, I feel like a castaway in my own street. It's all so *dreary* – not like when we first moved here. *Then* there were proper families, people one could take pleasure in knowing – dinners and bridge evenings and so on. Comings and goings. There was a lovely family in the house opposite. He was a solicitor and she and I used to walk our dogs together. They had a place in Shropshire, too.' She sighed. *Dem were de days, Joxer.*

'And what about the house at the end – Holland Lodge?'

'Ah, yes, that was Lord and Lady Daintree's house. Lovely people. They set the tone for the whole street. But they had a terrible tragedy in the eighties, when their son was killed, piloting a light aircraft, and of course they didn't entertain so much after that. But they were a proper, *old* family, not like the *nouveau riche* and the foreigners that buy up all our lovely houses nowadays. In fact, I think Lord Daintree was related in some way to the Holland family – you know, the owners of Holland House?' She looked to see if they did, in fact, know. Slider nodded encouragingly, glad that Atherton knew how to hold his peace. People like Mrs Havelock Symonds had to get to things in their own time. 'Holland Lodge used to be called Cope Castle Lodge when Desmond and I first came here in 1972. You know that Holland House was originally called Cope Castle, don't you?'

'Yes, so I understand,' Slider said smoothly.

'The Daintrees changed it in 1986, when the local council took over Holland House. I can't remember why. I think it was something to do with the lease. Desmond could tell you, if he were here. I believe the current owners want to change it back. But if Holland Lodge was good enough for the Daintrees, I'm sure it's good enough for *them*.'

'What are they like?' Slider asked. 'The current owners.'

'He's an *MP*!' she said, with a nod, opening her eyes wide as if that answered everything. 'I believe she's from a moneyed family but one never sees her. One doesn't see *him*, when it comes to it – just the car going past. And I wouldn't have any objection to him, whatever his politics, if it weren't for the *parties*.'

'The parties,' Slider repeated.

'That's what you've made complaints about, is it?' Atherton asked.

'Well, yes – as I thought you knew when you arrived here on my doorstep. Nearly every Saturday night. Occasionally on Friday, but most Saturday nights. Cars and taxis going down. You just don't know who's in them. And then the party starts. The lights. And the noise.'

'Loud music?' Atherton hazarded.

'I can hear it if I open my bedroom window,' she said severely. 'Especially when they're up on the roof terrace. I can't see much from my bedroom, but I can see the lights, and those outdoor heaters glaring, and people moving around and dancing, and I can hear the voices, and the music.' She fixed them with a stern eye. 'It's the rowdiness I hate most. The coarse voices and vulgar laughter. I don't know who they are but you can tell they're not nice people. I don't have any proof, but I'm sure they're taking drugs. I told the police they ought to come round unannounced and raid the house. I'm sure it would be worth their while – think of the fines they could impose! But they never come.'

Slider and Atherton exchanged a look. 'Noise nuisance is usually considered a matter for the local council,' Atherton said.

'Oh, and I've complained to them, too, umpteen times,' she said. 'First it was the construction work – the noise, the dirt, the disruption, day after day, hammering, machinery, lorries going back and forth. It was sheer hell for over a year! And no sooner was that over and done with, than the parties started. But nobody cares! You're the first people who have come to speak to me about it.' She looked at them, and realisation came back to her. 'And you haven't even come here about that, have you?'

'Only indirectly,' said Slider.

'Well, what *did* you want?'

'I wanted to ask you whether you had noticed any comings and goings last Saturday.'

'Last Saturday? Oh yes, they had one of their parties,' she said bitterly.

'Was it different in any way?'

'Not that I noticed. In what way?'

Slider didn't want to lead her. 'Do you remember what time it ended?'

'I couldn't say. It was going on when I went to bed at about eleven.'

'So you didn't notice any particular rumpus? Shouting or screams, for instance?'

'Not while I was awake. But I'd taken a sleeping tablet, to make sure I got my rest. I read for a while, about half an hour, I suppose, and then dropped off.' She looked hopefully at Slider, but he was deep in thought, so she turned to Atherton. 'So are you going to do something about it this time?' She seemed to have lost sight again of the fact that they hadn't come to sort out her noise pollution.

'We will certainly pass it along to the proper authority,' Atherton temporized.

'That's what they always say. But nothing happens.'

Slider came back with a jerk. He stood up. 'I'm very sorry you've been troubled with this, ma'am,' he said, 'and I shall certainly do everything in my power to see you aren't bothered again. I promise you I'm not just going to shelve it. Thank you for your time. We'll be going now.'

She talked all the way down the stairs to let them out, but it was the same things over again. She stopped at the door, and stood watching them down the steps and out of sight. The dogs watched too, from just behind her. Slider imagined they saw him go with regret. Their lives could not contain much variety.

Virginia Lamy did not seem to mind another visit from the police. The office looked too tidy to Swilley's sweeping glance. Perhaps the work had dried up in the wake of George's suicide.

'Oh yes,' she said, 'of course I know Mr Marler. He's our local MP.'

'And does he take any interest in the trust?' Swilley asked.

'He's a great supporter,' she said enthusiastically. 'He helps at our fundraisers, advocates for us in Westminster, writes a piece for our newsletter now and then. Brings in donors, too. It's very helpful for us to have an active, *connected* person like him to turn to.'

'Is he himself a donor?'

'Oh, in a small way,' she said.

'How much?'

She seemed to find that indelicate. Her smile stiffened. 'A hundred pounds here and there. I really couldn't say.'

'But I thought he was very wealthy,' Swilley persisted.

'Wealth is comparative, isn't it? And it's not for me to judge how people spend their money. His time and dedication are much more valuable to us.'

Swilley let that pass. 'So he's here quite a lot? He pops in and out of the office?'

'Oh, no. He's much too busy. I don't think I've ever seen him here.'

'You *have* met him?'

'I've seen him at fundraisers and openings and so on. I've only ever spoken to him face-to-face once, at a sponsorship dinner-dance. *Very* charming man. Quite delightful. An excellent dancer, too.'

'Did you dance with him?'

'Sadly, not.' She smiled. 'There was a lot of competition.'

'But he telephones here often,' Swilley said, not making it a question.

'Oh, I've spoken to him once or twice on the phone.'

'More than that, surely? He has telephoned Mr Peloponnos several times a week.'

Her cheeks coloured. 'I wouldn't know about that. George's line can be dialled direct. I would only know about calls that came in on the central line and I put through.'

'So you wouldn't know what Mr Marler and Mr Peloponnos talked about?'

'The trust, of course.'

'Anything else?'

'You don't imagine I listened in to his telephone conversations?'

Which meant, Swilley thought, that she had, once or twice, and felt guilty. 'It would be such a help,' she said, looking away casually, 'if you knew anything about a call Mr Marler made to your boss on Friday evening. About half past five.'

Mrs Lamy hesitated. 'We close at half past five,' she said. Swilley waited, receptively. 'As a matter of fact . . .'

Yesss! Thought Swilley.

'As a matter of fact,' said Mrs Lamy, trying to sound lofty, 'I did happen to take some papers into George's office at the end of the day, just before going home. There were some things that needed his signature, and while I was there, his telephone did ring.'

'How do you know it was Mr Marler?' Swilley asked.

'George had his hands full. He answered it on speaker, and I heard Mr Marler's voice say, "It's me." Then George picked up the receiver, so I didn't hear anything more, but I recognized his voice.'

'But you stayed in the room?'

'I was waiting for the papers.'

'So you heard what George said.'

'I didn't really pay any attention,' she said.

'I understand that. But please tell me anything you can remember, however small. It could be important.' She gave a woman-to-woman smile. 'I know you were fond of him – as a boss and a human being. You must want to know what really happened to make him kill himself on Monday.'

'I can't see how it matters,' Mrs Lamy said. 'And I really can't remember what George said, because it was only half a conversation, so it wouldn't make sense to me anyway. I don't think he said very much, actually – he was listening more. But I do remember he seemed a bit upset, or concerned at one point, and he said "Why?" and then, "But why me?" And then I suppose he saw me listening – not that I was, but perhaps I'd looked at him – and he turned away and lowered his voice, and he said, "Yes, all right," and then "I'll think of something."'

'And when he said that, you think he was upset?'

'Well – worried, perhaps, or anxious. As if Mr Marler was asking him to do something and he wasn't very happy about it.'

'What did you think it might be?'

'How could I possibly know?'

'Of course not – but you've obviously been wondering. What *sort* of thing did you think it was?'

She thought for a long time. 'George was a good man. He'd never do anything he knew to be really wrong. But suppose Mr Marler had asked him to be friendly to a bad person for the sake of getting a donation – that might be something he'd agree to do, but feel bad about, though it was for a good cause. I'm not saying that's what it was,' she added hastily. 'I'm just saying, that would be the sort of dilemma that might make him anxious.'

Swilley digested that for a moment, and into her silence Mrs Lamy said, 'You don't think . . . He didn't kill himself because of something Mr Marler said in that conversation?'

Swilley shook her head. 'Without knowing what was said, how could I say?'

'Because I was right there,' said Mrs Lamy. 'I could have asked him what was wrong. Got him to open up to me. If he could have talked to me about it, perhaps he wouldn't have felt the need to—'

'Whatever happened, it wasn't your fault,' Swilley said, more kindly than she felt. 'If it was bothering him that much, he probably wouldn't have told you anyway.'

Lamy gave Swilley a clear look. 'The detective who came yesterday, he said he thought George might have known someone who was mixed up in something you were investigating. Is that person Mr Marler?'

'Would it surprise you if it was?' Swilley countered.

'Yes, very much. He's a good person, a good local MP, and a tireless worker for our trust.'

And it doesn't hurt that he's good-looking and charming, Swilley thought. 'I know absolutely nothing against Mr Marler,' she said reassuringly. 'Can I ask you just one more thing? Do you recognize this phone number?'

She showed her the unregistered mobile number. Mrs Lamy shook her head. She checked on the office's directory, but found no match. 'Sorry,' she said. 'I don't know whose that is. I suppose the day may come when we recognize mobile numbers the way we used to recognize landline numbers, but we're not there yet.'

THIRTEEN
End of the Line

'Cope Castle,' said Atherton in the car. 'I missed that one. And Georgie's secret file was labelled Cope. I wonder if he had some dirt on Marler he was keeping in it?'

'Wonder all you like. Until we can get a look . . .' said Slider.

'You mean "unless". But I'm starting to think you may be right, guv,' Atherton admitted. 'You always thought there was a connection between Georgie and Marler, and that it had something to do with Kaylee. How's this? Georgie takes her to Marler's party—'

'In Marler's car?'

'If it *was* Marler's car. We can't be sure yet. But Georgie didn't have wheels, so say he borrowed Marler's. Or Marler had them both picked up.' He waved that away. 'Georgie gets a bit tanked, kills Kaylee, probably by accident—'

'How? And where?'

'Somehow. Somewhere. Are you going to keep interrupting my story?'

'When it needs interrupting.'

'*Anyway* – Georgie's scared stiff, asks Marler for help. Marler doesn't want bad publicity, so he helps Georgie dispose of the body. Then Georgie's overcome with remorse and tops himself, and Marler thinks the best way to distance himself is to pretend he's never heard of Georgie. Which ought to have worked. Except for phone records and number plate recognition, it would have.'

'Even when criminals *plan* crimes, they can't think of everything,' said Slider, 'and this has the hallmarks of the unplanned. After all, who could want deliberately to kill a nobody like Kaylee?' He was silent a moment. 'You don't want me to point out the holes in your theory, do you?'

'No, let me bathe in the glow of achievement for a minute. This isn't the way home,' he noticed. 'Where are we going?'

'The local police station. I want to find out why nobody ever progressed Mrs Havelock's complaints.'

They got passed to the uniform superintendent, Geddes, who was the most senior person on duty. He looked lofty, to begin with. 'Noise nuisance is a local government problem. We don't go out unless there's a danger of public disorder.'

Tell your grandmother, Slider thought. 'Oh, quite,' he said. 'I'm more interested in why no record was made of the complaints. There were many of them, and over a considerable length of time.'

'That's just it. This dotty old woman keeps complaining about nothing, you stop paying attention, don't you? I mean, you know the type – some old girl rattling around in a house too big for her, lonely, craves attention. All she wants is someone to talk to, but we haven't got the time to be nursemaids.'

'All that may be true,' Slider said, 'but still I'd have thought there would be something on record, just in case something happened further down the line. Suppose drugs *were* involved, and it came out later. I don't think she'd be the sort of person not to say I told you so – and to the press.'

Loftiness segued into annoyance. 'Oh, she's a troublemaker all right. There's plenty of them in this borough, I can tell you. Living in the past. Don't know the Empire's dead and gone. Think if they cock their little finger, you'll come running. Look down their noses at you and call you *officer*.'

'Yes, they can be a pain,' Slider said sympathetically.

'A *royal* pain,' the super amplified, apparently without irony.

'All the more reason,' said Slider, 'to keep your guard up against them.'

Now wariness took over from annoyance. 'Look,' he said, 'don't you realize who lives in that house? Holland Lodge, I mean?'

'Yes,' said Slider. 'Gideon Marler, MP.'

'Exactly! He's a VIP. Not just an MP, he's the chair of the Police Select Committee.'

'I know,' said Slider.

The superintendent placed both hands on the table and leaned forward slightly. 'I'll level with you, but this goes no further, do you understand? I'm only telling you because I don't want you trampling around and making trouble. We had orders not to record the complaints. Orders from a *very high place indeed*.'

'Why?' Slider asked.

If this had been a pub discussion, he probably would have got his nose punched at that point. The super breathed hard through flared nostrils. 'Ours not to reason why,' he said. With an obvious effort to be pleasant, he went on, 'There are matters of high strategy that don't concern those further down the chain of command. All you need to know is that Holland Lodge is not to be disturbed. It's off the radar. It doesn't exist. Got me?'

'Oh yes,' said Slider. 'That's very clear. Thank you.'

Outside, Atherton said, 'New theory. The parties are just a cover. It's high-level MI5 stroke MI6 work – top secret and radically sensitive. It'd be just the place for it – virtually no neighbours.'

'And Peloponnos and Kaylee?' Slider said.

'That was not the party they went to. It can't have been the only party happening in London on Saturday night.'

'Marler's car?'

'Not Marler's car. We don't have the full index. Georgie's connection with Marler is purely incidental, nothing to do with our case. Which, officially, is not a case.'

'Not a case, and not our problem for much longer. On Monday we'll have to drop it, and then we'll be perfectly justified in forgetting it, and going back to our proper work.'

'I wish you didn't care so much,' Atherton complained. 'You'll shorten your life, you know. Where now?'

'Back to the factory. I need a cup of tea.'

'I have ceased to resist your whacky theories,' Atherton said, when he came into the room later.

'I don't have any theories,' Slider said patiently.

'Never theorize ahead of your data, I know, Sherlock,' said Atherton, 'but you've been working all along on a connection between Georgie and Marler, and though for the life of me I can't see where Kaylee comes into it, meek submission to the idea has freed my mighty mind to roam over the available evidence.'

'And has anything emerged from the primordial swamp,' Slider enquired a little sourly, 'apart from gas?'

'A large bubble. If Georgie had become so depressed about something he wanted to kill himself, why didn't he use the pills? He had a good supply of downers and sleepers from his doctor tucked away in his medicine cabinet, and wouldn't an overdose appeal more to a – let's say – timid and unathletic type than being mangled – and possibly not killed but only painfully crippled – by a tube train?'

'How do you know he was timid and unathletic?' Slider objected.

'He still lived with his mummy at the age of forty-eight.'

'Perhaps he didn't want said mummy to be the one to find him dead.'

'He could have gone to an hotel room.'

'All right,' said Slider, 'supposing it is a surprising choice of suicide method, what then?'

'I'm wondering,' Atherton said, 'whether his suicidal feelings only came over him on Monday morning after he'd left for work – leaving, of course, the pills in the house. And if said feelings came over him so violently that he threw himself under a train, did something happen to him between the house and the station?'

'Such as?'

'Well, it occurred to me that he might have bought a paper at the station, or on the way, and seen something in it. Or the post came just as he was leaving and he took it with him and opened it on the way, and received a poisonous communication.'

'The post doesn't arrive before people leave for work any more,' Slider reminded him.

'Post office deliveries are so erratic, anything is possible. I'm going to find out, anyway.'

'Do,' said Slider cordially.

Mrs Peloponnos seemed to have shrunk – not only vertically, but as if she had collapsed together like a deflating balloon. She peered up at Atherton with an eye devoid of hope, even of interest, the expression newsreel cameras record on the faces of women in refugee camps. The anger that had sustained her was gone. Whether or not her good son had committed suicide, he had left her, and she was on her own, completely, and for ever. She shuffled before him into the kitchen with all the self-determination of a robotic vacuum cleaner, and none of the vim.

There was a film of dust visible on the wooden surfaces, and unwashed crockery in the sink. Not much of it – it looked as though she had subsisted for the past two days on toast – but it had an abandoned air, as if no one was ever going to wash it and put it away. When she ran out of clean plates, she would cease eating, and/or die, thought Atherton.

She didn't offer him anything, but sat in a chair at the kitchen table, folding her hands on it, and staring at nothing. Atherton walked past her to sit down facing her, catching a sour whiff from her of unwashed hair and body odour. Had she even undressed and gone to bed since it happened? he wondered. He had an image of her wandering about the house like a dust bunny blown hither and yon by random drafts, purposeless now that Yorkos would not be coming back. He had a further image of her dying here at the kitchen table, just collapsing forward one day over her hands. No one would miss her. Owing nothing, she would not be visited by bailiffs. No doorstep deliveries of milk any more. The services would be cut off when the red bills were not paid, but no one would come to check if she'd gone. She would lie there pretty much for ever, until she either mummified or rotted down to a skeleton.

He shook the thoughts away. He was turning into his boss. For one of them to be over-sensitive was a misfortune; two would look like carelessness.

'Mrs Peloponnos,' he said firmly, 'I want to talk to you about your son. You told us before that he had been worried and anxious for some time. About his work, you said.' She looked at him blankly.

'Now, last Sunday, did he seem more worried than usual?' She continued to stare. 'I want you to think back. Was he very upset about something – so upset he might have thought about killing himself?'

'He did not kill himself. It was accident,' she said, but it sounded automatic. There was no passion in it.

'So, how was he on Sunday?'

'Same,' she said listlessly. 'Quiet, a bit, maybe. But just the same he has been for weeks. Was in his study all morning, on his computer. Then I call him for lunch.'

'What did you have?' he asked. Perhaps the detail would pull her back.

'Lamb,' she said. She pronounced it 'Lemm'. 'I make lamb. Is Yorkos favourite – like his father. Roast, with plenty garlic. And rosemary potatoes.'

It worked. Just a hint of animation came into her voice. It was easier to talk about food.

'That sounds good,' Atherton said. 'I expect he tucked in to that.'

'He eat good,' she said. 'Always have good appetite, my Yorkos. You would not think to look at him, so tall and thin, but he eats well.'

'And he had a good lunch on Sunday?'

'Like I say. His favourite lamb. And apple pie afterwards. I make with raisins and cinnamon in the apple, and Greek yoghurt on top.'

'That does sound good. So there was nothing wrong with his appetite. And what did he do afterwards?'

She frowned. 'Cup of coffee. We talk a little. Then I say, Yorkos, you have jobs. Small jobs but a man must do man's work, like I do women's work.'

'What jobs?' Atherton asked.

'Fix hinge on kitchen cupboard. Fix tap that drips. Door to water tank upstairs does not close properly. Man's jobs.'

'So he didn't mind doing those things?'

'Why should he mind? Later I bring him cup of tea, piece of cake.' She almost smiled. 'Tell him to stop whistling. He is my good son, but he cannot whistle. Sounds like kettle.'

'And what did you do in the evening? Did he go out?'

'No, we watch TV, he does his knitting. I fall asleep, maybe, a little,' she admitted.

'He did knitting?' Atherton asked.

She gave him a look. 'Yes, knitting. Is not bad thing. In Greece all mens knit. Since he was little boy he made things. Made scarf for his poppa when he was six. He was making me sweater for my birthday.' Suddenly the realisation came back to her, her lips trembled, her eyes filled shockingly with tears. He would never finish that sweater now. In small things death is biggest.

Atherton pushed in the next question before she disintegrated. 'Did he have a newspaper delivered to the house?'

She shook her head, looking dolefully at him, like a dog unjustly punished. 'No newspaper. Why you ask?'

'On Monday, did the post arrive before he left?'

'What post?'

'The mail. Letters.'

'No,' she said. 'All rubbish in post – junk mail, he calls it. But it never come before afternoon.'

'Did he have a telephone call before he left for work?'

'No, no telephone.' She looked away from him now, the hopelessness sinking over her like a blanket of fog. 'Phone never ring any more.'

Another prime image to add to his unwanted collection, Atherton thought as he went away. The undisturbed dust gathering over the telephone – the telephone at which the skull of the skeleton at the kitchen table seems to be staring in entreaty.

I need to get out more, he thought.

Jason Conroy had a miniscule but private office in the back set of Shepherd's Bush Station, whose comforts included a proper coffee maker. He put it on and invited Atherton to sit down.

'I've got quite a collection now,' he said, indicating the DVD cases lined up along a shelf.

'A bit of a gruesome hobby,' Atherton observed.

'Well, everyone's got to have one,' Conroy said imperturbably. 'Anyway, you never know who might come back asking, as, for instance, yourself, on this present occasion. So, what's on your mind? You're not thinking it *wasn't* suicide, are you? Because I've watched that tape a dozen times, and I promise you he jumps. No one was near enough to push him.'

'It wasn't that. But there's something not right about it. He was perfectly all right on the Sunday night, and he didn't receive a letter on Monday morning before he left the house—'

'Who gets letters before they leave home?' said Conroy.

'Quite. Nor a phone call. So what suddenly came over him? And that woman, what was her name? Parkinson?'

'Carole Parkinson.'

'With an "e",' they said both together.

'She said that she just missed a train, but she also said Peloponnos was already on the platform. So that must mean he let the train go – he could have got on it, but didn't.'

'That's right,' said Conroy. 'I saw that on the tape. That's not unusual, though. They often have to think about it for a bit, gee themselves up for the effort. One bloke – that was before the refurbishment – he stood there and let train after train go. Eventually someone saw him on a monitor and went down and copped hold of him.'

'Stopped him doing it?'

'That day, yes. He came back another day, though, and went under.' Conroy shrugged. 'They might hesitate, but when they're determined, they do it eventually. Seems to be a fascination with the loco. It's almost . . .' He hesitated, and looked at Atherton to see if he would laugh at him for being fanciful. Atherton tried to look receptive and unsatirical. 'It's almost a sexual thing, you know? They want that loco like . . . like—'

'The consummation devoutly to be wished,' said Atherton. Conroy grunted agreement. 'So you've got him on tape letting the previous train go?'

'Oh, yeah. I've edited the whole thing now, like I said. I like to have the whole story on record. I've gone back and got him from the moment he arrives at the entrance up in the street.'

'Can I see it?'

'Course you can.' He got up and went to the shelf.

'I want to see if he buys a newspaper,' Atherton said.

'I can tell you that – he doesn't. Here it is. I file 'em by date order, so it's the end one.'

He put it into the slot, and the monitor came on. A moment of blankness, and then the movie started. There was no preamble, just the shot of the station entrance from the camera mounted opposite. 'There he is,' said Conroy, pointing. Peloponnos walked into view, paused a moment in the entrance, then walked on. The view changed to the ticket hall camera, showed him walking to the barrier, deploying his Oyster card. Other viewpoints watched him descend on the escalator, his face blank – grimly blank, not the switched-off look of the normal commuter but that of someone turned inward on an unpleasant landscape. Another camera received him walking onto the platform, and standing there as the train came in, somewhat buffeted by other passengers as they boarded and descended around him while he stood immobile.

It departed, and Peloponnos turned his head to watch it go. Then he walked a little further along the platform, and stood still, in the pose Atherton had seen before, staring at the wall, his hands by his side clenching and unclenching.

'Thinking about it now,' Conroy commented. 'Working himself up to it.'

'What was wrong with the previous train?' Atherton asked.

'Hadn't thought of it then. You can see.' He ran it back. 'See, he's staring at the ground at that point, as if he doesn't even know the train's there. Thinking about the trouble he's in. He's trapped in a situation, can't escape it. And *there*—' he tapped the screen as Peloponnos lifted his head to watch the train depart – '*there*'s where he sees his way out.' He spread his hands and let the tape run on. 'The rest is history.'

Atherton watched it in the interests of thoroughness, though he got no satisfaction from the last frames of Georgie's life. He declined to see the rest, the aftermath, and Conroy stopped it.

'Well?' he asked. 'Any help?'

'Can we go back to the beginning again?' said Atherton.

'Sure.'

They watched the opening frames. 'Why does he stop like that, in the entrance?' Atherton said.

'Suddenly realized it was his way out?' Conroy suggested.

'But you said that was the moment on the platform when he watched the train leave.'

'Yeah. Well, premonition, maybe. Goose walked over his grave or something.'

'Run it again.' Atherton watched. 'There!' he said. 'Take it back a couple of frames. And freeze.'

There was a man standing by the entrance, leaning against the side column, in fact, apparently reading a newspaper. As Peloponnos came level with him, the man raised his head and said something.

'Move on, frame by frame. You can see his lips move,' said Atherton. 'He says something, and Georgie stops. God, I wish I could lip-read! He says something else, and Georgie walks on.' Atherton peered at the screen, trying to make it tell him more. 'Don't you think his walk looks different? Sort of wooden?'

Conroy looked at him. 'No,' he said. 'What, you think this bloke put a curse on him or something? Hypnotized him and told him to go and top himself?'

Atherton ignored that. 'Can you isolate him, enlarge the image?'

Conroy obliged. 'Know him?'

'I don't think so. I don't know. Maybe he looks familiar. No, I don't think so. Email me that image, will you? I'll put him through the system.'

'Okeydoke. I'll see if I can enhance it any more, and zap it through to you.' He looked again. 'It might be nothing. He might just have been talking to himself. Or singing. Or talking on his Bluetooth.'

'I know. I wish you had him approaching, so I could see which direction he came from.'

'Don't have a camera pointing that way. But there are plenty of 'em around the Bush. You might find him on someone else's.'

'It's a long and tedious job,' Atherton said, 'and we haven't got the manpower.'

'It's always the way,' said Conroy, with sympathy.

Slider listened to Atherton's report with reserve.

'He was knitting a jumper on Sunday night?'

'And watching television with his mum, which is a cosy, domesticated sort of activity. He wasn't pacing the floor and biting his nails. And he whistled while he did his little jobs. I think it means he was not acutely worried, not to the point of considering suicide. He'd been worried for weeks, but it was more of a long-term thing.'

'But you can't know the rate of build-up. Everyone has their tipping point, and it often comes quite suddenly.'

'OK, but I'm just saying, I don't think suicide was on his mind on Sunday night, and since nothing changed, why should it have been on Monday morning?'

'Well, go on,' Slider said warily.

'And then he stops in the station entrance, as though he's been shot through the heart. As though the tipping point has just arrived. And why does he stop? Because the man he passes says something to him.'

'Really? You're going with this?'

'I'll show you the tape. You can see his lips move, and Georgie stops dead.'

'Does he look at him?'

'Georgie? No.'

'Then the man might not have been talking to him. He might have had a hands-free phone somewhere and be talking to that.'

'I don't think so. He looks at Georgie. You can see it for yourself. And I've got a good still of the man. I'm going to put it through the system, but even if he's not on record, someone who knew Georgie might recognize him.'

He produced the still with a flourish – ever the showman, Slider thought.

Slider took it. 'I know this person,' he said gravely. 'It's Marler's right-hand man. What was his name? Easter. David Easter.'

'Well,' said Atherton with enormous satisfaction, 'there's a coincidence.'

A movie of the complications that were about to arise flashed through Slider's mind. 'I almost wish it were,' he said.

FOURTEEN
Call Girl

Porson watched the monitor with disfavour. 'Coincidence. Marler lives just round the corner. He's probably waiting for his boss.'

'Holland Park Station's nearer for him,' said Slider.

'Not by much.' Porson did a couple of laps, then stopped in the middle and exclaimed, 'Oh, for God's sake!' A stray beam of sunlight from between the clouds backlit his head, toyed with the bumps on it for a moment and wandered away. 'You're suggesting he hung about outside the station just to tell Peloponnos to go stick his head in a train?'

'I think he passed on a message, sir, yes.'

'There's a handy new invention called the telephone.'

'Communication between Marler and Peloponnos was almost all through his office, where it could be explained away. I think they're just savvy enough to know we can get hold of phone records. And see how he doesn't obviously stop Peloponnos and talk to him, just speaks as he passes. He knows there's a camera somewhere about.'

'You're clucking at straws. Maybe he doesn't stop him because he doesn't *know* him – ever think about that?'

'Marler knew Peloponnos very well, so I think Easter must have too. He never seems to leave Marler's side.'

'Well, *thinking*'s not going to cut any mustard. Maybe there is some piggery jokery going on – nothing would surprise me less – but you've got to have some idea what it actually *is*.' He shook his head. 'Can't go with this. Go away and get more.'

Slider could see he was worried, which meant he thought there was something in it. He stood his ground. 'Peloponnos's home computer, sir. No obvious connection with Marler that anyone could object to. But the guarded files might have something material in them to give us a lever.'

Porson considered a moment, then nodded. 'All right. I'll go along with that. I'll get the warrant out.'

Slider turned away, and Porson called him back. 'How's Hart making out?'

'She's good. I wish she would stay permanently.'

'Fits in all right?'

'As if she'd never been away.'

'I'll have a word,' Porson said. He fidgeted. 'It's been suggested upstairs that we need to get more diversified.'

'Oh,' said Slider.

The fire came into Porson's eyes. 'But I'm damned if I'm going to let them think I'm willing to take on a totem black just to make their figures look right. I want to say I want her because she's good.'

'She is.'

'Exactly,' he said with defiant jaw. 'We don't care what colour anybody is – or what sex, come to that. We just care that they do the job.'

Slider smiled to himself as he went away. It wasn't only for Slider's faults that Porson would be denied promotion. If you didn't love statistics, quotas and targets, you'd never make the top.

When he got back, the office was bubbling like a cup-a-soup in a microwave.

'We've got a ping on Shannon's phone!' Swilley exclaimed, her receiver to her ear, listening as she spoke. 'Outside Kensal Rise Station. Oh.' Disappointed. 'She made one phone call and turned it off again.'

Slider addressed Mackay. 'Get on to Willesden. Get them round there, pronto.'

'Yes, guv.'

'Ask nicely. Send them Shannon's photo, ask them to do a run round the nearby streets, try and spot her.'

'Yes, guv.'

'Outside a station, most likely she got on a train,' McLaren pointed out.

'Not much we can do about that,' said Slider. 'We can't check every stop on the North London Line. But if she's used that station, she's probably staying somewhere in the area.' He turned to Swilley. 'Who did she phone?'

'I'm checking that, boss.' Fingers skittered. Then she looked up with a grin. 'Mobile phone registered to a Jessica Bale.'

'That's the friend the girl at the home told me about,' Connolly said.

'And we've got an address,' Swilley continued. 'Wornington Road, North Kensington.'

'That's just off Ladbroke Grove,' said McLaren, who came from round there.

'Half a mile from Kensal Rise,' said Atherton. 'If that.'

'Right. Let's go find Jessica, bring her in for a chat,' said Slider. 'Hart, you're the one, I think. You've got the street cred. She might open up to you.'

The house was one of a terrace of tall, shabby nineteenth-century family houses that had been chopped – minced, almost – into numerous lodging rooms and bedsits; a poor street, neglected and unloved, home to the shifting, the shiftless, the fractured and the refractory. The very sort of area, Hart thought as she looked for the number, to attract the benign attention of Peloponnos's trust. Legal and illegal immigrants, drug users, the hapless and hopeless naturally migrated to a place with lots of cheap accommodation and no questions asked. And girls thrown out of care homes, with no family to turn to – or none that cared, anyway.

The target house had four storeys plus the semi-basement. A jaunty spray of buddleia was growing out of the roof gutter like the feather on a fascinator. The window frame paint was so blistered and flaked it was impossible to tell what colour it had been, and one of the first-floor windows had a long crack across it mended with parcel tape. The rendering on the walls had fallen off in patches, exposing the brickwork underneath. It looked like a skin disease.

The front door stood open, and a large West Indian woman was sweeping the steps leading up to it. She stopped and leaned on her broom as Hart got out of the car. Her straightened hair had recently been in rollers and sat in fat cylinders around her head, waiting to be brushed out; her ample curves were confined in a tracksuit bottom and a sweater of sparkly turquoise knit; but her eyes were hard and noticing. She let Hart get all the way up to her before moving an elegantly economical step to block her passage to the door.

'Help you?' she said. She put her hand in her pocket and pulled out a packet of cigarettes, and proceeded to light one.

'I'm looking for Jessica Bale,' Hart said pleasantly. 'Is she in?'

The woman took her time. 'Never heard of her,' she said, blowing smoke out in Hart's face.

Hart did not flinch. 'You live here?'

'I'm the caretaker, honey, I live in the basement, take care o' the house, make sure there's no trouble.'

'Ain't gonna be any trouble,' Hart said. 'Not from me.'

'I promise you that,' the woman put in with a menacing smile.

'Yeah, and I promise *you* I'm gonna have a word wiv Jessica. Is she in?'

The woman considered. Hart stood her ground. 'She's at work,' she said at last, conceding the address, at least. 'What you want her for? She in trouble?'

'No, no trouble. I just wanna chat with her.'

'Cause she's a good girl,' the woman continued. 'Got a job, doin'
OK. I don't want her upset, you hear? These girls, it's easy to set
'em back. They fragile.'

'You care about her,' Hart accused.

The woman somehow withdrew without moving. 'I keep 'em in
order, honey, that's all. Don't want no trouble in ma house. I ain't
no social worker. I work for the landlord, and he's trouble enough
for *me*.'

'All right, ma,' Hart said with a cheeky grin. 'I believe you. I
ain't gonna cause no rumpus. I just wanna talk to her, that's all.
Where's she work?'

The woman gave her another long, hard look-over, and apparently
made up her mind. 'Agneska's in Westbourne Park Road. Don't you
go making a noise and gettin' her the sack, you hear?'

'I hear,' said Hart. She felt the eyes on her back all the way down
the steps. That was a woman you wouldn't cross, she thought, not
if she had any power over you.

Agneska's was, as it sounded, a Polish café off the Ladbroke
Grove. Notting Hill was rising, and the area was full of smart
restaurants, cafés and coffee shops, but there were still some of the
old sort left, plain-and-simple workmen's caffs. Agneska's was
obviously one of them, catering for the local Polish community of
cleaners, builders and gardeners. The menu was a mixture of the
indigenous sausage-and-chips culture and Polish staples like pierogi,
stuffed cabbage and dill pickle soup.

Inside it was plain and clean, with laminate-topped tables and
metal chairs, and the walls, innocent of decoration, were painted
mid-green below the dado line and cream above. There was a decent
sprinkling of customers, mostly head down and forking in the food,
one or two reading a paper, nobody conversing. They were working
people, with no time for frivolity.

The middle-aged man at the counter stopped wiping it with a
cloth and gave Hart a friendly smile, showing gappy teeth below
a threadbare moustache. 'What can I get you?'

Hart showed her brief. 'Can I have a word with Jessica? She's
not in trouble,' she added quickly as she saw the alarm enter his
eyes. 'I'm looking for a friend of hers, that's all. She might know
where I can find her.'

He nodded reluctantly. 'She's in the kitchen. You'd better go round the back and I'll send her out to you. Don't want to disturb the customers.'

There was an alley down the side and a gate into the small back-yard. The kitchen had a large window revealing cruel strip-lighting inside, and the door was open, letting out steam and a smell of chips, cabbage and sausages. There were voices inside and the clashing sounds of pans. Hart had only just closed the gate behind her when a small, skinny black girl shot out of the door as if squirted from a tomato-shaped sauce bottle. She was furious.

'Whatju want?' she demanded. 'Can't you leave me alone? I gotta job, I'm doing all right. These are nice people. They don't want the cops coming round, asking questions. If they sack me, I'm finished! Whatju *want* from me?'

The last was a wail, and her eyes filled with tears, part angry and part afraid.

'Cool it, babes,' Hart said. 'I ain't here to cause you trouble. It's Shannon I want to talk to, really.'

Her eyes widened. 'I don't know anyone called Shannon,' she said breathlessly.

'That must a'been a funny conversation you had on the phone this morning, then,' Hart said. The girl only stared. She seemed genuinely frightened. Hart took out her warrant card and showed it to her. 'Look, love, I'm the police, I'm one of the good guys. If Shannon's in trouble, it's better I'm the one who finds her. I ain't gonna hurt her.'

'I dunno where she is,' she said in a whisper.

'What she phone you for this morning?'

'To see if there was any news, that's all.'

'News about what?'

She didn't answer. She was twisting her fingers around each other. She was wearing a pink overall with gingham lapels and a matching pink bow was clipped in her blurred halo of hair, which Hart found for some reason unbearably pathetic. Her eyes looked too big for her thin face, as if she had recently been starving. Refugees and the recently clean, Hart thought. Well, she'd have the chance to put on a decent bit of flesh in a place like this. Potato pancakes and kielbasa. Egg, beans and chips.

'How long you bin clean?' Hart asked kindly.

'Three months.'

'Good for you. I ain't here to spoil your life, girl. I'm gonna make it clear to your boss that you ain't in trouble. But you gotta talk to me. Why'd Shannon run away?'

'She's scared.'

'Scared of what?'

'Them. She says Kaylee's dead, and they'll come after her next.'

Hart put a hand on her arm and felt her trembling lightly. 'I think you'd better come with me,' she said. 'We'll have a little ride to the station and have a chat where it's quiet.'

They put her in the 'soft room' and brought her tea and sandwiches, but she still looked like Marie Antoinette on the way to the guillotine. When she'd finished the sandwiches, Slider interviewed her himself, hoping she would respond to fatherliness, with Hart on the side for familiarity.

'So you know what happened to Kaylee?' he asked.

'I wasn't there,' she said. 'I didn't go any more.'

'Didn't go where any more?'

'To the parties. I didn't want to do that stuff any more. Anita told me I got to get out and get clean.'

'Who's Anita?'

'Anita. At the house,' she said, as if everyone ought to know who *she* was.

Hart intervened. 'Is that that lady, the caretaker where you live?'

'Yeah. She looks after us. This woman I met in a caff one night, she put me on to her when she found I didn't have anywhere to crash. Anita said I could have the room and she'd get me a job as well, but I had to clean up my act. No drugs, no drinking, and keep away from men. Otherwise, she said, next thing they'd be finding me in a skip. Well, I didn't want to do that stuff any more, anyway. Not after Tyler.'

Slider heard the name with relief, and an ache of sadness. On the plus side, they at last had evidence there was a connection between Tyler and Kaylee. The negative side was the nature of the connection.

'Tyler went to the parties as well?' he asked carefully.

'Yeah. We were mates at the home. Shannon got her in. She got me in, too. But she was cool with me leaving. She said she understood. She said as long as I kept my mouth shut it'd be cool. But then she come round the house Saturday night – well, it was Sunday morning by then. She rung me up from downstairs and I went down and let her in. And she told me Kaylee was dead, and they'd be after her next. So she had to go on the run. She had a couple of hours' sleep in my bed, and then she went.'

'Where did she go?' Slider asked.

'I don't know.' Her eyes were wide. 'Honest. She said it was better if I didn't know, and I don't. She said she was going into hiding, and she'd ring me sometime. She rung me today to ask if there'd been anything in the news about Kaylee, and that was it. I don't know where she is, I swear.'

'Who are these people who are after her?' Slider asked. Her answer was so low he couldn't catch it. 'What did you say?'

'Golden Eagle,' she said, still almost in a whisper. She shuddered. 'All of them.'

Slider reached for the file and took out the photograph of Peloponnos. 'Is this Golden Eagle?' he asked, handing it to her.

She took it with cringing fingers, as though it might be able to see *her*, like a two-way TV screen. Then her face cleared. 'No, that's not him.'

'Do you know that man?'

'Yeah. Otter, I think his name is.'

'*Otter*?' Hart almost snorted.

Slider threw her a quelling look. All the good names must have been taken – with a vengeance. *Otter*! 'How do you know him?' he asked. 'Where have you seen him before?'

'At the parties.' She put the picture down. 'He was there the night Tyler died. I never went again after that. I didn't fancy it any more.'

'I think you'd better tell us about the parties,' Slider said calmly. 'Take your time, start at the beginning. Would you like some more tea?'

She looked at him almost shyly. 'Can I have hot chocolate?'

She was so young, he thought. It would break your heart.

The parties were regular happenings at this big house, belonging to this rich bloke, and all these other rich blokes came.

'I think they were, like, business people,' Jessica said. 'But they all used these names, like Cobra and Panther and that. You never heard their real names. They were ever so hot on security and that. You couldn't take a mobile phone in, in case you took photographs. You had to leave your handbag downstairs when you arrived, and they, like, frisked you to make sure you hadn't got a camera or a bug or anything. That was all to stop anyone knowing who anyone was. But Shannon, she said she recognized some of them. She's, like, really smart.'

'And what happened at these parties?' Slider asked.

Jessica shrugged. 'Just the usual. Music and dancing and that. There was lots of drink, and charlie and weed. E as well – I never did that. And Viagra for the older blokes. And sex.'

'That was where you came in, was it, babes?' Hart asked.

'Yeah. That's what Shannon said when she got me in. You go along and there's lots to drink and fancy nibbles, and shedloads of drugs, and you have sex with these rich blokes, and at the end you get paid an' all. Paid for partying! Like, she said, it's win-win.'

'What sort of sex?' Hart asked.

'Well, some of 'em wanted, like, weird stuff, but mostly they just wanted to, like, shag. You never had to do nothing you didn't want. But like Shannon said, once you got in the party mood, you didn't care anyway. They were great parties. Like, I'd've gone without the money.'

'How much did they pay you?' Slider asked. A great rage was churning in his stomach, but it was part of the job to conceal that. He sounded merely pleasantly interested.

Jessica was blossoming under the atmosphere. She was not just willing to talk, she was eager. No one had ever taken so much interest in her before. Slider had got her details from the care home beforehand. It was the usual story. No idea who her real father was. Mother had taken up with a series of 'stepfathers', with the last one of whom she had been killed in a car crash on the M1 late at night, both of them drunk. Jessica, then ten years old, had been taken into care, until the system spewed her out and left her to cope on her own in a careless world.

'How much did they pay you?'

'A hundred pounds for the night,' she said proudly. 'You got that when you left. But sometimes one of the blokes would give you something as well. Like, a tip. I made two-fifty one night when I done a threesome with these two blokes. And all the drink and charlie you wanted. The only thing was you couldn't talk about it to anyone. They were real strict about that. Shannon said if anyone found out anything from me I'd be dropped, right off. But she said—' her lip trembled a bit – 'she said they might come after me as well.'

'Come after you?' Slider asked. 'You mean, hurt you?'

She nodded. 'That's what Shannon's afraid of. I dunno what she did, but she's really scared.'

'Because of Kaylee dying?' Slider tried.

'I dunno. She never said. She just said, "Kaylee's dead, and they'll come after me next."'

'Did she say how Kaylee died?' She shook her head. 'Didn't you ask?'

'I didn't wanna know. Shannon said right at the beginning, just enjoy yourself and keep your mouth shut. If you recognize anybody, never let on. The less you know the better.'

The hot chocolate arrived, and Slider let her sip it while he marshalled his questions.

'This big house,' he said. 'Where is it? Can you take us there?'

She looked scared. 'I couldn't. I don't wanna go back there.'

'We'll take care of you. You don't need to worry.'

'I dunno where it is. See, they pick you up in a car and drive you there. You can't really see, sitting in the back. I never really looked, anyway.'

'All the girls are picked up in the same car?'

'I think there's several,' she said vaguely. Obviously she was not curious about the arrangements.

'Tell me about the night Tyler died,' Slider said.

Her eyes grew moist. 'She was my mate, back at the home. She was a laugh, always up for it. I miss her.'

'What happened that night?'

'I don't know. I never see anything. I was up on the roof with a couple of blokes. Like, there was this great roof terrace where the party was, and downstairs in the house were all the bedrooms where you went to have sex. Tyler was in one of the rooms. The first I knew was when all the blokes and girls who'd been downstairs came out on the terrace. Some of 'em were, like, still putting their clothes on, and Golden Eagle sort of made an announcement asking everyone to stay up there until he said. And he asked one of the blokes, I think it was Cobra, to go downstairs with him. And after about half an hour they came back up and said everything's cool, carry on partying. But the next day Shannon rung me up and said Tyler'd had a heart attack while she was doing it with this bloke, she said Cheetah, and she died. But I was never to say anything about it. She said Tyler had probably done too much charlie – that can give you a heart attack. So that's when I decided to give it up. I didn't want to end up like Tyler.'

'So Golden Eagle was the big boss, was he?' Slider asked.

She seemed to shrink a little at the name. 'I think it was his house. I dunno if he arranged everything.'

'Do you know who he is?' She shook her head. 'If you know, you can tell us now. You don't need to keep it secret any more. We'll take care of you. They can't touch you now.'

'I don't know who he is,' she said in a whisper.

'You didn't recognize him from anywhere?' She shook her head. 'If I showed you some photographs, do you think you could pick him out?'

'I dunno,' she said. 'Can I go now? I got to get back to work, or I'll lose my job.'

'I think you'll have to stay with us a little bit longer,' Slider said. 'But we'll have a word with your boss and make it all right.'

'Babes, you're lucky,' Hart intervened. 'You're here with us, you're safe. Think about Shannon, out there on her own. We gotta get her in, before someone else gets to her. You must have some idea where she's gone.'

'I don't know. She said it was better if I didn't.'

Hart gave Jessica her card. 'When she rings again, tell her to call me. Tell her I can take care of her. She's not safe out there on her own. She's gotta come in.'

Connolly was waiting for him upstairs. 'I don't know if it's good news or bad,' she said, 'but it seems your man did go to the opera on Saturday night.'

Slider sat down wearily, 'Tell me.'

'I got onto this couple that had the next two seats. The female said she noticed him when he came in, because he was late and they all had to get up to let him past. She thought he must be a real opera lover because he was on his own, and most people go in couples or groups. But then she changed her mind because he was fidgeting all through like a flea on a shovel, and kept looking at his watch. She ended up wanting to lamp him. And at the end, they were all shuffling to the exit one behind the other, the way you do, and he was trying to shove his way through, and she thought how rude he was. Then when they got out on the pavement he was trying to wave down a taxi, and she thought, good luck with that, me boyo – or words to that effect.'

'So he was at the opera,' Slider said. 'They start at – what – seven thirty?'

'And the opera's about two hours long, so allowing for the interval and getting out at the end—'

'He'd be on the street about ten o'clock.'

'Not too late for partying.'

'And if he took a taxi—'

'Way ahead of you, boss. I've put the word out, and circulated his picture.'

'Get everyone together,' Slider said. 'I need to update you all.'

FIFTEEN
Noli Me Tangere

There was a thoughtful silence, and then Fathom said, 'I don't get it. Why all the secrecy – false names and warning the girls not to talk? It's not illegal to have parties.'

'The drugs are illegal,' Swilley pointed out. 'And the one thing they don't want is publicity.'

'And let's not forget,' said Slider, 'that Tyler was underage.'

'That's prob'ly why they panicked and dumped her,' Hart said. 'Which is also a crime.'

'And that's where all their troubles began,' said Atherton. 'Kaylee was also underage, and was also dumped. They've started to repeat their effects, like all criminals. That's where they fall down.'

'But they'd've got away with it,' said Mackay, 'if they hadn't done Kaylee. They *did* get away with it. Nobody was investigating Tyler, and nobody'd connected her with them.'

'So what happened to Kaylee?' Fathom asked. 'I mean, we still don't really know how she died – or even if she was at the party.'

'What a pity Georgie's dead, so we can't ask him,' said Atherton. 'And by the way, why did he kill himself?'

'What I don't understand is why Shannon thinks they'll be after her,' said Swilley. 'Why was it her fault?'

'Plenty of questions,' Slider said. 'What we want is answers.'

'Well, this party business makes sense of one thing that was puzzling me,' Atherton said. 'Georgie's list of names, the one marked "donors". I thought at first the dates beside the names were the dates he'd approached them for a donation, or maybe the date they'd made one. But then I did a bit of work with the calendar, and it turns out the dates are all Saturdays.'

'I should have noticed that,' Slider said.

'One of the dates was the 10th of January, and I remembered it was the presumed date Tyler died. And I knew that was a Saturday. That's what made me check. So now I'm wondering if there was a connection with the parties. Maybe they were potential donors that he hoped to meet there and put the bite on.'

Hart snorted. 'Bite? From an Otter?'

'Otters have sharp teeth. You wouldn't chuckle if you were a salmon.'

'Don't forget,' Slider said, 'we haven't established that the parties Jessica's talking about are the same parties that went on in Marler's house.'

'She mentions the roof terrace,' Atherton pointed out. 'I think you're being over cautious.'

'With a high-profile suspect, you have to anticipate every caveat,' Slider said. 'There are other houses with roof terraces. And unless Jessica IDs him as Golden Eagle, we've no firm connection with Marler at all.'

'We really need to find Shannon,' said Hart. 'She's the link.'

'Go back to her sister,' Slider said. 'Find out if there are any friends she might go to, or relatives. Impress on her that Shannon would be safer with us. And let's see if Jessica can give us the names of any other girls who went to these parties.'

Connolly used Atherton's 'donor' list and scoured the internet for images of them to present to Jessica, to see if she would pick any of them out. She found images of about half a dozen of them that were good enough. To the mix was added the best photo they had of Marler, plus a few random unconnected people, so that any future possible defence counsel couldn't say it was rigged.

Seated between Hart and Connolly, Jessica went through the whole lot without picking out anybody. 'Come on, girl,' Hart said. 'Have another look. You must recognize somebody.'

'I don't remember. It was a long time ago,' she said.

'Not that long. Three months.'

'There was, like, party lights, and smoke and everything. You couldn't really see.' She seemed close to tears.

'Just have another look. Take your time.'

'Don't be scared,' Connolly added. 'These people can't hurt you.'

'S'right, babes,' Hart agreed. 'They just say stuff to sound big. They can't really do anything. Go on, have another look.'

Jessica leafed through again, more slowly this time, but her expression was one of frozen fear. She didn't pick out Marler – but then she also didn't 'recognize' a TV presenter and show host who was virtually a household name. She did hesitate over an eminent heart surgeon, and eventually came back to him, staring but saying nothing.

'You know that bloke, love?' Hart asked.

'I dunno. I think it might be Cobra – like, the one Golden Eagle took downstairs to see Tyler.' She looked up with fearful eyes. 'But I dunno for sure. Can I go now? I got to get back to work.'

Afterwards, reporting to Slider, Hart said, 'I can't be sure she was really recognising him, or she thought we wouldn't let her go unless she picked at least *one* out. But if he's a doctor, it'd make sense Marler taking him downstairs to look at Tyler when she collapsed.'

Slider nodded thoughtfully. 'And there's the rod of Asclepius,' he said.

'You what, guv?'

'The staff with the snake wound round it. The symbol of medicine. A doctor might well choose a snake as his familiar.'

Hart gave up on that one. 'Well, it gives us someone else to pump, anyway. What about Jessica, guv?'

'Take her home. Make it all right with her boss. Urge her again to make Shannon get in touch with us – you know what to do.'

'Yeah, OK,' said Hart. 'I'll have a word wiv that Anita, too. She's a tough-looking cow, but whatever she says, I reckon she looks out for her girls.'

Slider thought of a North Kensington version of Mama Morton and shuddered.

Porson sighed. 'Every time you think you've come up with something, it goes off like a damp squid.'

Damp squid? Slider thought. No wonder they thought something smelled fishy. He enumerated. 'We know Marler had parties. We know he used the roof terrace. We've got Mrs Havelock Symonds for that. And now we've got Jessica describing parties in a big house with a roof terrace. And saying Tyler Vance died at one of them.'

'She won't ID the house and she won't ID Marler,' said Porson. 'And, frankly, she's not a credulous witness. A girl like that? The sort of counsel Marler could afford would turn her inside out. You know that.' He looked at Slider sadly. 'I wish you'd never got started on this. You could have left Kaylee Adams as a hit-and-run. Nobody missed her.'

Slider filleted Porson's expression and words. 'You think it *is* Marler.'

Porson didn't answer directly. 'High-oxytane parties, drink, girls – there's a lot of it goes on. OK, a bit of cocaine sniffing. Victimless crime. Nobody's interest to interfere.'

'Tyler Vance—'

'Died of natural causes. Kaylee – who knows what happened to her. But there'll be gnashing and wailing of teeth if this particular kettle of worms gets opened, I can promise you that. Have you thought who you'd be bringing down, if that list is a list of party-goers? The press would love it. They'd spread the lot of them all over the media, even if they'd done nothing wrong. Innuendo'd be enough for them.'

Slider was silent, waiting.

'This surgeon?'

'Sir Giles Canonbury,' Slider supplied.

'He'd just deny all knowledge.'

'Yes, probably,' Slider said. 'But it might rattle him. And he might rattle somebody else. That's when they make mistakes.'

Porson nodded without necessarily agreeing. 'What is it you want? I mean, where do you see this ending?'

'I want to know what happened to Kaylee.'

'Just that? You'd leave it at that?'

Slider avoided that one. 'I've got two more days,' he said.

'Anything you put up has got to be watertight. Airtight. Bomb-proof. Nucular shelter standard.'

Slider nodded, and turned away.

'And you can't interview Marler,' Porson called after him.

'I don't want to,' Slider replied. *Not until I've got enough solid evidence to make him squirm.*

Hart and Connolly were both supposed to be off on Saturday. 'I'll come in anyway, boss,' said Connolly.

'There's no overtime,' he reminded her.

'I don't mind. I'll take a day off in lieu sometime. I'd like to see it through.'

'Me too, boss,' said Hart. She was back from taking Jessica home.

Connolly had been visiting Dakota, who was just up and preparing herself for her evening's work. She'd said she couldn't think of anywhere Shannon might go. She had lots of friends, but Dakota didn't know any of them, apart from Kaylee, and that was only because she had come round to the house so often. Other girls had called from time to time, but Dakota didn't know their names or where they lived.

'All those little kids look the same to me, anyway,' she said. As for relatives, they'd never had any, apart from each other and their mum and their brothers.

Connolly had made a quick and unannounced visit to Shannon's mother Dee Walls, but Shannon was not there, and Dee seemed genuinely surprised that she was not at Dakota's. Connolly had asked the neighbours on either side, but nobody had seen Shannon in months.

'So unless she turns her phone on again, it all depends on Jessica persuading her to come in,' Connolly concluded.

'Nothing else you can do tonight,' Slider said, and sent them off home. And took himself off to Harley Street, where Sir Giles Canonbury had a consultation surgery until nine thirty p.m.

* * *

The consultation and waiting rooms were on the first floor of the fine old Georgian house, and benefited from the high ceilings, mouldings and Adam fireplaces. The handsome secretary said she would fit Slider in between patients, but he was alone in the waiting room, so presumably Sir Giles's sort of patients did not turn up before they had to. He was impressed by the silence in the room. The tall drawing-room windows must have been double glazed, for there was no traffic noise from outside, and the heavy, solid doors prevented any voices penetrating from other rooms. Slider sat with the heartbeat-slowing tick of the magnificent longcase clock in the corner for company. He didn't read any of the many publications thoughtfully disposed on a table, for fear that the rustling of pages would be too loud.

At last the inner door opened and a prosperous-looking man in his sixties came out, followed by a lean man in a suit so beautiful he could only be a senior consultant. They shook hands, and Sir Giles said, 'I'll let you know as soon as I've had the results, and we can schedule another talk.'

The prosperous man walked past Slider without a glance. Sir Giles turned a blank gaze on Slider and invited him into the sanctum with a voice so dry you could have mopped up spills with it.

Canonbury was not much taller than Slider, but he made the most of his height, and his slimness made him look taller. His suit looked breathtakingly expensive; his tie a daring but not vulgar splash of colour; his shoes – Slider was susceptible to shoes – looked hand-made, and were lovingly polished. His grey hair, sparked with silver, was elegantly coiffed and his face was tanned, showing off his sharp blue eyes. You would have classed him as handsome without ever examining his features. Slider, who examined them, thought there was something unpleasant about his mouth. It looked both thin and loose.

'Well, inspector, what can I do for you?' he asked, moving behind his desk and indicating the comfortable leather chair on the opposite side. The desk was heavy, mahogany, antique, and empty apart from a reading lamp, a desk blotter and a silver pen holder. The room smelled of furniture polish and thick carpets, and without the clock was even more silent. It was intimidating.

Slider decided to plunge straight in. 'I wonder if you'd like to tell me why you chose the name "Cobra".'

For a moment there seemed to be stasis in the authoritative face opposite him. Then he frowned. 'You mean the government committee, Cobra? The Cabinet Office Briefing Room committee? I'm afraid I've never been called to it.'

Deflection? Slider thought. 'You know I don't mean that. I'm talking about the name you took as an alias for the parties. I thought you might have chosen a snake because of the Rod of Asclepius.'

'The surgeon's staff? I see you are an educated man,' said Canonbury. 'But I still don't know what you're talking about.'

'Oh, I think you do,' Slider said pleasantly. 'I know the parties were supposed to be hedged about with secrecy, so that you could all feel secure, but you see, we have a witness – someone who was so disturbed by the death of Tyler Vance that they decided to come forward.'

The face frowned in innocent bewilderment, but Slider was sure there was something in the depths of the eyes – anger, or fear; something hard-edged, anyway. Or did he see it because he wanted to see it? That was always a risk when you got too involved with the victims. Was he making a monumental fool of himself?

'I'm sorry, but you're making no sense to me,' Canonbury said, sounding absolutely genuine. 'Is there a point to all this?'

In blood stepp'd in so far – nothing for it but to go on. 'Naturally enough, you were the one who went downstairs to examine her. I suppose you were the only doctor there. The fact that you are a heart surgeon was just luck. And it *was* later established that she died of natural causes. A congenital heart defect.'

Canonbury looked like a man clutching at a thread of sense in a stream of nonsense. 'Congenital heart defect? What did you say the name was?'

'Tyler Vance.'

'I'm sorry. I've never heard of her. She doesn't sound like one of my patients.'

Slider smiled. 'Good heavens, no. She was from the far other end of the social spectrum. She'd have been amazed to be examined by someone like you, if she hadn't been past being surprised by anything by then.'

Canonbury got to his feet. 'I'm sorry, but I have no idea what you're talking about, and I'm afraid I haven't time to sit and listen to nonsense. I have two more patients to see, and then I have to get over to Broadcasting House. I'm being interviewed on *Newsnight* about the Select Committee's report on the NHS. I have, as you know, been giving evidence.'

Nicely done. *I not only have connections to the media but to the government, and by the way I could buy and sell you.*

Slider rose, too. 'This won't go away, you know,' he said quietly. 'You've had a long run for your money, but you made a terrible mistake in disposing of Tyler the way you did. It's like an avalanche building up outside the door. When the evidence is heavy enough, the door will burst in and you'll all be swept away.'

Canonbury looked angry now. 'You sound as if you're quoting from a cheap thriller, but none of this means anything to me. I really think you must be delusional. Or drunk. Either way, I can't listen to you any longer. I must ask you to leave.'

Slider nodded, looking at him sadly. 'You haven't long. You can still help yourself by coming forward and telling what you know. Putting yourself on the right side. It's up to you.'

He walked out, leaving the door open. In the waiting room was a young woman, expensively dressed, but with a pale, fatigued face. It was tough when it got them that young, he thought. As he closed the outer door, he heard Canonbury's voice, urbane but a little strained, saying, 'I'll be with you in just a moment, Mrs Taylor, but there's a rather urgent telephone call I must make first.'

And he smiled.

Joanna was home for the evening, a rare pleasure these days. The orchestras were going through a phase where there was plenty of work, and like all freelances, they had to take everything they could get while they could get it, to guard against future dearth.

She'd invited Dad and Lydia to eat with them, and Dad had immediately offered to do the cooking. 'You and Bill are both working full time. I've got nothing to do but enjoy myself,' he rationalized. Dad's cooking was no hardship – he had had to learn when Slider's mother had died untimely, leaving her husband and son to fend alone.

So Joanna was hands-free to greet Slider as he came through the front door. She saw at once that he was tired, too tired even to talk, so she made him a gin and tonic, sat him down on the sofa and told him about her day instead. Slider sipped and listened. Trained as he was to hear the subtext, and the subtext to the subtext as well, he not only knew that she was entertaining him to take his mind off his troubles, but that she was enjoying being back at work, and busy. As a human being, and as Bill Slider, he was glad for her. As a man, he couldn't help a little twinge of wistfulness that being his wife and mother to George wasn't enough for her. And then as Bill Slider again he knew that sort of thinking was selfish and not to be indulged in – certainly never to be voiced.

It was complicated being a man in the twenty-first century. A bit like being a land-mine disposal expert. Somebody had to do it, but you were quite likely to get blown up for your pains.

She was talking about the programme for a concert. 'This is the concert tomorrow night, is it?' he asked, to show willing.

'Tomorrow night at the Festival Hall, and the repeat on Sunday afternoon in Croydon,' she said, with a faint frown. 'Weren't you listening?'

'Just checking. You won't have a rehearsal on Sunday, then?'

'No, thank God.'

'So we can have a proper Sunday lunch together?'

'As long as it's earlyish. It's not a demanding programme – well, not for me, anyway. There's that fiendish two-bar bassoon solo near the end of the finale of "Beethoven Four". And to think I nearly took up the bassoon! Then my music teacher warned me not to choose an instrument there's only two of in an orchestra. Less chance of getting work in the first place, and more chance of your mistakes being cruelly exposed.'

'You're enjoying being back, aren't you?' Slider said, to show he was listening.

'It's like I've never been away,' she said. 'Do you know, the main topic of controversy is the same now as it was six months ago?'

'What's that?'

'Sleeveless dresses. The men resent having to wear heavy tail coats in overheated concert halls, when women can wear flimsy dresses, and they want the board to pass a rule that our long blacks have to have long sleeves. They say it's about having a uniform look up on the platform, but it's really just jealousy.' She grinned. 'We call it "The Right to Bare Arms".'

Over supper they talked about ordinary things: George's progress; Dad and Lydia's next holiday – if, when, and where; the desirability of adding a conservatory to the house and whether, now that Joanna was working again, it could be afforded. Joanna had perceived that he didn't want to talk, and tossed the conversational ball back and forth between her and Lydia; Mr Slider added the occasional comment, and watched his son with a countryman's eyes. It was from him that Slider had learned the art and practice of observation: to tell from small signs what creatures had passed, and when, and why; to wait patiently and silently in the dusk to see the badgers emerge from their setts, or the deer come down to the pond to drink. Joanna looked from one to the other as she talked, and thought how alike they were. That was how Bill would look when he got old, she thought; and the knowledge made her feel warm and loose inside.

Slider listened with the top half of his brain. The underside was miserably churning over the consideration that he had made a horrible fool of himself with Sir Giles Canonbury, that the man *really* hadn't known what he was talking about, had thought he was mad, and might well put in an official complaint about him to the IPCC; and from there his self-critical organ burst into life with the suggestion that the whole 'case' was a mare's nest full of cockatrice's eggs. All he really knew about Gideon Marler was that he was a good man who worked tirelessly for his constituency, supported local charities and was fighting for the police budget in a select committee. And this was the man he had been persecuting, on what evidence? That Peloponnos had rung him immediately after ringing Kaylee. He wanted to groan and bury his head in his hands. What had he been *thinking*?

He didn't usually watch television in the evening, but he put it on for *Newsnight*, in the manner of one probing a mouth ulcer with the tip of the tongue. After the opening spiel, the presenter said, 'Later in the programme: what's in the future for the NHS? We were to have interviewed Sir Giles Canonbury, the eminent heart surgeon, who has been giving evidence to the Parliamentary Select Committee, but unfortunately we've been told that he's indisposed, so instead we'll be hearing from . . .'

Slider stopped listening. It might be nothing, but the cold weight in his heart told him it was something.

Hammersmith rang him horribly early, and he was summoned to a meeting with Borough Commander Mike Carpenter at half past eight. Everything about that was wrong – that the big boss should come in on Saturday was bad enough, but that he would get out of his warm bed for half past eight was ominous. Slider dragged himself in. Joanna gave him a look that told him she knew something was wrong, but, blessed woman that she was, she also divined that he didn't want to talk about it, and refrained from asking him questions. She made him breakfast and watched him eat while she fed George his egg, and only picking a thread off the shoulder of his suit as she kissed him goodbye expressed her concern. But that was eloquent.

Slider was there at eight twenty, and Carpenter's PA said he was already in. Indeed, his door was closed, and through it Slider could hear the sound of someone talking on the telephone, though he could not make out the words. It was SOP to keep the miscreant waiting for his thrashing. Slider sat, working the mouth ulcer like a man possessed.

The PA must have felt pity for him, because she said, 'Sorry you've had to come in so early, but Mike's down for a round of golf this morning so he's had to fit several things in beforehand.' Carpenter liked his staff to use his first name. On paper, it was supposed to make him more approachable. But since everyone in the Job knew the last thing a commander really wanted was to be approached, only the civilian staff availed themselves of the privilege.

The telephone voice within ceased, and the intercom buzzed. 'Is Slider there?' the voice squawked. 'Send him in.'

Slider went in. Carpenter was a big man, well over six feet and muscular in proportion. Even sitting down behind his desk he seemed to tower over Slider. He was writing something and didn't look up as Slider entered, but gestured with his free hand for him to sit. It was a power-ply Slider was familiar with. It was meant to make him feel small and insignificant, not even as important as that note that was being written. It was all wasted on him – he felt small and insignificant anyway.

Finally Carpenter stopped trying to make him a better person and looked up, putting down the pen and scowling. 'I don't know what the hell to *do* about you,' he said abruptly. 'Have you got a death wish, or something?'

'Sir?' Slider said, with what he hoped was maddening innocence.

If you're going to get eaten by the lions, sticking your tongue out won't make things any worse.

'Don't give me "sir"!' Carpenter snapped. 'You were told, categorically, not to go after Mr Marler. To leave well alone. Do not touch. Well, weren't you?'

Obviously he wanted an answer. 'Yes, sir.'

'And what do you go and do? You deliberately confront Sir Giles Canonbury in his own consulting room and accuse him of – well, I don't know exactly *what* you think you're accusing him of, but he seems to think you suspect him of some sort of illegal conspiracy with Gideon Marler. He wasn't clear what, but he certainly doesn't like having some low-grade policeman prance in and throw dirt at him. What the *hell* were you thinking?'

Slider rightly guessed that this was not a question and kept schtum.

Carpenter raged on. 'He complained to Mr Marler, who you might be interested to know is a personal friend of the AC. Mr Marler told the AC exactly what he thought about this "persecution" of him and his friends – his word. The AC has been raising Cain on his behalf from Scotland Yard downwards, ending up with me. I don't like being rung up at home by infuriated top brass, Slider. He had me on the carpet, and I don't take kindly to my officers putting me in embarrassing positions. So what have you got to say for yourself?'

Slider let the echoes cease before answering. 'I didn't mention Mr Marler to Sir Giles, sir.'

Carpenter was caught up short. 'What are you talking about?'

'I didn't mention Gideon Marler.'

There was a silence. The implications slowly filtered through Carpenter's brain. The layout inside the heads of commanders and above was very different from ordinary policemen, and it took a few moments, but he got there.

'You must have,' he said flatly.

'No, sir. I'm very clear that I didn't. The only name I mentioned was Tyler Vance. If he immediately complained about that to Gideon Marler, it means that there *is* something to investigate.'

'I'm well aware of what it does and doesn't mean, thank you. I don't need you to teach me my job!' Carpenter thundered. His brow was worried. Slider was not without sympathy. When you were at the bottom, like him, the brown shower got up more momentum. But those nearer the top, like Carpenter, got it freshest and hottest.

After a moment, he asked in a more normal voice, 'What do you think Sir Giles had to do with Tyler Vance?'

Slider explained. Carpenter listened with increasing fidgetiness. 'You've got nothing but a second-hand report from this *girl*.' For *girl*, read *slut*, Slider thought. 'You don't know that this Golden Eagle is Marler, or that Canonbury is Cobra.' His downturned mouth expressed his disgust at the silliness of using code names. 'Or that either of them had anything to do with the Vance girl.'

'But isn't it interesting, sir, that when I ask Sir Giles Canonbury about Tyler Vance, he goes straight to Gideon Marler, and Mr Marler complains to the AC?'

'Interesting is not the word I'd use.' But Carpenter was thinking. There was a long silence. Then he said, 'I don't know what to say to you, Slider. We're facing horrendous budget cuts and loss of personnel, and you seem set on demonstrating that we're overstaffed by investigating things that don't need investigating, and opening up cans of worms all over the damn place in the process.'

'I'm just doing my job, sir.'

'*Don't lecture me about the Job!*' Carpenter exploded. It was at this moment that seniors in the good old days would shout that they were in the Job when you were in short pants, laddie. But in fact Carpenter was younger than Slider and had come in through accelerated promotion on account of his university degree. That verbal weapon was marked U/S in this case.

He seemed to make up his mind, turning his head away slightly as though tiring of the whole thing. 'I can't waste any more time on you,' he said. 'This is not an argument or a discussion. I'm giving you a categorical order to leave Mr Marler alone. There are ramifications that are well above your pay grade, things going on that you don't need to know about. It's enough for you to know that this comes from the very top: do not contact him, attempt to interview him, do not investigate him – *or* any of his influential friends. Do I make myself clear?'

'Quite clear, sir,' said Slider.

Carpenter did not entirely relax. He stared at Slider minutely, looking for cracks. 'You've plenty of proper work you ought to be concentrating on,' he said. 'Our clear-up rate is not what it ought to be.'

'Sir.' Slider took himself to be dismissed and turned away.

Carpenter called after him, 'And you can take this as a general warning, Slider. Any more infractions from you, and you'll be looking at suspension, possibly dismissal. Keep your nose clean.'

'Yes, sir,' said Slider, and went.

Outside the PA looked up at him with sympathy. She may not have heard the words from within, but she'd have heard the tone. Slider met her eyes, and she said in a low voice, 'Not a nice way to start a Saturday.'

Slider was grateful for the kindness; but afterwards he thought she might have been referring to Carpenter's Saturday. He was going from here to play golf, and having to bellow at junior ranks first thing could put him off his game, poor fellow.

SIXTEEN

Billingsgate on a Warm Day

Porson was not in, thank God, which meant that Slider didn't have to report to him yet what Carpenter had called him in for. There was no need to telephone the old boy at home and spoil his whole Saturday. He'd find out soon enough.

He'd reckoned without Carpenter's zeal. Carpenter had rung Porson at home, and Porson arrived while Slider was still taking his coat off.

He shut the door of Slider's room behind him, but he didn't roar, which was sign in itself of the seriousness. 'What's going on?' he asked, rather than barked.

Slider told about his visit to see Canonbury, and how Canonbury had gone straight to Marler, despite Slider's not having mentioned his name.

Porson looked grave. 'These parties . . .' he said at last.

'They're going to a lot of trouble to protect them,' Slider said.

'They don't like their privacy being trammelled on.'

It was Atherton's 'sense of entitlement' argument – and it carried a lot of weight. But Slider said, 'Tyler Vance was fourteen. Kaylee Adams was fifteen.'

'Vance died of natural causes,' said Porson. 'Adams – well you don't know how she died.' Slider didn't point out the obvious. Porson knew as well as he did that disposing of a body was a serious offence, worth good jail-time. And now Porson looked sad, which was unnerving. Slider could cope with him bellowing and pacing, but not this. 'It's serious this time,' he said.

'I know, sir,' Slider said quietly.

'I've stuck up for you over the years, because you've been right and protocol's been wrong. We're not here to make ourselves popular, we're here to do the Job. That's always been my viewstand. But the Job's changing.' He stared at Slider for a long time with melancholy eyes. 'It's not me so much. I've got a secured pension. Could have been more if I'd got the promotion, but there's only me now the wife's gone. I'll manage. But you've got a family. You've got to think of that.'

'Yes, sir,' Slider said.

'I'm serious. These people mean business. There might be something behind all this or there might be nothing, but either way they don't want you sticking your nose in. They don't want stones lifted. And they have ways to stop you.' He searched Slider's face for a sign that he was taking it all in. 'They could invoke the Official Secrets Act, you know. Have you thought of that? That could be two years in the slammer. Do you know what they do to police officers in jail?'

Slider didn't need to answer that. He had gone cold all down his back.

Porson sighed. Which was worse than the sad look. 'I can't protect you any more, not on this one. You've got to leave Marler alone. And his friends. That's my final word on it. Got to be.' He looked around him, like a man saying goodbye. Then he became brisk. 'What are you doing in, anyway? This isn't your weekend on.'

Slider played the game. 'I had some things to catch up with, sir. Paperwork.'

'Get it done and go home,' Porson said. 'See your family. Take the kids to the park.'

'Yes, sir,' said Slider.

*　　*　　*

It was Atherton's day on, and he was there, at his desk, and looked up as Slider re-opened the door. 'Trouble?' he asked quietly.

'A final warning. Leave Marler alone, or . . .'

'It's your arse?'

'At least.'

Atherton studied him. 'It's serious, then?' Slider nodded. 'What are we going to do?'

That 'we' warmed him. But he said, 'I shall do what I can to find out how Kaylee Adams died, without, if possible, brushing up against Mr Marler or any of his friends. But nobody else should get involved. It could lead to disciplinary measures.'

Atherton digested that. Then he shrugged and said lightly, 'I always said I wasn't cut out to be a policeman.'

Hart and Connolly arrived together. Slider explained before they could take their coats off. 'You'd better go home again,' he concluded.

Connolly was indignant. 'What about Jessica? What about Shannon? We can't just abandon them.'

Hart only shrugged. 'There's plenty we can do wivout breaving on Mr Marler's works. I vote we stay. I'm only here temporary, anyway.'

'Disciplinary action would follow you wherever you went. I don't want you to jeopardize your careers. Go home.'

Now Hart grinned. 'I ain't here anyway. S'my day off.'

'Mine too. We'll just be careful, so,' Connolly reasoned. 'Walk like the cat. I'm going to follow up those other names on the donor's list, see what there is about 'em on the internet. What harm?'

'I'm gonna see if I can find where Shannon's brother's gone to. Maybe she went to stay with him,' said Hart.

Swilley, who was also officially on, appeared in the doorway, a vision of loveliness in beige slacks and a jumper in a shade of blue that brought out the colour of her eyes. For years she had been hunted relentlessly by what had sometimes seemed like every male in the Job in Hammersmith, and their lack of success had forced them to label her a lesbian. The fact that she had now married her long-term boyfriend and had a daughter with him did not much diminish the power of the rumour. If a woman wouldn't go to bed with you, she *must* be a lesbian, right?

All this tumbled through Slider's mind in a micro-second, and he said, 'How's your little girl?' They'd called her Ashley. Swilley's husband's name was Tony Allnutt, and Slider was so sensitive to the fact that the child was called Ashley Allnutt that he always referred to her as 'your little girl'.

'Oh, she's fine, sir,' Swilley answered, only slightly surprised by the question. There was a wisdom that said there was no point in wondering why bosses said the things they said. You just rolled with it.

'Who's looking after her while you're at work?' Slider asked, thinking of George. Not everyone was lucky enough to have a parent in a granny flat.

'Well, Tony's home today,' she said, and seeing he wanted more, said, 'When we're both at work, she goes to nursery, and I've got a neighbour who fills in the gaps. We do all right.'

Slider nodded. 'You must miss her, though.'

'Of course. But she's well looked after.' Swilley's look said clearly, that's enough of that. 'Boss, we've got the report on Peloponnos's home computer. Apparently, ludicrously easy to open the password protected files, considering what was in them was porn.'

Slider winced at the contiguity of the subjects. He wished now he hadn't asked her about Ashley. 'How bad?' he asked abruptly.

'Not the worst, but bad enough,' Swilley said. 'Underage girls.'

'Boys too?'

'Just girls.' She made a *moue*. 'I'm wondering if that's what his mother's hiding. Maybe she walked in on him one day and saw what was on the screen. Or maybe he printed something off for later – bedtime reading, so to speak – and she found it.'

'It's possible,' Slider said. He pondered a moment. 'It doesn't help us really. I was hoping for something implicating Marler, or at least confirming the parties.'

'Yes, boss,' Swilley said, 'but at least it gives us a reason to go on looking at him. And if his path happens to cross that of some other, eminent people . . .'

'Don't take risks.'

'No, boss. Who would have thought old George was one of those? He seemed such a mild-mannered nobody – and his PA obviously loved him. It just shows you never know – this blasted porn business goes deep and wide.'

Slider nodded. 'It's a cesspool,' he said. 'All right, pass it on to SCD5. They'll know what to do with it.' That was the specialist child abuse investigation team.

Atherton poked his head round the door. 'I think you'd better come and have a look at this,' he said.

They had a television set in the corner of the outer office, which was on all the time, with the sound turned down, tuned to a rolling news programme. Everyone was standing round it. Atherton turned up the sound, but Slider had already spotted the name 'Canonbury' on the moving ribbon at the bottom.

'Sir Giles Canonbury, the eminent heart surgeon, was found dead this morning in his Buckinghamshire home. Sir Giles, 69, is best known for pioneering the use of replacement heart valves sourced from pigs. He was a consultant at the Royal Free hospital and had many well-known entertainers among his patients, giving rise to the nickname "heart surgeon to the stars". Sir Giles, who was unmarried, was also a noted big game hunter, though his weapon was a camera rather than a rifle, and several of his photographs have appeared in international exhibitions. Most recently he had been giving evidence to the Parliamentary Select Committee considering the future of the NHS.' Pause. 'The Prime Minister is today to visit . . .'

Atherton turned the sound down. 'Well,' he said. 'Now that's what I *call* fishy.'

'Found dead,' said Swilley. 'That could mean anything.'

'Usually means something untoward,' said Atherton, 'otherwise they'd have said "died".'

'But *when* did he die?' Slider asked. 'He was supposed to appear on *Newsnight* last night, but they said he was indisposed. Does that mean he was already dead? Or did he feel ill, call off and go home?'

'What you really mean is, was it your visit that made him feel ill?' said Atherton.

'Don't be cute,' said Swilley. 'If it was suicide . . .'

'He lived in Chalfont St Peter, didn't he?' Atherton asked. 'Do you want me to ring Buckinghamshire police?'

'God, no!' said Slider. 'What part of "do not investigate Gideon Marler or his friends" didn't you understand?'

'There's no reason anyone at Buckingham would shop us. They're not Met.'

'You just don't know how far Marler's influence goes. Remember he seems to be protected by the AC. No, we'll have to find out some other way.'

'Sir,' said Connolly cautiously, 'maybe we shouldn't try. I mean, after the warnings.'

Slider didn't answer, but Swilley knew him better. 'We have to know,' she said – meaning Slider had to. You go and interview a man to stir him up, and you stir him into death. That's not nice to live with. 'Boss, what about the local journos? They generally know everything.'

'Good thought,' said Slider. He looked at Atherton.

'I'll do it,' he said. 'A short life and a merry.'

'Be discreet.'

'Always.'

Canonbury's house was outside the village and most fortuitously only a hundred yards down the lane from a pub, which meant that the press camped outside the gate could take it in relays to escape the boredom and the drizzle for a warm and a wet in the Jolly Cricketers. And that meant that Atherton could stay put and have the sources come to him. There was no trouble about getting anyone to talk, and for the price of a pint they were as happy to talk to him as to anyone else.

The basic facts had already filtered down from the attending doctor, who had once been snubbed by Sir Giles at a village fete and had therefore been all the more eager not to respect his privacy.

'Overdose of narcotics,' said the man from the *Buckingham Gazette*.

'Barbiturate,' said the man from the *Bucks Herald*, who considered himself a harder-nosed newshound. The *Gazette*, in his view, was a property-and-car-ads rag and didn't do proper news at all, so their man shouldn't even *be* here.

'Same thing, innit?' said *Gazette*.

'The question is,' said Atherton, 'was it accident or suicide?'

Gazette stared at him. 'Not likely to be an accident, is it? Not when it was an injection. Ain't you 'eard?'

'Must have missed that bit,' said Atherton.

'Massive overdose,' said *Herald*. 'Felled him like a horse. Half the amount would have done it, the doc said.'

'Wanted to make sure, didn't he?' said *Gazette*. 'He was a doctor, he didn't want any mistakes.'

'So they found the hypodermic by the body, did they?' Atherton said innocently.

'Right there, laying on the coffee table,' said *Gazette*.

'Who called it in?'

'Housekeeper,' said *Herald*. 'Tommy Carling, he's a copper, friend of mine, he told me. His mate Danny Ryan was the first one on the scene. This housekeeper came in the morning like usual and found him in his lounge on the sofa, dead as a herring, with the hypo on the table in front of him.'

'On the sofa?' Atherton queried. 'So when did they reckon it happened?'

'Oh, I can tell you that,' said *Herald*, happy to be the source of all enlightenment. 'Tommy said the doc reckoned he was dead eight to twelve hours, so he must have done it when he got home last night.'

Blast, Atherton thought. That wouldn't make the guv happy. 'Do they know what time he came home, then?' he asked.

Another journalist had just come in, damp of hair, smelling doggily of wax jacket. He had a face lined with too much knowledge of humanity, and a sardonic eye. 'Hello, my merry lads, what's all this?'

'Oh, bow the knee, boys,' said *Herald* sourly, 'it's the national press. Who dragged you in, Purser?'

'Eminent heart surgeon,' said Purser. 'It's national news. Who's buying?'

'This gent,' said *Herald* tersely, indicating Atherton.

'Concerned member of the public, are you?' the newcomer said, looking Atherton over and obviously clocking him as a copper.

'Something like that,' said Atherton. 'Pint?'

'Always. Now,' he said, settling an elbow on the bar, 'the interesting bit is, Canonbury was supposed to be on *Newsnight* last night, but he cancelled. Then he comes home and tops himself. What's that all about?'

'You tell us,' *Herald* invited, miffed at having his spotlight nicked.

'You'll have to do your own sniffing around. I'm not going to spoon-feed you. Oh, ta very much.' He received his pint from Atherton, and turned to face him so that his back was to the other two. He took a long draw from the top and said quietly, 'What's the police interest in this?'

Atherton smiled. '*I* bought *you* a pint, remember?'

'I'll tell you what I know if you tell me what you know.'

'I can't at the moment,' Atherton said. 'But I will promise to ring you as soon as the blockers come off the story.'

Purser looked at him keenly. 'Something big, is it?'

'It could be very big. But I'm not allowed to say.'

Purser nodded. 'Here's my card,' he said. 'Don't forget a friend when the time comes.'

'I won't. So what do you know? It was suicide, wasn't it?'

'That's what it looks like,' said Purser. 'But the doc said he couldn't think why Canonbury would use so much when he must know as well as any other medical man what the lethal dose is. Also, the doc lives down the end of the lane, and he says he heard a car go past about a quarter to midnight. That lane doesn't go anywhere else but Canonbury's house.'

'Any bruises on the arms? Any sign of a struggle?' Atherton asked quietly.

'Woah! What are you suggesting?' said Purser with mock alarm. His eyes gleamed with the excitement of the chase. 'It looks as though Canonbury was sitting on his sofa drinking whisky. The scenario is, he was making up his mind. But if there was someone who wanted him out of the picture . . .?' He looked at Atherton hopefully.

'I'm not allowed to say.'

'Ah! That means yes. Well, I'll tell you. No bruises, no sign of a struggle. But the doc says his bed had been slept in, and his pyjamas were lying on the bedroom floor. And Canonbury was in trousers, underpants and shirt, nothing else. So it looks like he'd gone to bed already, and got up again. Got up and got dressed to commit suicide. Does that make any sense?'

'Maybe his bed was unmade from the previous night.'

'No, the doc knows the housekeeper. She makes the bed every day. Makes the bed, folds his jimmy-jams and puts them under the pillow. And she says he's very tidy, never drops clothes on the floor. When he gets dressed in the morning, he leaves them lying across the bottom of the bed.'

'Did she tell the police that?'

He shrugged. 'She thinks it was a sign of how upset he was. And between you and me, I'm not sure the police want to know.'

'I wouldn't be a bit surprised.'

'Ah, like that, is it? Well, now you have got me intrigued.'

'I haven't told you anything.'

'I know. That's what makes it so tasty,' said Purser.

Slider looked as though he'd eaten a bad oyster. 'This gets worse and worse,' he said.

'Wait, wait,' said Hart, 'you're saying they came round, broke in, killed him in his bed, then dressed him and took him downstairs to make it look like suicide?'

'If they'd broken in, the police would have to have noticed that,' said Swilley.

'Maybe he come down in his p'jamas when they rung the door-bell,' said McLaren, who was also officially 'on'. 'And they dressed him after so it'd look more like suicide.'

'But no bruises on the arms,' Atherton reminded them.

'Thick, padded gloves,' said Slider. 'If they did it quickly enough, he wouldn't have had much chance to struggle.'

'Grab him and jab him?' said Atherton. 'How quick could it be? They'd have to have rolled his sleeve up.'

'If he only had pyjamas on, they could have done it through the sleeve,' said Slider.

'That's nasty,' said Hart, screwing up her face.

'I just wonder why he cancelled *Newsnight*,' said Swilley.

'He was shaken by the guv's visit,' said McLaren. 'Couldn't see himself talking calmly on telly with all that on his mind.'

'But he'd already complained to Marler, to have it dealt with,' Connolly pointed out.

'Maybe Marler told him to cancel and go home – couldn't trust him to bring it off,' said Atherton.

'Yeah,' said Hart, 'and then they thought about it and reckoned they couldn't trust him in the long run, so they sent the heavies round.'

'Or it could have been suicide,' Slider put in.

'Well,' said Atherton, 'I suppose we'll never know, if the local police aren't disposed to enquire any further. *We* certainly can't. And another potential witness to Tyler Vance's story is gone beyond recall.'

'Which leaves us with – what?' Connolly asked glumly.

'The other people on the donors list,' said Swilley, 'who we're not allowed to talk to.'

'And Jessica – who won't identify anyone,' Hart added.

'It might be worth getting her in again,' said Atherton, 'and seeing if she'll give us the names of any other girls. Names, descriptions, anything we can trace them by. I know she's scared, but she's all we've got.'

'I'll think about it. Give me a little while,' said Slider. He didn't want any more bodies on his conscience.

'A little while is all we've got,' Atherton reminded him.

SEVENTEEN

More Clubbing Than the Inuit

H art drew a blank on Shannon's brother. His name didn't come up on any register. Restlessly she checked on the monitoring of the girls' phones. Shannon's was still not switched on. Jessica's was stationary, and the triangulation made her still at home. Given that Saturday was likely to be the busiest day in any café, she wondered why she hadn't gone to work. And then a horrible thought came over her – what if it was stationary because she was dead? Could they have got to her during the night? It would not be difficult for them to discover that she had been taken to the station the day before for questioning. Would they think her enough of a threat to eliminate her?

Having thought the thought, she couldn't shake it, so she went round to Wornington Road. The front door was closed this time, and ringing Jessica's bell got no response. She went down the area steps and hammered on the caretaker's door.

Anita appeared, cigarette drooping from her lips, one eye screwed up against the smoke, which gave her a sinister, Robert Newton look. All she needed was the parrot.

'You again!' she said. It was not a cry of welcome.

'I'm worried about Jessica,' Hart said without preamble.

'Oh, worried now, is it?' said Anita with broad irony.

'She's not answering her doorbell.'

'Maybe she's not in. Ever think of that?'

'I know she's in because her phone's in there. She wouldn't go out without her phone.'

This obviously had the force of truth for Anita. The normal teenager was surgically welded to her mobile. She'd as soon venture outside without it as without clothes.

'Maybe she don't want to talk to no one,' Anita said, but with less force.

'You got a pass key?' Hart said.

The enquiry alarmed her. 'You think summing's happened to her?'

'I don't know. Probably not, but let's just make sure she's all right, OK?'

Anita grumbled, but went to fetch a ring of keys, and led the way up to the front door and then inside. The windowless hallway was dark, and the stairs and landing lights were of the lowest wattage and on the shortest timer. Hart followed the sound of Anita's breathing – she was a big woman – as she heaved herself up the stairs, and stood behind her on the landing while she knocked at a door and called out, 'Jessica! You in there, honey? It's Anita. Open the door.' When there was no response from inside, she rattled the bunch of keys. 'F'you don't open up, I'm coming in, honey. To see if you're all right. Jessica? I'm coming in now.'

She had the key in the lock when the door slowly opened, and a sorry-looking Jessica stood there, in a vast, baggy jumper and bare legs, bed hair, smeared make-up and panda eyes that spoke of weeping. She opened her mouth to speak, spotted Hart, registered alarm and tried to slam the door shut.

But Hart had her foot in the way. She said, ''S'all right. I'm just worried about you, babes. Wanna have a little talk, OK?' But as she forced the door further open with a practised shove, she saw that Jessica was not alone in the room. There was someone in the bed, and the mid-brown, corkscrew hair on the pillow, which was all that was showing, gave her the clue. She smiled with satisfaction. 'Oh, good, Shannon's here. Did you give her my message, love?'

Jessica stared at Hart with mad, scared eyes, but she only whispered, 'She's asleep. Don't wake her. She's ever so tired.'

Not only tired, it turned out, but hungry. She'd been on the move ever since she left Jessica's room the previous time, sleeping rough, afraid to stop anywhere. She'd had a night's respite with another friend in Willesden, but had moved on again for fear of getting her into trouble. Finally she had lost the determination to go on, and had come back to Jessica's late last night, and begged shelter. They had sat up for hours, talking about their situation and crying together over what might happen, until Shannon had fallen asleep in sheer exhaustion. Jessica had been afraid to leave her to go to work. She was sleeping so heavily, even Hart's ringing at the doorbell hadn't roused her.

Woken at last, Shannon seemed less alarmed by Hart's presence than resigned to it. Hart guessed she had reached that stage of flight where the effort of going on overcame the fear of giving up.

'Come on, love,' Hart said. 'You'll be all right wiv me. Get some clothes on – you too, Jess – and we'll get you both some breakfast.' The prospect of food got them going, and muted the threat she posed. If she was going to feed them, she couldn't be meaning them harm, could she?

Hart rang it in while they were drooping about, listlessly pulling on clothes, so by the time she pulled up outside Andy's Caff in Goldhawk Road, Connolly was waiting there for them, just in case the energy rush from breakfast caused either of them to bolt. Hart might be able to collar one, but she didn't think she could collar both simultaneously.

Shannon engulfed bacon, egg, two sausages, fried slice, beans, chips, double toast and two mugs of tea with an avidity that suggested she'd been on short commons while on the run. Jessica had the same, but picked at it. She avoided the eyes of both policewomen, but kept looking at Shannon, like an amnesiac actor glancing into the wings for a cue. Shannon didn't intercept the looks, or offer any of her own. When she wasn't eating, she stared blankly at the wall, waiting for anything to happen that she could do something about.

Then it was back into the car and round to the station, and up to the soft room, where Slider was waiting.

Shannon registered his adult, male presence with a return of alertness. 'You arresting me?' she asked bluntly.

'Have you done anything to get arrested for?' he asked.

'Not s'far as I know.'

'There's your answer, then. Why don't you sit down, make yourself comfortable, and we'll have a little chat.'

She gave him a look with just a hint of wry humour in it. 'That's what they all say. It never stops at a chat, though, does it?'

Connolly took Jessica away to see if she could get any more names out of her, of girls or partygoers. Shannon sat on the sofa, clutching the bottle of water they had provided for her and fiddling with the cap. She sat sprawled and knock-kneed, and had the leggy charm of a Great Dane puppy. She seemed very thin, too thin for it just to be the result of her six-day flight. To Slider it looked like a cocaine-and-vodka thinness. But though she was down, she was not out, like Jessica. She had hauled a brush through her hair, and it stood out round her head in a kinked aureole like a Pre-Raphaelite angel, almost blonde at the margin where the light shone through it.

'How old are you, Shannon?' Slider asked, to get her going.

'Seventeen,' she said. And then, as Slider continued to look at her. 'Nearly. Coupla weeks, all right?'

'You understand that you're here voluntarily, to help us by answering a few questions?'

'Didn't have much choice, did I?' she said, with a look at Hart, sitting quietly to the side taking notes.

'You can leave any time you want,' Slider said. She didn't get up. She looked at him warily. 'I mean it. You're free to go. But we need your help. Two girls have died, and I don't want any more to go the same way.'

'I don't know anything about that,' she said.

'You've been on the run for nearly a week. If you help us, we can take care of you, keep you safe. If you leave, you're on your own.'

'Been on my own a long time,' she said sassily.

'And how's that working out for you?' Slider enquired quietly.

She looked down at her thin, grubby fingers twisting the bottle cap open and closed. 'What happened to Kaylee?' he asked.

She jerked her head up with a look of panic. 'I didn't see anything. I wasn't there. I don't know what happened, all right?'

He'd hoped to surprise it out of her, but she was evidently too scared. He'd have to take her further back.

'Tell me about the parties,' he said comfortably, as if it was no big deal. 'How did you start going to them in the first place?'

'Parties?' she said warily.

'Jess told us about the parties, babes,' Hart said. 'No biggie. How'd *you* get in?'

She relaxed a little. 'It was me and this other girl, Debbie. She lived down the road from me – when I lived with Mum. We went to school together, but she was, like, a year older than me. Then one night we went clubbing up the West End, and we missed the last train, so we started walking, and this cabbie pulled up and said we shouldn't be walking that time of night and said he'd take us home.'

'Don't you know girls get in trouble that way?' Hart said.

She looked impatient. 'That's mini-cabs. This was a black cab. And he seemed like a nice bloke. Anyway—' she shrugged – 'it turned out all right. He just drove us home, he didn't do nothing to us. And on the way he got chatting, about us and what we liked and stuff, and he said how'd we fancy going to some really hot parties, and probably making a bit of money as well. And he give us this card and said give him a ring if we fancied it. So we did.'

'What was his name?' Slider asked.

'He just said to call him Mick, but the name on the card was Shand Account Cabs.' She looked up from her fiddling. 'That's the one they use all the time. There's about six different drivers but you always get one of 'em. They're all right. There was one, he tried getting in the back of the cab once with us, but we told . . . um, someone, and he got thrown out.'

Hart and Slider exchanged a look. It seemed an unnecessary step to save the girls from corruption. Perhaps it was more a matter of trust: if you break the rules we'll cut you loose.

'So it was the cab drivers who brought new girls in?' Slider asked.

'Some, but we brought our friends in once we knew it was a good gig.'

'Did they encourage that?'

'Yeah, as long as they were the right sort.'

'And what made a girl the right sort?'

'Well, pretty – you know. And up for it. And she had to be able to keep her mouth shut.' She looked worried.

'Did they threaten you?' he asked gently.

'Well,' she said, 'mostly you kept quiet because you didn't want to be dropped. But if anyone got a bit – you know – well, they said if you told anyone, it'd be the worse for you. One girl, she went to the police, and they found out somehow, and they beat her up. So you knew – you knew they meant it.' She was silent a moment.

Slider said, 'What did she go to the police about? Having a party isn't illegal. Was it the drugs?'

She looked up, examined his face, troubled. 'No, not that. There was never any hard drugs, anyway, only weed and charlie and E, and everybody does them.'

He didn't pursue that. 'What was it, then? What did she go to the police about?'

She evidently didn't want to answer, but he waited in silence, the silence that the amateur eventually feels obliged to fill. 'Well, like, the girls – they like 'em to be young. Me and Debs, she was fourteen and I was thirteen when we started. They asked us to find girls like ourselves, or younger. Like, twelve was about right. That was what they wanted.' She shrugged. 'So we did.'

Hart was too good a policeman to show her feelings about that. But she asked, casually, 'So what happens when you get older? Do they chuck you out?'

'Well, some. It's all right if you're skinny, like me, so you look younger. But other girls, they just said thank you and told 'em not to come any more. That's what happened to Debbie. I don't know where she is now. I think she got a job.'

She said it as though getting a job was the same as fading out of life.

'So you got Tyler into it,' he said, not making it a question. 'How did you know her?'

'Well, she was fostered with this couple round the corner from us – when I lived at Mum's.'

'Didn't she go to the same school as you?' Hart asked.

'That was after. The fostering didn't work out, and she got sent back to the home, and they sent her to a new school at the same time. A fresh start, they said.' She grinned reminiscently. 'She was a riot, Tyler. A real laugh. They couldn't handle her, the foster parents. She used to sneak out at night, and we went clubbing, so I told her about the parties and she like begged me to get her in. So I did. She was really popular. She really loved charlie, that girl, and when she was high she was up for anything. I didn't like anything too kinky, but she thought it was all a laugh, so they all wanted to go with her.'

'What happened the night she died?' Slider asked.

'I don't know. I only know what they told me.'

'But you were there.'

'Well, she was in one of the bedrooms and I was in the one opposite, with this bloke.'

'Who?'

'We never knew any of their names. They had, like—'

'Nicknames, I know. But didn't you recognize any of them?'

'No,' she said flatly. Her voice and her eyes were dead.

'All right, what was the nickname of the man you were with?'

'Otter. He was all right. I liked him. He was keen on Tyler, too – he liked the very skinny, young ones. Liked 'em flat-chested. That was why it was funny when—' She stopped.

'Yes?' Slider encouraged.

'Oh, nothing,' she said, looking away.

He waited. But she didn't go on. So he primed her. 'You were with Otter. Who was Tyler with?'

She seemed to hesitate. 'Cheetah,' she said at last, and stopped again.

'Go on,' he prompted. 'What happened?'

'Well, there was this ruckus, like, outside in the corridor. Otter got up and went to look, and I heard someone say Tyler's name, so I went as well. The door of the other room was open and Cheetah was standing there stark naked, saying, "She's dead." I tried to run across to her, but Golden Eagle come up, and he stopped me. Told me and Otter to go back in the room and shut the door.'

'And did you?'

'Well, we did at first. But Otter, he was, like, terribly upset, 'cos he liked Tyler a lot, like I said. So he said, "Go and open the door a crack and see if you can see anything." So I did.'

'And what did you see?'

'Well, I see Golden Eagle come back with Cobra, and Cobra went in the room and shut the door. And then he see me watching, and came over and threw the door open and told Otter and me to get some clothes on and go up on the terrace. So we had to. Everyone went up there, and we had to wait there until Golden Eagle said. Most of 'em didn't know what was going on, and I didn't dare say anything, and Otter, he was too upset to talk. So we just stayed schtum, until Golden Eagle come up and said we could carry on. Otter didn't want to go back down, so I was hanging around, wondering what to do, and Golden Eagle comes over to me and says Tyler'd had a heart attack, and it sometimes happened when people took too much coke, and he said it was all being taken care of, and not to talk about it to anyone.' She took a deep, slightly shuddering breath. 'And that's the last time she was ever mentioned.'

'The care home reported her missing,' Hart said. 'Didn't you see the fuss in the papers?'

'I don't read the papers,' she said simply.

'Well, it was on the telly as well.'

'I never watch that stuff, the news and that. Got better things to do.'

'So you never wondered what happened to her afterwards?'

'She was dead, that was it. What else could happen to her?' Shannon said harshly. 'Anyway, I was told not to talk about it.'

'But you did talk to someone. You told Jessica.'

Shannon looked uncomfortable. 'She was my mate,' she said at last.

'Why did you tell her?' Slider asked.

She sighed. 'She was scared. She thought maybe someone had done Tyler in. She didn't want to come any more. I told her it was just an accident, from too much charlie, and there was nothing to worry about. But she was still scared. I s'pose she thought the same would happen to her. So she said she was giving it up, and I said as long as she never told anyone anything about the parties or anything, she'd be all right. So I told Golden Eagle, and he said the same, it'd be all right if she didn't talk.'

'Golden Eagle,' said Slider. 'He's the boss, is he? The one who runs it all?'

'Well, I think it's his house, and he, like, runs the parties, but I don't think he's the boss.'

Slider and Hart exchanged a quick look. So there was a Moriarty behind it all, was there?

'Do you know who Golden Eagle is?' Slider asked.

'I told you, we never knew their names.'

'But you might know anyway. You might have recognized him.'

'Well, I didn't. I don't know him,' she said in that same flat, dead tone that denial seemed to require.

'We're trying to help you, babes,' Hart said. 'We can't help you if you won't be straight with us.'

Shannon set her jaw and stared at the wall.

Slider said easily, 'How do you know that Golden Eagle isn't the boss? If it's his house . . .'

''Cos I've heard him asking Cheetah stuff sometimes, like asking for instructions, or if something's all right. And I've seen Cheetah giving out to him – like, telling him off.'

'So you think Cheetah's the big boss?'

She looked alarmed. 'I never said that.'

'Yes, you did, darlin',' said Hart. 'I just heard you.'

Shannon tried looking pathetic. 'My mouth's ever so dry. Can I have a drink of something?'

She had forgotten the water bottle in her hand. But Slider felt they both needed a break – the rage he was holding back was giving him a headache. And they were going to have to talk about Kaylee next, and that would not be easy.

'Would you like a cup of tea?' he asked.

'Yeah,' she said. And then: 'Please.'

He was touched by the word. He nodded to Hart, who went to ring for it. Shannon got up from the sofa, stretched her skinny limbs, and walked over to look at one of the deliberately bland prints on the wall.

Then she turned abruptly and looked at Slider with less attitude than he had yet seen. She seemed very young to him. He thought of his own daughter, Emma, just of an age to be interesting to the likes of Peloponnos, and who would have loved to get dressed up like a hooker and go clubbing, if her mother and stepfather had not been so boringly old-fashioned and strict. A gripe of sheer terror seized his bowels at the thought of what could happen to her, if vigilance slipped for an instant. How had they, the nation, got to this point? What had gone wrong? Who was to blame? The culture, the zeitgeist, the internet, the entertainments industry? How did it come about that the only activity teens embraced with enthusiasm was meaningless sex? Whatever happened to stamp collecting?

'What's going to happen to me?' Shannon asked bluntly.

He knew what she was asking: *Am I in trouble with the law?* His mind ran rapidly over the things she had done that were infractions: procurement, the drugs, not reporting illegal activities – and whatever was to come with Kaylee, whatever her part in that had been.

But he said, 'Nothing. You're the victim here. We're going to look after you.'

She held his gaze steadily for a moment, as if testing him; and then her eyes dropped, and she sighed. 'Yeah, but you can't, can you. Once I go out of here. They'll know I grassed, and they'll come after me. You can't be with me every minute, can you?'

'We'll take care of you,' he said. 'I won't let them get you.'

'You promise?'

It was a child's question, a little child's. It hurt him to answer, 'I promise.'

And it hurt him more to see that she knew exactly how much a grown-up's promise was worth.

EIGHTEEN

Slouching Towards Kensington

'So the whole thing was an under-age sex ring?' Atherton mused. 'I suppose they paid good money for it. If Georgie's list of "donors" are the customers, they're all big men, well-off. They could afford to pay for their pleasures.'

Slider made a face at the word 'pleasures'. 'See what you can find out about Shand Account Cabs,' he said. 'They could be the weak link.'

'That's the company whose number appeared in Georgie's phone records,' said Atherton.

'It looks as though they were recruiting girls, as well as driving them to the house. If we can get them on procurement, they may give up the organisation to save themselves,' Slider said.

Atherton read between the lines. 'We need a more credible witness than Shannon?'

'It couldn't hurt,' Slider admitted gloomily. 'Is Mr Porson still here?'

'No, he went home hours ago.'

'Better give him a ring, bring him up-to-date,' Slider said. 'He might want to come back in.'

It was that serious.

Hart had taken Shannon to the loo, and ordered her coffee and sandwiches.

Slider returned, and they resumed. 'So tell me what happened to Kaylee that night.'

'I don't know,' she said quickly. 'I never saw nothing. I wasn't on the roof.'

'How do you know it happened on the roof?' Slider asked.

She looked from him to Hart and back, as if testing how far she had betrayed herself. 'You dunno what happened to her?'

'She died as a result of a fall from a height,' Slider said.

Shannon seemed relieved. 'Yeah. She fell. That's what they said. She was drunk and fooling around, and she fell over the . . . what you call that wall?'

'Parapet?'

'Yeah, like that.' She folded her hands in her lap and stared at them.

Slider watched her, plotting his way in. 'So, that Saturday – Otter rang her and asked her to come to the party. Was that the usual way?'

'No,' she said quickly, looking up. 'Mostly they ask you when you're there for the next time. Sometimes they'd ring me, if it was someone I'd brought in, like Kaylee or Tyler. I s'pose the drivers'd fix the ones they brought in.'

Limiting communications, Slider thought. They were cautious – but not cautious enough. Anxious to protect themselves, but believing they were invulnerable.

'So Otter ringing Kaylee was unusual?'

'That never happened. You weren't supposed to have anything to do with them outside the parties. So when Kaylee told me, I said there's something screwy about that. But she wanted to go. She was saving for the deposit on a flat and she needed a bit more. Anyway, she said she trusted Otter. She rang him back to ask if he was going, and he said he'd be there. But he wasn't,' she said bitterly. 'I think it was a plot.'

'A plot?'

'To get her there. They knew she'd go if he asked her 'cos she'd been going a lot with him recently. Which was weird because she wasn't his type. He liked 'em flat and boyish, and she was, like, a big girl. But he'd been picking her ever since—'

'Since what?'

She bit her lip. 'Since Tyler died.'

'You think it had something to do with that?'

'Well, they was both upset, her and Otter. But – well, I think it was something else as well.'

'What?'

'I don't *know*,' she said, frustrated, and a bit tearful. 'Her and Otter were always talking together, like, privately. And I was scared for her. She'd been asking a lot of questions, and I'd seen them looking at her, like, suspicious. You weren't supposed to ask questions.'

'What sort of questions was she asking?'

'Like, trying to find out who the blokes were. Their real names. I told her to knock it off. I said she was drawing attention to herself. And I think she'd got a bit scared too, because she said she was giving it up, she wasn't going to go any more. So I said, good thing too. So I told Golden Eagle she was leaving, and he said that was cool. But then she rung me to say Otter had rung her and asked her to come. He said someone was asking for her special.'

'Who?'

'He didn't say.'

'How did he get her number?'

'I dunno. Maybe she give it him. We weren't supposed to do that. Like I said, we weren't supposed to have anything to do with them except at the parties. I told her not to go, but she said it'd be OK, she trusted Otter. She said it'd be the last time.' She shrugged her shoulders, acknowledging the irony.

'She was picked up by a car – a black SUV,' Slider said. She nodded. 'You didn't go with her.'

'I had to go and get a new girl I was bringing in, Savannah. We got picked up by a Shand cab. Generally they pick you up outside a tube station. But sometimes you got the car.'

'Whose car is it?' Slider asked casually.

'I dunno,' she said indifferently.

'So what happened when you got to the party? Did you see Kaylee?'

'Yeah. Everybody was up on the roof, like, partying, and she was well away already. I said to her, you going for it? And she said it was her last time, she might as well make it a good one. She was drinking vodka an' cranberry, and she'd had a coupla lines already. I said, where's Otter, and she said he'd not turned up yet, and she weren't waiting for him. She was going with the richest bloke she could find, she said. Sometimes they give you a tip,' she explained.

'Yes, I know. And who did she go with?' He asked it casually, almost holding his breath.

But she said, 'I dunno. I had to, like, sort out Savannah, and then I went downstairs with a bloke. She was still on the roof and I never see her again.'

The last part was said in a flat, empty tone. It could have been grief or shock; but from the tightness of her face muscles, Slider took it for a lie.

He tried a switch-hit. 'You know Otter killed himself?' he asked after a pause. She barely nodded, not meeting his eye. 'Why do you think that was?'

'How should I know?' she said resentfully. 'I didn't know the bloke.'

'Remorse?' She looked blank. 'He was sorry because Kaylee was dead,' he translated. She stared at him, ungiving. 'He felt guilty, couldn't live with it, so he killed himself.'

'He wasn't even there,' she said.

'But he was the one who made sure she went to the party. And she died. So he felt responsible for her death.'

'Otter never did nothing to her. She liked him. She said a lot of the time she went downstairs with him, they just sat talking. It wasn't him killed her.'

'So she was killed, was she? It wasn't an accident.'

She went rigid, realising what she'd said. She looked at him, scared. 'I never—' She licked her dry lips.

Now he knew. His heart contracted with pity. 'You were there,' he said, not making it a question. He kept his voice even and unemphatic. 'You saw what happened.'

Very slowly, she nodded.

He took a moment to gather himself. 'I know you're scared,' he said. 'But I'll take care of you. Just tell me what happened. You'll feel better when you've told me everything.'

'It was Cheetah,' she said in a husk of a voice. She licked her lips again. 'I saw her with him on the roof at the start. He was, like, getting her going, giving her drinks, and lines and that, and she must've gone downstairs with him. She was really spaced, or I don't think she would've. We didn't like him, 'cos he liked rough stuff. He used to go with Tyler a lot because she was up for it, but Kaylee and me, we didn't go in for that. But he give the biggest tips, and she was, like, going for broke.' She shook her head slowly over her friend's foolhardiness.

'Go on,' Slider said, wishing they could both stop there, and never have said what was coming next.

'I was there when they come upstairs,' she said. 'They didn't know I was there. I was in the bar getting a drink of water. I'd just finished with my bloke and I was on my own. The bar's, like, this sort of glasshouse on the roof. It's got that glass that you can't see in from outside. Golden Eagle was there, outside, I mean, sitting on the parapet, on his own. He had his phone in his hand. He looked like he was waiting for something. Then Cheetah comes out. He had Kaylee by the arm, like dragging her. She looked like she was well drunk. Her legs were sort of sagging, and he was sort of holding her up. She was—'

'Yes?'

'She was naked,' said Shannon, screwing up her eyes. Somehow, he saw, that had made it worse. Perhaps it had brought home to her the disrespect with which they were viewed. They had seen it as fun, but they were just a commodity.

And Slider thought, they dressed her afterwards. In haste. Hence the pants being inside out. 'Go on,' he said.

Shannon resumed. 'Then he says something to Golden Eagle, and he says something back.'

'What?'

'I couldn't hear. But it sounded angry – Cheetah did, anyway. And Golden Eagle stands up and it's like he's arguing with him, but more worried than angry. And then . . .'

She was looking beyond him now, into space – into memory. Her eyes were wide and terrified.

'Go on,' Slider said grimly.

Her voice sank to a whisper. 'Cheetah, he picks up Kaylee, just picks her up like she was nothing, and—' she had to swallow – 'he threw her, right over the wall. She never made a sound. But I heard . . .' A long pause. 'I heard when she landed.'

She closed her eyes and put her face in her hands. Hart went to her and put her arm round the thin shoulders.

'So Doc Cameron was right all along,' said Atherton. 'A fall from a great height, not an RTA.'

'Drunk as she was, she went down like a sack,' said Slider. 'It accounts exactly for the injuries.'

'That poor kid,' Swilley said. 'Shannon, I mean. She must have been out of her mind with terror.'

'All she could think of doing was hiding,' said Slider. 'She waited in the bar until the two men left the roof then went downstairs and hid in one of the bathrooms. When she finally came out, there were sounds of partying on the roof. She crept up there, found several couples having a good time, and joined in as best she could. She didn't see Cheetah again – I suppose he was putting some distance between himself and the scene – but Golden Eagle came back, seemed completely calm, as if nothing had happened. She had to stay until the party broke up, so as not to draw suspicion to herself. But she kept thinking Golden Eagle was "looking at her funny". So as soon as she got home, she grabbed a few things, wrote her sister a note, and legged it.'

'But if they *had* seen her in the bar,' said Swilley, 'she'd have known it by the end of the evening, surely? Given they let her go home, why did she run?'

Slider shrugged. 'She's sixteen. She's just seen her friend killed. She thinks she'll be next.'

'In her case, I'd've left Usain Bolt standing,' said Hart. 'Bloody hell, it's a miracle she held it together that long.'

'Did you get any names from Jessica?' Slider asked Connolly.

'Yeah, boss, but it's first names only, so it's not much help. And she doesn't know where any of the girls live. It looks as though the way they run it, it's like separate cells. Whoever brings the girl in runs her, no one else has any contact. Keeps it nice and tight.'

'And minimum phone records,' Hart added. 'They were careful.' She grimaced. 'Lotta reputations to be busted wide open, if that "donors" list is anything to go by.'

'Jessica wasn't much help there,' Connolly said. 'She wouldn't recognize anyone from the photos.'

'Couldn't, or wouldn't?' Atherton asked.

'I'd say she's too scared. Wouldn't pick herself out from a row o' mirrors,' said Connolly.

'We'll have to see what Shannon can do,' Slider said. He stood up and stretched crackingly. 'I'd better get back in there. Don't want her to go off the boil.'

'Do you want me to come with you, boss?' Swilley asked.

'No, I'll keep Hart. She's used to her now. Are you all right, Hart?'

'Yeah, boss,' said Hart. 'Gotta see it through. I want to get these bastards.'

They had managed to get photographs – not all of the best quality, but still – of all the people on the donors list, plus Marler and Peloponnos. Shannon leafed through them, blank-eyed, not really looking. 'I don't know any of them.'

'I know you're scared, love,' said Hart, 'but you got to help us. We got to put these people behind bars, so they can't hurt anyone else.'

Shannon's lip stuck out, and she stared defiantly at the wall. Slider could see she was trembling lightly.

'Jessica's already helped us,' he said. 'We know most of them now. We just need your confirmation.' He used a matter-of-fact tone, as though it was hardly important. 'For instance,' he said, drawing out Gideon Marler's picture, 'we know this is Golden Eagle.'

For a moment his whole universe held its breath. Despite his convictions, what if he had the wrong man, the wrong house, the wrong parties?

And then Shannon expired a sigh, like someone letting go of a long-held pain. 'Yeah,' she said.

Slider controlled his own breath. 'And this,' he said, showing Peloponnos's, 'is Otter.'

'Yeah,' said Shannon. She touched the picture with a forefinger. 'Did he really jump under a train?'

'Yes,' said Slider.

She pronounced his epitaph. 'He weren't a bad bloke.'

'Now, how about these others,' Slider said briskly. She still seemed reluctant. He pushed Giles Canonbury's photo towards her. 'What about this man?'

She sighed one last time. 'That's Cobra,' she said. She seemed to have given up now. She went through them slowly, almost wearily. Some she recognized, but did not know their code name. Some she wasn't sure about – thought she recognized them, but wasn't sure. And one she looked at a long time, her lower lip between her teeth.

'Who's that?' Slider asked. 'Who's that, Shannon?' Her answer was inaudible. 'Say it again, please.'

'Cheetah,' she said.

Slider heard Hart take a sharp breath. He made a small movement of his hand to still her.

And then, her voice stronger, Shannon cried, 'That's Cheetah. That's the bastard that killed Kaylee.' Large tears welled up in her eyes. 'Who is he?' she demanded shrilly. 'Why's he wearing that uniform? What is he, an airline pilot?'

It made sense, Slider thought dully, not only of how they had kept the thing so secret so long, but of why it had been so extra, super necessary to do so. Cheetah, it seemed, was Assistant Commissioner Derek Millichip. It might well spell the worst trouble he had yet been in.

Porson was stationary with horror. He had come in after the first news, in time to hear from Slider's own lips the latest evidence from poor Shannon Bailey.

'Oh my good Gawd,' was all he said, but it was the way he said it.

'We can't let this go,' Slider said, when the silence had extended itself too long.

Porson looked at him sharply. 'It's not up to you, is it? This is way above your pay grade, laddie. Mine too. We can't touch this. This is a tanker-load of toxic waste. This'll burn your hands off right down to your socks.'

'Sir—'

Porson thumped his fists down onto the desk and leaned on them, poking his jaw aggressively at Slider. 'Don't "sir" me! Do you know what you're suggesting? A child abuse sex ring made up of all the top names in society, protected by an assistant commissioner of police? Can you even begin to imagine the shitfest this'll cause? The media storm? Do you think these people are going to lie down and take it from a CID inspector with a *teenage crack whore for a chief witness*?' His voice went off the scale, and he had to bring it back down again. 'Do you seriously think the CPS would contemplate bringing a case like this? Even if you had Gandhi, Albert Schweitzer and Mother Teresa swearing on a stack of Bibles they were actually there and saw it all, they still wouldn't touch it. And do you know what they would do to the officer suicidal enough to bring it up?'

Slider waited for the reverberations to stop before saying quietly, 'They have to be stopped.'

Porson breathed heavily through his nose. 'They'll be stopped, all right – a sharp word from the right direction in the right ear. Without bringing the whole smelly mess out into the light. Without trashing the reputation of the service. Think of the public confidence crisis! There's MPs here, a High Court judge. "Not in the public interest", that's what the CPS'd say, if anyone was mad enough to let you present this bucket of nucular waste as a case.'

'We can't let them eliminate Shannon, the way they eliminated Kaylee,' Slider said. 'And other girls will come forward. You know these abuse scandals can't be contained once they start to leak out. Look at Dolphin Square. The more we try to contain it, the worse we look when it all comes out. That's the real public confidence crisis.'

Porson regarded him for a long time, and seemed to grow older as he did it. 'Let's cut to the cheese. You're not going to let this go, are you?' he said quietly.

'I can't,' said Slider.

'You'll make sure the press find out. Even if it means your job.' Slider didn't answer that. 'Very well,' Porson said without joy. 'Get your stuff together, everything you've got, line it all up. Make it good. And be ready to duck when the spit hits the spam.'

Slider stood his ground. 'Sir,' he said, 'it's Saturday. There might be another party tonight.'

Porson's eyebrows shot towards where his hair had once been. 'Good God, you're not thinking we ought to mount a raid?'

'There'll be underage girls being abused, not to mention illegal drugs. Can we really turn a blind eye towards all that?'

Porson seemed to withdraw inside his face, and became cold. Official. 'Leave it with me,' he said.

All of them who had come in worked frantically to get the evidence together in a coherent narrative. Connolly and Hart took statements from the two girls. Atherton assembled the Peloponnos connection. Swilley collated the telephone records. Slider put together Mrs Havelock Symonds's complaints and what Superintendent Geddes had said about orders from on high to ignore them.

McLaren brought his ANPR results. 'I've got Marler's SUV early hours of Sunday, all the way down the A40, from the West Cross roundabout to the Denham roundabout, where he turns off.'

'But that's the way he'd go home,' Slider pointed out wearily.

'Yes, guv, but there's a good, clear image from the Denham roundabout camera where you can see into the motor, and it's not Marler. It's that sidekick of his driving – David Easter. He's on his own in there.' He looked hopefully at Slider. 'It's suggestive, guv, innit?'

There was a lot that was suggestive, Slider thought, but suggestion didn't feed the bulldog. There were too many holes. And when it came to Kaylee's death, all they had was Shannon; and the opposition would call her an unreliable witness. A raid on tonight's party – if there was one – would be the solution, give them all the evidence they needed, net all the guilty in one snatch. But he hadn't the power to authorize that. Porson would have to take it higher up for the Fiat to go out.

'If we'd had time to get after those cab drivers . . .' Atherton said.

'You can be making a start,' Slider said. 'Take McLaren with you.'

'Don't you want to wait and hear what the commander decides?'

Slider didn't answer directly. 'Any evidence you manage to gather won't be wasted.'

His stomach was churning, thinking of what might happen, and what he might have to do. The very fact of sending the stuff up to Hammersmith could result in an alert going out. You didn't know who knew who, or what. They might cancel tonight's party, cutting off the chance to bag the villains. They could shut down the ring and start it up somewhere else – they might even have done that before. And as for Shannon; as the only person who could implicate Millichip, who in turn was the only person whose removal would expose the rest to prosecution, what chance would she have on the outside? And he had promised to protect her.

The lure of the option to do nothing had never been stronger. And anyway, who did he think he was – the Caped Crusader?

Again he thought, how did we get to this place? Where men in positions of responsibility would have sex with children simply to scratch a lascivious itch, careless of what it did to the children?

And if he and people like him turned away . . . What was it Yeats said? 'The best lack all conviction while the worst are full of passionate intensity.'

Porson had urged him to think of his family, but that was the trouble – he did. And his daughter in particular. Every man subconsciously dreaded the deflowering of his daughter, even when it came garlanded with respectable marriage to a nice boy. But this . . . He thought of Kaylee, fuelled by vodka and cocaine and the excitement of thinking she was all grown up. Kaylee, whom nobody had ever taught better. And Tyler. And Shannon. Unloved girls, there just to be *used*. He couldn't bear it. It made him want to . . .

He found his fists painfully clenched, and deliberately relaxed them. Then he pulled a file towards him, looked up Mrs Havelock Symonds's number, and reached for his phone.

NINETEEN

And Besides, The Wench is Dead

Porson, back from Hammersmith, sent for him. He looked grave, and Slider's heart would have sunk if it was not already more scuppered than the *Belgrano*.

'I've passed the whole thing on to Commander Carpenter,' he said. He seemed inclined to leave it like that, but Slider's sturdy attention made him add, 'He wasn't best pleased.'

Slider could imagine it. To the man who loved spreadsheets, good crime figures, positive reports and shining for his superiors, Porson bearing this gift would have been as welcome as Herod in Mothercare.

'And?' he asked.

Porson was irritated. 'You can't expect a snack decision on a thing like that! Good God, man, don't you realize what's entrailed? If they take it forward, it'll involve the DPP, the CPS, the IPCC, SCD5, the Home Secretary – a special task force'll have to be set up—'

'Did you say "if" they take it forward?' Slider interrupted.

Porson, for once in his life, looked shifty. 'I can't tell you what they'll decide. Not my providence – nor yours either. There are imprecations, considerations, got to weigh up what's in the best interests—'

'You mean they're going to bury it?'

Porson scowled. 'Don't go jumping to conclusions! That's just like you, Slider, always thinking everyone's out to shaft you.'

'Not *me*, sir.'

'Oh, what then? Justice?' Porson sounded ironic. 'Leave justice to the bloody lawyers, that's not our business. Law enforcement, that's what we're in.'

'Then let's enforce it,' Slider said. 'A raid on the party house tonight—'

'You know I can't authorize that. Besides, there may not be a party.'

Slider stared at him. 'You mean,' he said at last, 'they'll be tipped off?'

'Oh, what do you care,' Porson snapped, 'as long as it's stopped?' Slider didn't answer that. Porson knew what he cared, and cared the same himself. 'My hands are tied,' Porson went on. 'I've done all I can do, and so have you, bringing it to their attention. Now someone else has to make the decisions.'

'And what about Shannon?' Slider asked.

Porson sighed, but held his gaze. 'They know we know,' he said. 'If anything happened to her, they'd know we'd be straight after them.'

'It would be too late for her, though, wouldn't it?' Slider said. And he doubted, in any case, if that were true. If they weren't to be called to account for Kaylee, why Shannon?

'Look,' said Porson, 'you're getting yourself all airiated for nothing. They probably *will* take it forward – or some part of it, anyway. It'll be put a stop to, you can bet on that. And certain people will be out of a job.'

'Out of a job? We're talking about *murder*, sir.'

'You don't know that. No good evidence for that. Look, there may be prosecutions, I don't know. Just let it go, now, laddie. You've done your bit, now leave it for others to look into.'

'Sir,' said Slider woodenly.

Porson cocked an eye, in which kindliness and exasperation held equal sway. 'That's official,' he said. 'They'll look into it, you forget it.'

'Sir.'

'Go home, Slider,' said Porson. 'You shouldn't even be in today. Go home to your family, see your kid, have a drink, watch some telly. Veg out. That's what I'm going to do. Bar the kid, bit,' he added, with an attempt to lighten the atmosphere. His only daughter was married and lived in Swindon. Well, somebody had to.

'Sir,' said Slider a third time. He turned and trudged to the door.

'You *are* going home?' Porson asked sharply as he reached it.

'Just a couple of things to tidy up first,' said Slider.

Hart took Shannon and Jessica home. Shannon said she wanted to stay with Jessica, and thinking how easy it would be for a strange man to enter Dakota's flat, Slider thought it a good idea.

Hart saw them inside, warned them not to answer the door to anyone they didn't know, gave them her card. 'You worried about anything, any time, you ring me. I'll have a car round here before you can say Jack Robinson.'

'You think they're gonna come after us?' Shannon asked. She looked almost too exhausted to be scared.

'No, I don't think so. It's just a precaution, just for a few days. Once we round 'em up . . .' She had heard, of course, about the commander's command, to forget the whole thing, and had a healthy cynicism about whether there would be serious action taken. But words would be had and warnings would be issued. The cloud would pass over.

And besides, if Shannon's statement wasn't taken seriously, she

would be in no danger, would she? Hart left them, and went downstairs to the basement flat to engage Anita's help in watching over
the girls, which Anita was more than willing to do. She even eyed
Hart with respect when she suggested it.

'I got a baseball bat in mah wardrobe,' she said with relish.
'Nobody gonna get past *me*.'

Shand Account Cabs had around thirty drivers, some full-time, some
called in on a more casual basis when work was heavy. Atherton
and McLaren had done little more than get a list of them all, and
talk in roundabout terms to the boss and the dispatchers who were
on duty, trying to get a feeling for whether anyone knew anything
about the parties and the girls. It would be a long and painstaking
job to interview every one of the drivers. Atherton phoned in to see
if they should start that job tonight, given that it was after six already,
and Slider called them back in.

'That's enough for today.'

'OK,' said Atherton. 'If you don't mind, I'll head straight home.
I've got a date tonight, and theatre performances start early.' He
expected Slider to ask who it was this time, or rib him in some
way, but Slider only said fine, he would see him on Monday. 'Are
you all right?' Atherton asked.

'Of course. Why not?'

'You sounded a bit distracted. Any word from on high?'

'Nothing definite,' said Slider, and rang off.

Everyone had gone home. The department took on that unnerving
feeling, when the phones don't ring, and the occasional distant
sounds are magnified to significance. Slider was alone, sitting at his
desk, in the glow from his desk light. Beside him, the open door
into the dark main office yawned like the mouth of Erebus.

He went over and over the accumulated paperwork, seeing the
larger pattern, trying to work out how more and better evidence
could be obtained to fill in the gaps and make it a proper case. Of
course, if there was an official investigation, more girls would come
forward. The ring members would be identified. But Shannon
remained the only witness to Kaylee's death – Kaylee, where it all
started. He felt, as he so often did in these circumstances, a responsibility to her. He had taken up the cudgels on her behalf, and now

he was being asked to lay them down unused. It would have been better, of course, if he had not allowed idle curiosity to lead him out to Harefield in the first place. She would have gone down as an RTA – and who would have cared? Then the shit storm he could sense heading his way would not have happened.

Joanna was doing a concert; George was long in bed, with his father and Lydia sitting in, probably on the sofa by now watching something. They both liked quiz shows – fortunately there never seemed a moment of the day when there wasn't one showing – and between them they knew all the answers. Once he had said, 'You're so good, why don't you go on?' and Dad had given him a look and said, 'We don't do that sort of thing.' 'But you'd win the prize,' Slider had said. 'I'm happy earning my way,' Dad had said. 'I don't want prizes.'

There was no comfort for him at home, not yet.

He phoned Mrs Havelock Symonds. It rang a long time, and he thought she must be out, but she answered at last. 'Oh, I was going to call you,' she said. 'I've been standing by the bedroom window, watching. Behind the curtain, so I can't be seen,' she added, as though he'd asked.

'And?'

'Nothing. All quiet,' she said. 'There are no lights on the roof terrace, no music, no movement up there. It's too early for guests to arrive, but there's been no coming and going at all – in fact, there's only one light on in the whole house, so I think we can be sure there'll be no party tonight, because they would have been setting up by now. I don't know if it's your doing, but I'm most grateful for a quiet Saturday evening for once,' she concluded. She sounded almost wistful. The parties, and objecting to them, must have given her an interest in life.

When he had rung off, he sat in thought a while longer, then fetched his coat and headed down and out to the car. It was folly. It might be his equivalent of Peloponnos putting his head in front of a train. But it seemed to be something he had to do.

Abbotsbury Walk was deadly quiet, the houses dark. Mrs Havelock Symonds's curtains were thick and heavy enough to keep her light in, and only a faint gleam, through the fanlight over the front door suggested her presence. At the end of the road were the tall, forbidding walls, the gates, and Holland Lodge, quiet and dark, except for a glow of light-behind-curtains on the first floor. The SUV was parked at an angle on the gravel. A security light popped on and caught him as he approached the gate, and the call button on the panel lit up. The light decided him. He had half been thinking of staring at the house and going away again, but the spotlight had been turned on him, and he felt obliged to perform.

He pressed the button. It made no sound, and he stood feeling foolish, wondering if it had worked. But after a while one side of the gate swung silently open. He stepped through and it began to shut again at once, almost catching him. He trudged across the gravel, feeling absurdly exposed in the open space, as though he were in a film and someone was going to shoot him down. He reached the handsome, square house – 'very Kensingtony': he recalled those words from somewhere, some society lady's verdict on Osborne House, if he remembered rightly. In the porch was another panel, another button, and this time there was almost immediately a buzz of a door release, and he pushed his way in.

The hall was dim, lit by a light coming down the stairs from above; handsome stairs, broad, polished wood, starting straight ahead and folding round the height of the hall. He got an impression of a few pieces of fine antique furniture, a large flower arrangement, a smell of polish; but then Marler appeared, coming down the stairs, and his attention was painfully riveted.

Marler was in smart trousers and loafers and a cashmere sweater with the sleeves pushed up to the elbow, very casual and at his ease. His charming smile was on display. 'Well, well, you again,' he said as he reached the turn of the stairs. He came no further. 'Come on up. Have a drink. I'm on my own tonight, so company's welcome.'

Was there a message in that for him, Slider wondered as he mounted towards him. Marler stuck out a hand. 'Slider, isn't it? What do they call you? Bill, is it?'

Slider didn't want to shake hands with him, but in his inferior position on the stairs he felt vulnerable. He touched hands as briefly as possible, and said, 'Detective Chief Inspector Bill Slider, sir.'

Marler beamed – was there a touch of malice in it? 'Oh, please, not "sir". Call me Gideon – a burden of a name, by mine own. I hope this isn't an official visit? Never mind, whether it is or not, come on up to the drawing room and have a noggin.'

Noggin? Slider wondered. Who said that any more? He followed, faintly bemused, up the stairs, across the landing, and in through the tall, beautiful door to a tall, beautiful drawing room, dressed in keeping with the house and its age, but made human by a real log fire in the grate. A room in whose mouth butter wouldn't melt. A room you could entertain ambassadors in. He thought of the bedrooms above, and the roof terrace, and what happened there. If this room found out, it might die of shame.

Marler glanced at the fire. 'I know it's not really cold outside, but I don't care for central heating, and these big rooms can be chilly at night. And besides, it's for comfort. Grab a pew – take that one, over there – and I'll get you a drink. What's your poison?'

Pew? Poison? It was like a theatrical performance, Slider thought: Marler was the hale fellow, well met in about 1955. What did he know? What had he been told? Had someone from Hammersmith rung him – or had word gone via a more involved path up to the AC and back? Or had there never been going to be a party tonight? In which case, why was he alone here? Surely a man like him, in his position, didn't have evenings alone at home? Slider felt unease, adding to his existing nervous tension, churning an acid storm in his stomach. *Poison?* He didn't mean it literally, did he?

Marler was hovering by a table on which stood a massive silver tray bearing bottles, glasses, a vast ice bucket. His smile was unwavering, his eyes genially crinkled. 'Whisky? Gin? Vodka? I've got most things. You are allowed to drink, aren't you? Or are you on duty?'

'Whisky, please,' Slider said. 'No ice.'

'Wise man. Care for a single malt?'

Slider could not allow himself to be beguiled. 'Anything's fine,' he said, though in any other circumstance it would have hurt him to say it. He took the chair Marler had indicated – one of those huge, square, buttoned-leather 'club' chairs, facing another just like it, the two flanking the fire and the composition completed by a matching chesterfield. He perched on the edge of the seat; Marler handed him a cut-class tumbler heavy enough to club seals with, and took his own drink to the chair opposite, in which he sat well back, ostentatiously at ease.

'So, what can I help you with tonight, Bill?' he said. The 'Bill' seemed to come in inverted commas, and there was again, Slider thought, that gleam of malice in the smiling eyes.

'I want to talk to you about various things,' Slider said. 'The parties. Cobra, Cheetah and all the rest of it. The girls, the drugs. Tyler Vance. Kaylee Adams.'

'Is that all?' he asked, almost merrily.

'That'll do for a start.'

Suddenly, shockingly, the geniality was gone. Slider saw what he looked like without the PR façade. His face seemed thin and hard, his eyes pouched. He was less handsome; he even looked less young. Slider remembered the magician's use of the word 'glamour' – a spell which caused the subject to see something not as it was, but as the practitioner wanted them to see it. Now he saw Marler without his glamour.

'I know about you,' Marler said, his voice clipped and without warmth. 'You're the loony one, always throwing yourself at lost causes. Only got your promotion to keep you quiet – and long after everyone else shot up the ladder. And you'll never go any further. Some people think you're a nutcase. Others think you're just trouble. Why should I talk to you?'

There was no good reason. 'To satisfy my curiosity,' Slider said.

Marler's smile was feral. 'You *are* a nutcase. Drink your whisky – or do you think I've poisoned it?'

'You wouldn't do that,' Slider said, but he didn't drink. He needed to keep his head clear.

'So,' said Marler, 'what do you want to know? Nothing I say to you is evidence, you do understand that?'

'I know,' Slider said.

'You're alone. If you tried to repeat anything I said, I'd deny it. And I don't need to remind you who they'd believe, do I?'

'You have the ear and the protection of Assistant Commissioner Millichip,' Slider said.

Marler looked slightly surprised at having him named. But he recovered himself. 'Well, if you know that . . .' He waved a hand. 'Knock yourself out. What do you want to talk about?'

'The death of Kaylee Adams,' Slider said.

'That was an accident,' said Marler.

'No, it wasn't,' said Slider. 'But I don't think it was meant to happen the way it did. What *were* you intending to do with her?'

He didn't think Marler would answer, but he said quite easily,

'She was going to be the victim of a hit-and-run. Get her drunk, bundle her in the car, out to the sticks somewhere where bad driving is traditional. Only someone had a different idea.'

'Someone, meaning Cheetah,' Slider said.

Marler looked sour. 'He wanted to have the little slut first. He was angry with her. Her nosiness was threatening the whole set-up. And besides, she'd always shrunk away from him, and that annoyed him. So he took her downstairs first.'

'You remained on the terrace,' Slider said, remembering he'd had his phone in his hand, 'waiting for him to tell you he'd finished. To tell him if the coast was clear.'

'He was supposed to take her down the back stairs to the car. Instead he brought her up to me, wanting to know how much she knew, saying we ought to get it out of her before we dealt with her. We argued. He lost his temper.' He shrugged.

'And threw her over the parapet.'

'You could never prove that,' Marler said. 'Officially, she was the victim of a hit-and-run. It looked just fine the way it was – until you started poking about. I really ought to be very cross with you.' He wagged a finger jokingly, then took a swig of his whisky. Slider saw that he was enjoying himself: he felt absolutely safe, and wanted to boast about it. There would be no one else in his life he could brag to about his cleverness. Slider was his perfect audience – informed, and helpless.

'Tyler,' Slider began.

Marler waved a hand. 'That *was* natural causes.'

'If you can call an excess of cocaine natural,' Slider said.

He shrugged. 'Cheetah wanted her disposed of. There'd been some rough sex. And of course, she was underage, so we couldn't exactly call an ambulance, now could we? Not that it would have helped. She was dead as a herring.'

'She had a congenital heart defect. Her mother had it too,' Slider said.

'Yes, we heard about that afterwards, when she got washed up. That was just bad luck. The river police tell me most of 'em get taken right out to sea, or unrecognisably eaten.'

'Bad luck, you call it?' Slider said.

Marler eyed him, took another swig. 'Oh, are you going to get all self-righteous on me now?'

'About organising a sex ring for abusing little girls? Yes, I think I might.'

'Abusing!' Marler exploded. 'Get real, will you? No one forces these girls to come to the parties. They love it! The little sluts are gagging for it. They get exactly what they want: drink, drugs, sex and a bit of pocket money at the end of it. Hell, we don't even really need to give them money. We've never had any trouble recruiting. Once they know what they're getting, we have to beat them off with sticks! There are no victims here, Bill, get that through your thick head. These little whores would spread their legs for anyone. If it wasn't us, in nice clean beds, they'd be doing it up against the wall with a pimply youth from school.'

'I'm glad to have all that made clear,' Slider said. He had to put down his glass to hide the fact that his hand was shaking. 'I was afraid there might be something admirable about you, however small.'

Marler grinned. 'You can't touch me. Not emotionally or in the law. And, by the way, I know you aren't wearing a wire, because everyone who passes through the porch is scanned by the latest equipment. We're not amateurs, you know. The girls are all screened, they have to leave their phones and devices in the cloakroom, switched off, we never used proper names inside the house. There are a lot of people with reputations to lose, and we take care of them.'

'Like Cobra? Did you take care of him?'

'What do you mean?' he seemed genuinely puzzled.

'After I'd talked to him, he rang you, and you sent someone round to kill him, in case he blurted it all out.'

Marler tried laughter, but it was brittle. 'You've been reading too much gangster fiction! We're not the Mafia, you know.' Underneath, Slider saw he had been taken aback. He didn't know – it hadn't occurred to him that it might not have been suicide. He recovered himself, and managed to sound confident at least while saying, 'That was nothing to do with me. Cobra killed himself. You must have scared him badly. He did ring me, and I told him there was nothing to worry about, but it seems I wasn't reassuring enough. He gave himself an overdose rather than risk exposure.'

'And Otter,' said Slider.

'What about Otter?' Marler said impatiently. He got up and refilled his glass.

Slider sensed he was tiring of the game, and thought he'd better get the rest of his answers quickly. 'You knew Kaylee had decided to drop out, but you couldn't trust her to keep quiet,' he said. 'You used Otter to get her to come to one last party, because you knew she trusted him. And you told him not to come, because you'd seen symptoms of a friendship between them, so you didn't want him around in case he intervened.'

'I told him to get out for a change, enjoy himself. Apparently, he took me literally and went to the opera.'

'I expect he thought it was an order, coming from you.'

'You flatter me! Well, I hope he enjoyed it, anyway.'

'I don't think he did. He must have been wondering what was going on. What I don't understand is why he killed himself.'

'Oh, you don't think that was me, then? You're willing to believe that was a suicide?'

'But he wasn't suicidal on the Sunday. Or, apparently, on the Monday morning. It was only after David Easter spoke to him outside the tube station. What did Easter say to him?'

'You work it out,' Marler said, drinking again.

'He told him Kaylee was dead,' Slider said slowly. 'He said, you did well, getting her to the party, and now we've got rid of her. Told him if it ever came out, he was implicated, he was as guilty as the rest, so he'd better keep his mouth shut. And the guilt of it, and the realisation of what he'd got into, was too much for him.'

'Sounds reasonable to me,' said Marler.

'You fixed him so that his hands were red. You didn't trust him to keep quiet. Why?' Slider said.

Marler shrugged. 'He wasn't really one of us. I only brought him in because he was useful. I needed him to get my planning permission through, but he was nosy about some of my, let's say, more specialized alterations. Then I found out he was hot for little girls, and I had him. After that, he was my creature. I got him into the trust, so he could do some specialized work for me there. Rewarded him with the girls, while making it impossible for him to split on us. But I was worried about his apparent fondness for Kaylee. So I had to make doubly sure of him.'

'You were right to be suspicious. He was keeping a log of your guests. Their names and the dates they attended your parties. It looks as though he was planning to shop you at some point.'

Marler had scowled at the mention of the list, but the scowl cleared and he said, 'Well, he's out of it now, anyway. Dead men don't grass. And I think I've given you enough of my time. Much as I hate to end our lovely evening, I'm going to ask you to go, now.' He stood up. 'I'll see you out.'

Slider stood too. 'You don't have one scrap of remorse? Kaylee Adams was only fifteen. She had her whole life before her.'

'Life? You call that life? You know what sort of girl she was – you must do. Probably the best thing that ever happened to her was falling off the roof. Imagine what she'd have been like at thirty – a drug-raddled old bag. We saved her from that.'

He sounded almost self-righteous. That was the nearest Slider got to hitting him.

He made Slider walk down the stairs in front of him. Slider felt the hair rise on the back of his neck, half expecting the sudden shove that would send him flying to a broken neck. But all he got from behind was the voice, genial again, in complete control of the world.

'By the way, if you think I'm not going to report your visit to your commander, you're living in a fool's paradise. You really are finished, you know that? We didn't go into this without making sure our rear was protected. There are a lot of important people involved, and I don't just mean at the parties. You'd have done well to think about that before you went blundering in with your size twelves.'

Slider reached level ground with gratitude, and walked towards the door without looking back.

'You should have weighed it up first. The most powerful people in society on the one hand, versus a completely replaceable slut.' A snort of laughter. 'And a dead slut at that!'

Slider found the door latch, opened it, let himself out into the cool evening. A little prickle of rain touched his face. His stomach felt scoured, and there was a hot pressure behind his eyes, as if he might cry. But his mind scurried like a mouse on a wheel. An alternative strategy? We might get him yet, he thought.

Across the gravel, his crunching footsteps seemed to say, '*Al Capone. Al Capone.*'

TWENTY
It Was AI All the Time

S lider and Joanna sat up into the small hours at the kitchen table, talking, over relays of tea. She didn't reproach him. She might have said all manner of things along the lines of 'what were you thinking?' But they had always granted each other autonomy.

Anyway, he could do that bit himself. 'Why did I do it? I'm not that person,' he said. 'I'm not the "maverick cop", for God's sake. I'd have to be a sad loner with a drink problem – and this would have to be New York, or LA. You can't make that work when you live in Chiswick with your wife and child and your dad in a granny flat.'

'I can see how you had to,' Joanna said. 'What you've told me – it's beyond appalling. How can people be so utterly inhuman? We live in a sick age.' Her eyes were shadowed – she'd done a hard evening's work and he shouldn't be keeping her up like this, upsetting her. He reached across the table and closed his hand over hers. She gave him a wan smile and said, 'You're the only bright thing in this story. You and your belief that most people are like you, not like them.'

'You should believe it, too,' he said. 'If most people weren't good, life couldn't go on.'

'Do you really think it will be hushed up?' she asked.

'It looks as if they mean to. I don't think he'd have been so confident if someone hadn't already reassured him.'

'Then it will have to be leaked to the press,' Joanna said. 'Once it's out there – you can't put the genie back in the bottle.'

'If they could prove I leaked it, I could be sent to gaol,' he said soberly. 'They could invoke the Official Secrets Act.'

She was frightened for a moment into silence. 'Then it mustn't be you that leaks it,' she said at last.

'Darling, for these purposes, you count as me,' he said.

'Someone else, then,' she said stubbornly.

'Well, there might be another way,' he said. 'Anyway, we've got a little breathing space. Tomorrow's Sunday.'

'Today,' she corrected.

'And they'll hardly bother themselves until Monday, so let's try and enjoy it.' He yawned. 'We could start by going to bed.'

'OK.' She sighed and stood up. 'You're such a worry to me, Bill Slider.'

'But you love me?'

'That's why you're such a worry.' She reached for his hand and drew him towards the door. 'It's late. I'm cold. The heating's gone off. You'll have to hold me very close in bed. Very close *indeed*.'

He underestimated them. There was a phone call at a quarter to nine, and a car arrived at half past to take him to Hammersmith.

The car was an impressive detail. 'What do they think, you'll do a runner?' Joanna asked, but he could see she was upset.

'Try not to worry,' he said.

'What do I tell your father?' she asked following him to the door, George tottering behind her, holding on to her trouser leg.

Slider shrugged. 'Everything. No point in trying to keep anything from him – he always finds out somehow.'

'He'll worry.'

'He's tough.'

It was strange riding in the back of a big leathery car with a uniformed police driver in front. West London in its Sunday morning quiet bowled by. It was a cold, bright, breezy day – very Aprilly, he thought. He was aware of a renegade strand of hilarity in him, the thing had always made him want to giggle when he was a child and on his way to the headmaster's room. They were not pleased with him – the magnitude of their not-pleasedness was manifested in sending a car for him – and he was probably looking at six of the best, at least. It was no laughing matter. Other possible consequences crowded into his mind and killed the giggle stone dead. The prospect of prison was terrifying. Death would almost be preferable to that. Each person had one unfaceable fate. He could understand why Canonbury had killed himself.

*   *   *

He was afraid he might have to face the AC, but Millichip was not there. The borough commander saw him alone, which gave Slider a slight lift of hope. If it was a formal disciplinary meeting, there would have had to be witnesses, a representative for Slider, someone from HR, someone from the IPCC if it were serious enough.

Instead, Carpenter raged at him solo. 'What's the matter with you? Have you got a death wish? You were told to leave well alone. I *personally* told you not to speak to Mr Marler. Only yesterday you were told to drop the whole business, and the next thing – the *very* next thing you do is go round to Mr Marler's private residence and accuse him of murder.'

'Actually, not—'

'*Be quiet*! There are things going on here that are well above your pay grade, Slider. Things you don't know about. This whole business is desperately sensitive, don't you understand that? It has to be handled by people of very senior rank, people with the skills and experience to defuse the situation carefully. If it were to blow up, it could do untold damage to the whole service. You were told other people would deal with it. What the hell were you thinking?'

It was a rhetorical question, but Slider answered it. He was wondering, above all, how much Carpenter knew, how much he was implicated. Whether he was just a useful idiot, or he was actively protecting 'important' people – for the sake of his career, or the status quo, or some perception of larger public order, the 'fabric of society' . . .

'I was thinking that it was going to be buried and forgotten, sir. I was thinking there was going to be a cover-up.'

Carpenter blinked, but he reacted quickly. 'Cover-up of *what*?' he said, managing some exasperation. 'There's nothing *to* cover up. You have no evidence, no evidence at all, that anything was going on.'

'We have an eyewitness to the murder of Kaylee Adams—'

'The unsubstantiated testimony of a girl of no character, high on drugs and drink,' Carpenter said with contempt.

'Three separate girls have told us about the sex ring, the underage girls, the drugs.'

'Nobody is going to believe them, rather than people of position.'

'Sir Giles Canonbury didn't think that,' Slider said.

Carpenter glared. 'You don't do well to remind me of that. You went to see him, alone and unauthorized—'

'I don't need authorisation to interview a potential witness,' Slider said. He found himself, now, completely calm. Carpenter *didn't* know, he thought, and the belief soothed him. 'Sir, I'd like to know what *is* going to be done. Something like this – you can't keep a lid on it. It'll come out, and the more there's perceived to be a cover-up, the worse it will look. Look at Saville. Look at Dolphin Square.'

'Don't presume to lecture me!' Carpenter said hotly. 'Do you think I don't know what's right? Nobody's talking about a cover-up.' He stopped, his eyes puzzled. Slider thought he had just realized that that was exactly what was being talked about. It was only a second's pause. He rallied. 'The matter will be dealt with, and dealt with properly, at the appropriate level – which is not you, however much of a white knight you believe yourself to be. And I'm warning you, Slider, if this gets out into the press, I'll know exactly where to look for the leak.'

'Is that an official warning, sir?'

'*I'm* warning you,' Carpenter glared. 'That's enough for you to know.'

'Sir,' Slider said quietly, 'there may be another way.'

'Another way what?' Carpenter snapped.

'Another way to get at them. A way to get Mr Marler on the ropes without mentioning the sex ring. And I'm pretty sure a lot of the others are implicated as well.'

'What are you talking about?'

'Financial impropriety,' Slider said.

Al Capone, his mind whispered.

'I think we ought to look into Marler's pet project, the North Kensington Regeneration Trust. I think there's a lot of suspect financial activity going on there, and it may well involve the most powerful members of the sex ring. You see, Peloponnos dishonestly got Marler's planning permission through, and was rewarded by being moved to the trust at a larger salary. And Marler told me last night that he'd recruited Peloponnos to handle certain sensitive matters for him there. There are protected files on Peloponnos's work computer, including one named Cope, which is the old name of Marler's house. I think we ought to look at them. It occurs to

me to wonder, you see, how Marler could have afforded to buy
Holland Lodge, and do the alterations to it.'

'He has a rich wife,' Carpenter said, but Slider could see his
attention was caught.

'Not that rich. We're talking multiple millions. But you know very
well that urban regeneration is wide open to bribes and backhanders
from developers and other powerful "investors". A lot of people get
very rich that way. If we can go after the financial crime . . .'

'This is all pure supposition.'

'Then let me look at the files and see. Let me take the trust apart.'

Carpenter slapped him down, but there was a telling beat before
he opened his mouth, a second of thought. '*You* will do nothing.
You have been guilty of disobeying orders, and seriously unprofes-
sional conduct. I shall be convening a disciplinary hearing on
Monday and we'll see what happens to you then.'

'But if there's a hearing, everything will come out,' Slider said.
It was a delicate moment. If the Official Secrets Act was invoked,
he would not be able to defend himself without committing a breach
which would lead to imprisonment. But he sensed in Carpenter no
real appetite for the hunt. Something was going on which he was
being obliged to defend, without knowing exactly what was in it.

'You don't want to take that attitude,' Carpenter said loftily. 'An
official hearing goes on your record, whatever the result.' He thought
a moment, and went on: 'However, if you agree to let me deal with
it . . .' He looked away, across the room, as if the whole business
meant nothing to him.

'Sir?' Slider said.

'You know I can't let this go. Where would my discipline be if
it was known you ignored my orders and got away with it? We're
talking suspension, at the least.'

'Sir,' said Slider, his heart sinking.

'Four weeks' suspension.' A pause. 'With pay.' He frowned,
looking awkward, as though too many things were tumbling through
his mind for him to concentrate.

Slider considered. Suspension with pay was a good let-out. It
meant no guilt was imputed to him. There would be nothing on his
record. On the other hand, he would not be in his office to pursue
the case.

'And what about the rest of it, sir?' he asked.

Carpenter jerked back to the here and now. 'Don't push your luck,' he growled.

'But will you look into the trust? Let my people look into it?'

Carpenter thought a long moment. 'It would have to be done discreetly,' he said.

Slider's heart leapt. 'I've got a good team,' he said. 'But it would have to be done without telling the AC,' he suggested.

'If what you've been implying is true,' Carpenter said, 'he won't be long in finding out.'

'But I don't believe he'd be able to interfere, sir. Not in something like that. How would it look?'

Carpenter nodded. 'And what if you don't find any impropriety?'

'That's a chance we'll have to take.'

'*You'll* have to take,' said Carpenter. 'If this doesn't work, the shit is really going to hit the fan.'

Slider was almost immune to fans by this time. 'Meanwhile, sir,' he said, 'can my team also interview some taxi drivers. Very discreetly.'

Carpenter looked at him a long moment. 'I can't understand why someone hasn't murdered you long ago,' he said wearily.

'Look on it as a holiday,' Porson said. 'With Easter coming up as well, you lucky pup. Four weeks off with your family. Have a rest, forget the whole sheboodle, come back refreshed blah blah blah.'

'Unless someone changes their mind meanwhile,' Slider said.

'Well, you're not out of the woods yet,' Porson agreed. 'What the hell made you do it? No, don't tell me, you thought they were going to cover it all up.'

'Don't you?'

Porson sighed. 'Sometimes there are things you can't do anything about.'

'But not this, sir,' Slider pleaded. 'Not something like this. You have a daughter yourself . . .'

'Oh, get off it,' Porson snarled. 'You can't carry the woes of the whole world. Anyway, you're not the only copper in the barrel,' he added cryptically.

'I'm depending on you to tell me everything,' Slider said to Atherton. 'Daily reports. It's going to drive me nuts otherwise.'

'I shall be as permeable as a moth-eaten sieve with extra holes,' said Atherton. He eyed his boss curiously. 'Do you really think Commander Carpenter didn't know?'

'I think he's a career man who does what he's told without asking questions, when the telling comes from high enough,' said Slider. 'But I may be maligning him.'

He left Atherton to figure that one out while he want to talk to the rest of the troops.

Connolly rang him up one evening. 'I thought you'd want to know, boss. Karen Adams died early this morning, in hospital.'

'Karen Adams?'

'Kaylee's mother. Multiple organ failure, after the drug overdose.'

'Oh. I'm sorry.'

'So am I. Not for her, for Julienne. She's in care, o' course, but now she'll never come out. Rotten thing for a kid her age.'

'Yes,' said Slider. Look what had happened to Tyler Vance.

'She's just the sort,' Connolly began, and stopped. 'If they don't break up that ring, what are the chances she'll meet a taxi driver one day? She's got her sister's example in front of her.'

'Her sister was killed.'

'But she had a good time first, and made some jingle,' said Connolly. 'That's what Julienne will see. I wish I could—'

'But you can't,' Slider said firmly.

'No. I know. Can't rescue every dog in the pound.'

Atherton came to dinner. 'Things are turning out very interesting at the trust,' he said, on the sofa with a gin and tonic while Joanna finished off in the kitchen. 'Enough so that Mr Carpenter's authorized the seizure of all the papers. Not that there'll be anything untoward in them – it'll all be hidden on the computer – but it'll make sure there isn't any doctoring done while we look.'

'Carpenter actually decided that?'

'Well, it was Mr Porson who said it, but he hinted it came from higher up. So our tails are up. Meanwhile, we're interviewing cabbies. And one of the dispatchers is a woman, and she's started to look uneasy. I think we might be able to lean on her.'

'Good. Excellent.'

'How's the holiday?' Atherton asked, examining him curiously. 'You seem unusually relaxed.'

'I'm doing my best. It's strange having to sit on my hands while someone else conducts the orchestra. But underneath I'm a raging volcano.'

'Try not to think about it.'

'Easier said than done.'

'I'll give you something else to chew over,' Atherton said. 'I had drinks with Emily, had a long talk. She wants to give it another shot.'

'She's staying in London?'

'She's been wanting to move back for a while. And there's a job going with CNN's London newsdesk. And—' his grin became indecently wide – 'she's been missing me. Little me! Who'd a thunk it?'

Slider looked worried. 'But won't you just be back where you were before? She'll start wanting commitment, and you'll start feeling trapped.'

'Oh well,' Atherton said with an airy shrug that didn't entirely fool Slider. 'The ride'll be fun, even if the destination's wrong.'

Serious financial improprieties were discovered in the running of the trust, implicating not only Marler but developers, builders, property funds, large investors, even a charity. Peloponnos had assembled a coherent account in the file name COPE, and many of the names on the 'donors' list were involved. The report was being collated, ready for the DPP to bend his mighty brain over.

And then the Holland Lodge sex ring scandal burst into the news with all the impact and unexpectedness of a V2.

A large house in West London, the private residence of a prominent MP, is claimed to be the centre of an alleged paedophile ring. Claims concerning long-term sex abuse of underage girls at drug-fuelled parties by VIPs and politicians are as wide-ranging as they are shocking. The most serious allegations, involving a murder, have emerged from an abuse victim given the code name 'Wendy'. She told of years of abuse at the hands of eminent men including senior politicians and members of Britain's establishment. 'Wendy' came forward first to an independent investigative journalist, giving the names of 'VIPs' allegedly involved in the abuse.

Atherton rang while Slider was still staring open-mouthed at the newspaper.

'It's all over everywhere,' he said. 'TV, radio, the internet. The media's going mad.'

'I don't doubt it.'

'They haven't exactly named Millichip yet, but there are hints that a senior Scotland Yard policeman is involved in a cover-up. Mr Porson wants you to come in for a little chat. In your own time. Meaning now, if not sooner.'

'It wasn't me,' Slider said.

'I never thought it was. But you'd say that even if it was, wouldn't you?' said Atherton.

'Not to you,' said Slider.

It was strange to be back. He'd forgotten the smell of the place, which seemed very strong after an absence. He'd forgotten the subaural hum. His team looked at him with a mixture of pleasure and wariness that touched his heart. He wanted to be back with them. He wanted to know what they were all doing, how his ground was faring without him.

Porson was actually sitting down, but he got up as soon as Slider appeared, drew his eyebrows down like a couple of tatty old grey comforters, and said, 'All right, cards on the table time. Was it you?'

'No, sir.'

Porson made an exasperated sound and began his usual pacing. 'Look, I know you'd say that whatever, but I want the truth. Your secret's safe with me, but I want to know.'

'I didn't leak it, sir. And nor did my wife.'

'How do you know?'

'I asked her. She doesn't lie.'

The eyebrows relaxed. 'Well, whoever it was, it's done our job for us. Can't shut the stable door once the genie's out of the bag. The only question is, how far will it go? But I had it this morning from HQ that the Home Secretary's been on. Something this big, there'll have to be a full police operation. They've apparently given it a code name. Operation Neptune.'

'Neptune?'

Porson shrugged. These names were taken from a list of what were supposed to be neutral words when investigating a major crime.

'Giving it a name means they're committed. Well, they couldn't back off, given the media storm. So it'll be out of our hands now.' He looked carefully at Slider. 'You understand. We're all off the hook. It'll be properly looked into, every aspic. It's a result.'

'I'm glad, sir,' Slider said. But he felt a dissatisfaction all the same. He would have liked to finish it himself, though he knew it was not possible, not with something this big. But he'd have liked to witness the arrest of Marler and of Millichip in particular. These operations could take years – sometimes many years before anyone came to trial. And unless Marler turned on his erstwhile protector, they still only had Shannon as a witness to Kaylee's murder. Most probably the defence – if it ever came to trial – would accept that it was more likely that the drunken girl had fallen to her death. The disposal of the body was harder to explain away, but might not result in jail time, even if they pinned it on anyone. And it was Kaylee where it all started for him.

Porson was still talking, about the taxi drivers, the probability of other girls coming forward, some of the big names turning Queen's evidence in return for a non-custodial sentence. 'And there's still the bribery, corruption and fraud in the North Kensington Trust,' he said, almost rubbing his hands. 'We haven't even got started on that. Of course, they'll take that away from us as well, seeing as it's connected. But we'll have some people on the task force. Mr Carpenter's suggested it'll be at least three from here.'

'Three?'

'Not you,' Porson said quickly. 'You can't expect that. I'm going to suggest you give them Atherton, for one. Put your best player in.'

'Good idea,' said Slider. 'And what *about* me?'

'Oh, I think that's all blown over. You'll have a clean record, don't worry – though I wouldn't cross Mr Carpenter again in a long while, if I were you.'

'So I can come back?'

The eyebrows shot up. 'Not *now*. Bloody hell, take your holiday first! You don't get offered a free one that often.'

'I thought I could just come in for a few hours a day, work myself back in gently. With three of the team away with the task force, we'll be short-handed. And Hart's time is up soon.'

'I've had a word with her. She'd like to come back permanently, if you want her.'

'Yes, I want her,' Slider said. 'That's good.'

'All right. I'll put that through, then. And I'll put in for some more personnel while we've got people away at the task force. Probably won't get it, but no harm in asking.' He made a note on his desk pad, then looked up. 'You know, this is a very delicate business. And it's not over yet. Big heads might roll, and when they do, a lot of the blood'll spurt this way. You want to keep your head down for a bit. Don't draw attention to yourself.'

'Yes, sir.'

'I don't think HQ really knows what to think about you,' Porson said thoughtfully. 'Whether to love you or hate you.'

'I can live with that, sir.'

'Frankly, sometimes, neither do I.'

On the television news, footage of the arrests of Millichip and Marler. Millichip being escorted into his local police station, tall, powerful in a dark overcoat, his grey hair cut very short. A momentary glimpse of his face turned camerawards, skull-like in the grey early morning light, his expression grim, very grim.

Marler coming out of his house and getting into a police car, bravely hoisting the tattered standard of his PR smile one more time for the assembled press.

Both men later released without charge on police bail, pending further investigation. It was just the beginning – more, much more to come.

Another day, another funeral. The weather had turned clear and sunny, though still cold, with a wind coming down from the northeast with the Arctic steppes in its breath. Hammersmith cemetery had been cleaned up and made beautiful by the council some years back, a place of velvet grass, mature trees and old, serene headstones. Charing Cross Hospital staff often went there in their lunch hour for a bit of green peace and quiet.

Kaylee Adams had been kept on ice all this time, awaiting someone's say-so to bury her, but there had only been her mother, and once she went into hospital it was obvious she couldn't make a decision. Now she was gone too, and the council was having to inter both of them, mother and daughter, since there was no one else to arrange and pay for it. Buried 'on the parish', as the old term was. They were being cremated at the same ceremony, and the ashes interred together. It was as dreadful an occasion as Slider could imagine.

There was no need for him to go, but he went anyway, and Joanna, thank God, went with him. 'I don't think you ought to be alone,' she said.

Connolly also went. 'I can't help thinking about Julienne,' she said.

Julienne was there, accompanied by a social worker, who looked as though it was about the worse day in her life, too. Julienne, thin as a stick, her face old with sorrow, was wearing a dark green tartan skirt and a black anorak, which had the air of having been drawn from a common wardrobe, and had her hair tied back with a bit of black velvet ribbon. Her skinny legs in thick black tights stuck out from under the short hem like well-gnawed bones.

When she saw Connolly, she broke away from her escort and ran to her, and buried her head in Connolly's stomach. Connolly sat with her through the short service. Slider thought that if it had been a film or a TV series, Connolly would have adopted the troubled child and become her role model and saviour. But real life wasn't like that.

The two coffins slid away along the conveyor belt, one behind the other in silent procession, like buses easing along the Cromwell Road, and the shutter came down behind them. Julienne gave one convulsive sob, and it was all over. Joanna squeezed Slider's hand, and they got up and fled to the cold sunshine outside. Slider was as surprised as delighted to see Freddie Cameron seated near the back of the little Gothic chapel, neat in a fitted black overcoat over a dark suit. He nodded to them, and went outside to wait for them for a chat.

'Freddie! It's nice of you to come,' Slider said, with a heartfelt look.

Cameron shook his hand, and kissed Joanna. 'Thought I should, given that I started the whole thing off,' he said.

'No, that was me,' Slider said. 'Going to Harefield in the first place, when I had no business.'

'Just as well you did, as it turned out.'

'I don't know. The shit storm is only just beginning. Are we really any better off?'

'Don't you start doubting,' Freddie said. 'How are the rest of us to cling on?'

'You can't put it all on me,' Slider said, alarmed.

'Man with no self-confidence,' Joanna remarked. And to Cameron: 'You've seen the newspapers, of course?'

'Yes,' said Cameron. 'Damned nasty business. Of course, everyone around my office is wondering how the thing came out. Must have been a leak.'

'Don't look at me,' Slider said hastily.

'Oh, I wasn't,' said Freddie. 'In fact, one or two of my underlings have been looking at *me*, given I was the one who examined the corpse. I was able to head them off with an appropriate look of innocence. But I did hear something of interest.' He paused and looked curiously at Slider, as though wondering whether to go on or not.

'About the leak?' Slider asked.

'Mm,' said Freddie. He looked at Joanna, and then away at the trees, just coming into leaf. The cold weather had held everything back. There were some Japanese cherries amongst them, covered with blossom that looked like crumpled, pink-dyed tissue paper.

Out of the corner of his eye, Slider saw Connolly emerge from the church with Julienne attached like a barnacle to her hip. They stopped, and the social worker hurried up to make a threesome. He thought painfully of Hollis's plain children, bewildered and clinging together. And Hollis was still dead. That was the worst thing about death, that you could never rewind. Then suddenly, shockingly, he thought of his mother's funeral – something he rarely revisited, in memory or dream. That had been this time of year, too. They'd had a dog, then, a black and white collie called Ben. Dad had left it at home, but it had broken its lead and followed them, and when Slider came out of the church it had been waiting in the porch, head low, eyes upturned, looking guilty at one end and so, so glad at the other to have found them again.

He shook himself. 'Come on, Freddie. You can't drop great clunking hints like that and not tell us. *What* did you hear?'

Cameron turned his head back to them. 'I don't know if there's anything in it. You know the witness went to an investigative jour-nalist, who passed it anonymously to the various news desks, all at the same time.'

'That's what I heard,' said Slider.

'Nobody knows who the journalist was, but rumour says was a female,' Freddie said. 'British, but she's been working in the States for a while. That's what I heard, anyway. Just come back to the home country to take up a new job. It made me think how much kudos it would have given her with her new bosses to take them that story as an exclusive. She must have had some pretty powerful reason to go the altruistic route instead.'

'Perhaps,' said Slider, his voice seeming to him to come from a great distance, 'she thought the whole business was too shocking to want to make personal gain out of it.'

Cameron nodded kindly. 'No doubt that's what it was,' he said.